BLOWN

Also by Chuck Barrett

The Savannah Project
The Toymaker
Breach of Power

Non-Fiction:

Publishing Unchained: An Off-Beat Guide to
Independent Publishing

BLOWN

CHUCK BARRETT

SP
SWITCHBACK
PRESS

Blown is a work of fiction. Names, characters, places, and incidents are products of the author's imagination or are used fictitiously. Any resemblance to actual events, locales, or persons, living or dead, is coincidental.

Cover design by Mary Fisher Design, LLC, http://www.maryfisherdesign.com
Edited by Debi Barrett & Cheryl Duttweiler

FIRST EDITION
ISBN: 978-0-9885061-6-9 (Print)
ISBN: 978-0-9885061-7-6 (Digital eBook)
Library of Congress Control Number: 2015900067
Barrett, Chuck.
      Blown / Chuck Barrett
      FICTION: Thriller/Suspense/Mystery

Published by Switchback Press

www.switchbackpress.com

For Debi.

I will always place the mission first.
I will never accept defeat.
I will never quit.
I will never leave a fallen comrade.

CHAPTER 1

New Year's Day
Baalbek, Lebanon

FOUR HOURS.

That was all the time he had to stalk his prey, kill his target, and leave the country.

There was no fame or recognition for what he was about to do, only right and wrong. He didn't have to justify the targeted killing; it was sanctioned well above his pay grade. The decision had already been made—the world must be purged of this evil.

All that mattered was completing the mission and getting the hell out of there.

If he failed, he did not exist. That's why he was chosen for this clandestine operation.

The moonless night was selected deliberately and the cover of the olive grove offered the assassin an advantage. His orders were unambiguous; the commander's killing must look like a political assassination and not a random killing.

A warning must be sent.

A shot across the bow.

The message to the Sheik must be clear.

Less than one kilometer from the Roman ruins of Baalbek, the apartment home belonged to Commander Hassan Bin

Riyad, both a member of the inner circle and younger cousin to Hezbollah Sheik Hakim Omar Khalil or as the Sheik preferred to be called, Çoban.

The assassin's vantage point provided an unobstructed view of the garage next to the commander's apartment building. Equipped with enhanced night vision goggles, he monitored all activities around the building. Camouflaged in full black, with gloves and a balaclava, only his cold brown eyes were visible.

By morning, news of the assassination would have reverberated across the Middle East. Fingers would be pointed. Blame would be placed. The assassin, though, would be hundreds of miles away in Greece.

As a lone set of headlights approached the small apartment building, he crouched even lower behind the tree's twisted trunk. After the car passed, he rushed forward from the olive grove. Always mindful to remain in the driver's blind spot, he waited for the right moment to strike. When the car entered the unlit garage, the killer slipped in behind him.

The commander turned off the engine and opened his door.

The assassin grasped the terrorist by the arm and neck and ripped him from the vehicle.

Hassan Bin Riyad was short, thin, and weaker than expected. A spindly man used to giving orders, not taking them. The dossier said Riyad was a cruel man with an evil intellect and a reputation of a savage military style. He expected defiance and resistance, yet got neither. Instead, the man in front of him seemed somber and resigned.

He placed the Ruger Mark II .22 LR with its integrated suppressor against the commander's forehead and pushed the man to a seated position against the rear tire. He saw shock on the Riyad's face turn to panic as the terrorist stared up the long barrel of the handgun.

When the man's feeble attempts to talk and bribe his way out of death failed, he did something unexpected given his callous reputation.

He began to sob.

CHAPTER 2

Eight Months Later
Little Rock, Arkansas

HE WAS FOLLOWING ORDERS.

Officially, he wasn't there. Wasn't even in this country.

Gregg Kaplan walked across the street toward the restaurant reflecting on his handler's final instructions, *Disappear until you locate the woman.*

The restaurant was exactly where his friend had described, a few blocks south of the Arkansas River and just west of downtown Little Rock on Rebsamen Park Road. From the outside it appeared to be a small building with an unexciting front exposure. In reality, it was not small at all. Like a row house, it was narrow and deep. A striped awning, faded from too many years in the sun, hung from the cracked and weathered façade. Four empty tables with open umbrellas were arranged behind a three-foot high wrought iron fence guarding the street level entrance. Now, on a late August evening, with humidity at eighty-five percent and the temperature still hanging near ninety, it was no wonder all the tables outside were empty.

In the South they were called the *dog days*, that period from July until mid-September when the sultry days were fraught with high temperatures, high humidity, and hot, suffocating breezes. That is, if there was any breeze at all. The *dog days* seemed to last longer now, what with climate change seeming to become a reality. They came sooner and stayed later.

He reached for the doorknob and hesitated. Something inside his gut urged him to run like hell and put Little Rock in his rear view mirror.

But he didn't.

Perhaps his instincts were wrong. They had misled him before, but only when he got too close. He looked up and down the street surveying for any sign that might explain this feeling. Nothing *looked* out of the ordinary in this small corner of Little Rock, it just *felt* wrong. Or, maybe he was just tired. It had been a long day, after all. He entered the restaurant anyway knowing his decision would prove to be uneventful, destiny, or plain old bad luck.

It didn't take him long to figure out which it was.

Within minutes after he set foot inside the restaurant and sat down, he recognized the impending threat. He'd seen similar situations before. Several times. And each time, somebody died.

He should have listened to his gut.

He had no reason to get involved; yet without his help innocent people might die. He possessed the skills and knew he couldn't sit idly by and do nothing. He never could.

Protect and defend was the oath he took when he joined the Army. And even though it had been decades since he left Special Forces for a career on the civilian side of the government, that oath had become part of his ingrained psyche and he had to get involved.

Even if it meant blowing his cover.

It was the right thing to do.

Kaplan sat at a corner table near the front door allowing him full view of the open-air dining room. Full view of anyone entering or leaving. A force of habit developed from years of specialized training. The same force of habit that compelled him to subconsciously evaluate everyone in the room, assessing each one for potential threats.

Mental programming, courtesy of the United States government.

A finely honed skill infused into an integral part of his everyday life. Every thought process, every observation became a situational analysis. It might seem like a paranoid existence to many, but if truth were told, it had saved his ass on more occasions than he cared to remember.

The Cajun restaurant was divided into two basic sections, the dining room and the bar, separated by a waist-high wooden rail. The dining area had a row of booths against the wall, a row of tables in the middle, and another row of booths along the rail. Every table jammed close together to maximize seating capacity in the long, narrow space.

Dark wooden floors along with the faded cedar paneled walls gave the restaurant its rustic appearance. Pictures of the unique culture of New Orleans, such as Zydeco bands and jazz musicians, flanked each window. Acoustics were loud, voices carried, and the tantalizing aroma of spicy Cajun food filled the air and permeated his clothes.

On initial scan, Kaplan counted twenty-three other patrons, an even two-dozen counting himself. Then there were the hostess, the two overworked waitresses who were both dressed in matching khaki shorts and t-shirts, a bartender, and no telling how many kitchen workers in the back.

Nine couples sat at six different tables. None of them

caused him any concern.

To his left was a table with two men, one mid-thirties, in jeans and a sports coat accompanying a silver-haired senior wearing khaki slacks and a dark blue tropical print shirt. To Kaplan's trained eye, he could tell the younger man was probably law enforcement. It wasn't the clothes; he was dressed like many men who had been in their clothes all day. Shirt wrinkled, top button undone, tie pulled loose around his neck, creases in the back of his jacket from sitting in a chair too long.

The *tells* were his body language and grooming. The way he held himself with a calm, confident demeanor, head high, back straight, feet flat on the floor, direct eye contact, and a strong voice. Put together, they screamed *LEO*. Law enforcement officer. It also didn't hurt that Kaplan had grown accustomed to recognizing LEOs over the years, domestic and abroad.

Both men were eating, drinking, engrossed in casual conversation, and seemingly lulled into a false sense of security. They were unaware of what was going on around them.

The older man had the LEO laughing. His features suggested Italian heritage—olive skin, dark sunken eyes, and the nose. When he spoke, the man's right hand was always gesturing, palm turned up, thumb touching his first two fingers, and his wrist moving up and down. Like he was holding a pencil upside down. Kaplan expected the old man to touch his fingers to his lips and say something like *molto buono.* Very good.

The bar was to Kaplan's right, across the dining room from the old man and the LEO, and on an elevated platform perhaps six or eight inches higher than the dining room floor. It was u-shaped with a television suspended above it on the upper corner wall. Behind the bar were mirrors and a counter full of liquor bottles and glasses. Strings of small lights outlined each mirror. A bartender with a white cloth draped over his shoulder stood behind the bar sink washing glasses, drying them, and putting them back on the shelf.

Three men sat at the bar. All about the same age. Fortyish. All overdressed for the weather outside. It was those men who had sounded Kaplan's warning bells, especially the way they continually glanced at the old man and his companion.

Kaplan held the menu in front of him so he could see over the top, closely scrutinizing the men at the bar. They wore black pants, black shoes, and black leather jackets, the kind that could easily conceal a weapon. All three had dark hair, one with too much grease, and they looked Italian. If Kaplan were to paint a picture of stereotypical mob men, these thugs fit the canvas.

From the reflection in the mirror he could see one of them had a prominent scar on his left cheek. Another seemed nervous. They were all sturdy men and probably had Italian names like Vito, Sal, and Nico. They weren't talking, just watching the old man and his companion.

Kaplan's instincts, profiling skills, and training told him the men were trouble and that the Italian man in the tropical print shirt was most likely a target. But Tropical Shirt and the LEO were talking to each other and not paying attention to the impending threat. Assuming, of course, he really was a LEO.

Kaplan was certain he was.

One of the two waitresses, the older one, approached his table and blocked his view of the three Italian men in jackets. Deep lines etched across her face, her dark skin was leathery, and he could tell she was a lifelong heavy smoker before she reached his table by the yellow circles under her hollow eyes. When she spoke, her raspy voice and the smell of smoke in her clothes confirmed his suspicions.

"What would you like to drink, honey?"

"Water. Half ice. No lemon."

He feigned a smile and leaned to one side to see around her. Tropical Shirt raised his arm to signal his waitress. The young, college-aged waitress walked over to Tropical Shirt's table. Kaplan overheard the old man ask for the check and her phone number. The young waitress handled Tropical Shirt as if she'd done it dozens of times. She smiled, shook her finger at him as if playfully scolding, and said something Kaplan couldn't hear. Whatever it was made both men laugh.

At that moment, he saw one of the Italian thugs nod and all three men reach a hand inside their jackets. A bulge in Scarface's jacket revealed the outline of a handgun. Kaplan was right. This was a takedown and the old man in the tropical print shirt was the only logical target.

As he watched the scene unfold before his eyes, he knew staying off the grid was no longer an option and blowback from tonight's events might very well drag him back on the radar, something he desperately wanted to avoid.

Kaplan felt a tingle shoot down his spine. *It's happening now.*

There wasn't enough time to make anything more than a cursory initial assessment and now he must engage based on gut instinct.

By the time the Italians turned around and pulled their weapons from underneath their jackets, Kaplan had already pushed his waitress to the floor and charged Tropical Shirt's table. If Tropical Shirt's companion was indeed a LEO he might perceive Kaplan as the threat, not the men across the room, and open fire on Kaplan. A risk he had to take.

In his peripheral vision he saw the Italians raise their

weapons. He was cutting it close. He dove at the space between the young waitress and the old man, snagged one with each arm, and bulldozed them toward the floor.

Bullets flew before they hit the hardwood floor. Kaplan managed a glance at Tropical Shirt's companion. The man had already pulled his weapon, a standard law enforcement issue Glock, and taken a firing stance toward the Italian thugs. Attached to his belt was a badge.

Kaplan was right—a LEO.

Within seconds, the dining room erupted in pandemonium. Patrons screamed. Some ran for exits while others ducked behind tables and chairs. Although the Italians paid no attention to them, three were still mowed down in the crossfire. The thugs' true quarry was lying on the floor and Kaplan was on top of him. The old man was smaller than Kaplan, perhaps five-ten, a hundred-eighty pounds with some extra padding in the middle. He was in good shape for a man his age but a little soft. Probably spent most of his day behind a desk.

Kaplan flipped a table on its side and instructed the young waitress to lie face down on the floor. "Cover your head with your hands, turn away from the gunfire, and don't move until I tell you it's safe."

She nodded.

He flipped over another table and shoved Tropical Shirt behind it. "Is this about you?"

Tropical Shirt hesitated. His hands were trembling. Finally, he gave Kaplan a nod.

"Stay down and out of sight," Kaplan said. "I'll deal with you later... if we get out of here alive."

"Who are you?" Tropical Shirt asked.

"The guy who is trying to save your ass. Now stay down

and shut up."

Bullets pierced the side of the table. Kaplan ducked, instinctively aware of all the firearms in the room and from which direction they were being fired. In the LEO's hand, a Glock. Across the room, the unmistakable muzzle blasts of two Smith and Wesson M & P .45 caliber handguns and what sounded like a Beretta Px4 Storm .45—just like the one locked under the seat of his black Harley-Davidson Fat Boy. What he wouldn't give to have it in his hand right now. Instead, all he had was the pocketknife hidden inside the customized pouch in his boot. He didn't like traveling on his motorcycle without locking his handguns under his seat. Too much explaining in the event he got pulled over and searched. A lesson he'd learned the hard way on one of his yearly pilgrimages to Sturgis, South Dakota.

Long shot odds—three against one. How long could the lone LEO hold off the assault?

Then he heard one Italian grunt followed by the distinct clunking sound of the man's gun bouncing across the floor. It stopped halfway between Kaplan and the LEO but remained within the line of fire of the remaining Italians, both of whom had taken refuge behind the bar. When he looked up, the dead Italian's body was draped over the wooden rail.

Gunfire filled the air with its burning stench as round after round fired across the restaurant. Windows shattered. Glass rained down on the floor. Injured patrons moaned. With every gunshot, a hysterical woman screamed. He heard another woman chanting a prayer and two others crying. A cloud of smoke coalesced with clean air by the slow moving ceiling fans.

After a momentary pause, the LEO and two Italian thugs resumed volleys of gunfire.

Two against one.

Better odds than before.

The LEO ducked behind his overturned table and glanced at the gun and then at Kaplan. He was noticeably unsure how Kaplan fit into the scenario. Kaplan understood the man's dilemma and gave him as much of a reassuring *I'm-on-your-side* kind of look as he could.

Maybe it was intuition, instinct, or sheer desperation but the LEO nodded. He held up three fingers and Kaplan readied himself to make his move. The LEO counted down with his fingers and at the balled fist he raised and fired. Kaplan sprang from his crouched position and dove toward the gun, grasping it in one smooth motion as he rolled into position next to the LEO. Both men ducked as another volley of gunfire emanated from the Italians.

"Who are you?" Asked the LEO.

"Someone in the wrong place at the wrong time."

"Bullshit. You knew something was going down before I did. I want to know how."

Kaplan didn't want to answer questions. No one was supposed to know who he was, what he was, or that he was even here. "Look, I only stopped to get a bite to eat. I was just passing through. Maybe it was my Special Forces training. I don't trust anybody so it doesn't matter *how* I knew, what matters is we don't end up dead."

"Army?"

Kaplan nodded. "Delta. 'A' Squadron."

"No shit? I was 'A' Squadron too. Kuwaiti Resistance. Purple Heart landed me on the civilian side."

More shots rang out. Both men ducked. "Let's see about getting out of here alive," Kaplan said. "Then we can chat."

"You know, Delta," the LEO said. "I almost shot you when you charged the table."

"Glad you didn't."

Kaplan pointed at the man's belt badge, a silver star. "Marshals Service?"

The man nodded. "WitSec."

CHAPTER 3

WITNESS SECURITY.

Some people called it witness protection. Technically, they were wrong.

Unexpected, but it made perfect sense. Tropical Shirt was a witness.

And that meant the U. S. Marshals Service didn't consider Little Rock a *danger area* for the witness otherwise Tropical Shirt would be tucked away somewhere in a safe site and this guy would be delivering food to him instead of escorting him out in public.

It also meant Tropical Shirt was probably in his *relo area* waiting to testify in a federal trial.

And since the relocation area was known only within the agency, it meant the United States Marshals Service had a leak.

"WitSec, huh? What's up with wearing the star around a witness?"

The deputy looked down, "Oh crap. I forgot to take it off and put it in my pocket when we left the hotel. See, that's another reason I know you're not a drifter. Only insiders have that kind of intel. Who do you work for?"

"Nobody," said Kaplan. "Lucky guess, that's all." Kaplan ejected the magazine, checked the number of bullets remaining, and then clicked it back in place. It was a Beretta. Exactly like his. "Four rounds, three in the mag, one in the chamber."

The deputy held up his Glock, and ejected the magazine. "Seven plus one."

"Spare mag?"

"Already spent."

Kaplan surveyed the layout. Not much to hide behind. "They're reloading. We don't have much time," he said. "Divide and conquer."

"What?"

"*Divide et impera.* Latin for divide and conquer. In warfare, it means a tactical maneuver to efficiently deal with an opponent."

The Italians resumed firing. Bullets ripped through the tabletop. Both men dropped to their bellies.

"I know what it means, Delta." The deputy gave him a discerning look. "Plan?"

"Spread out, divide their attention. And their fire power." Kaplan pointed toward where Tropical Shirt was hiding. "I'll go that way, you stay here."

The deputy grabbed Kaplan's arm, "How accurate are you?"

Kaplan thought about his response. "Better than most."

"Swap firearms." The deputy held out his Glock. "Shrapnel in my shoulder left me with hand tremors. Barely pass my quals as it is and that's with no one shooting back."

Kaplan understood and appreciated the deputy's honesty. He swapped handguns and readied himself to make the fifteen-foot dash across the unprotected space.

When the firing slowed Kaplan said, "Go."

The deputy raised and fired two rounds at the Italians.

Both Italians ducked below the bar.

Kaplan dove headfirst, tucked and rolled until he was back behind the table with Tropical Shirt.

The deputy fired his last two rounds then ducked behind the table.

The Italians rose up from the bar and resumed shooting, mostly in the deputy's direction.

The deputy looked at Kaplan, picked up a chair, and waited for the signal. Kaplan nodded, rose, and fired. The deputy hurled the chair toward the firing Italians.

The chair cleared the bar, smashed into the mirror, and then tumbled through two shelves of bottles before crashing to the floor. Kaplan heard glass break, shuffling and whispering. The room went quiet. He waited. One Italian, the one with the greasy hair, rose up from behind the bar and looked in the direction of the deputy.

Mistake.

Kaplan squeezed the trigger and the bullet struck the man between his dark bushy eyebrows. Blood and brain splattered on the remnants of the broken mirror. Kaplan heard the last Italian yell then stand and run toward the door. *Not so fast.* Kaplan squeezed off two more rounds striking the last man in the chest with both. The man fell.

Silence.

Kaplan looked at Tropical Shirt and the waitress, "You two stay put." They both nodded in unison.

He stood and crouch-walked toward the bar, leading each step with the barrel of his Glock, his eyes and gun moved as one. Any threat would be met with another bullet.

He heard rustling from patrons on the floor. "Everybody stay down," he yelled.

He stepped over the rail separating the two levels one leg at a time. He moved to the side for a better angle before he advanced toward the Italians. The first man was lying over the rail, dead. A shot to the head had a way of adding finality to one's life span. He rounded the open end of the bar and saw the remaining two men. The first, Greasy Hair, dead with a bullet hole in his forehead. The other was slumped against a mini-fridge behind the bar in a pool of his own blood, gun still in his hand. Shards of broken glass littered the floor.

Kaplan stepped toward him maintaining eye contact. The eyes were the best gauges of the man's intentions. If the last Italian thug were going to make a move, he'd see it in the man's eyes first. Kaplan kept his gun aimed at the man's head.

He stopped five feet from the Italian. "Release your weapon."

The man didn't move.

Kaplan pushed his gun forward as a threat. "Who do you work for?"

Nothing.

Kaplan stepped forward and pressed the toe of his boots against one of the man's chest wounds. "I asked you a question. You better answer or this will get a lot worse." He put more pressure against the gunshot wound.

The Italian grimaced, his expression full of pain. "All right." Then he muttered two words, "Four eyes."

Two words that held no meaning. "Wha—"

Kaplan saw the skin flutter around the Italian man's eyes and then his hand moved.

"Don't do it," Kaplan yelled.

The bleeding man raised his gun.

Kaplan squeezed the trigger. *Two in the chest, one in the head works 100% of the time.* His old Delta Force mantra.

Kaplan returned to the deputy to give him the all clear. The man was lying on his back, blood oozed from his neck and chest. He must have been shot when he threw the chair. The deputy's bloody belt badge lay on the floor next to him. Somehow it was knocked loose during the gunfight. Kaplan picked it up and stood over the man. He dropped to one knee and placed the badge in the deputy's hand, and closed the deputy's fist around it. There was nothing he could do for him now; the deputy was going to bleed out.

The dying man clutched Kaplan's arm. His grip was weak. "Be honest, Delta, how bad is it?"

"Not good, soldier." Kaplan grabbed the deputy's hand and placed it against his neck. "Hold pressure. We need to slow the bleeding."

"Just another shitty day in paradise, huh, Delta?"

Kaplan feigned a smile. "Same shit, different country." Kaplan looked at the hole in the deputy's chest. It couldn't have missed his heart by much and by the way it was bleeding, it must have hit a major vein. He grabbed a handful of napkins lying on the floor and pressed them against the chest wound. "What's the deal with the old man?"

"Listen, Delta," the deputy pleaded, "you have to get him out of here. It's not safe. I don't know how they found him, but they did." Blood oozed from the corner of his mouth as he spoke.

"Try not to speak. Save your strength." Kaplan sat down next to the deputy and cradled his head. "Only one explanation, his cover was blown because WitSec has a leak. I'll call the cops," said Kaplan. "They'll keep him safe until your deputies arrive. I can't stick around and babysit the old man."

"Please, I know these cops…they're good ole boys. This is out of their league. All they'll do is either get killed or get him killed…or both. I watched you. You know how to handle yourself, Delta. You might be passing through, but you're certainly no drifter. You can keep him alive. You can get him to a WitSec safe site."

"Look, I don't have time for this," Kaplan insisted. "If the locals can't do it then I'll call the fibbies." Kaplan referenced the FBI. "Hell, they're going to get called here anyway."

"No." The deputy coughed. Blood splattered on the dying man's face. "Don't trust anyone except WitSec." The deputy's eyes wandered.

"Hang in there, soldier," Kaplan said. "Suck it up. Be strong."

"Promise me you'll take care of him, Delta. I screwed the pooch. You have to deliver him to WitSec. And only WitSec… do it as a favor for a fellow Delta comrade. I don't want to be remembered as losing a witness. You have to fix this for me. Promise me, Delta. Promise." Kaplan thought it was ironic that a man who had sacrificed so much for his country might now have the memory of all that forgotten. The deputy was right about life being defined by the last chapter. It was an injustice he couldn't allow happen to a fallen Delta comrade.

"All right, all right. Where's the closest safe site?"

"Stay…off…the…grid." The deputy's speech faded and his hand fell away from his neck.

"Come on, soldier. Stay with me." Kaplan shook the man's shoulders.

The deputy's gaze locked on the ceiling above him. Then his head fell to one side.

Kaplan placed his fingers on the deputy's neck and checked for a pulse. Nothing.

Stay off the grid, the deputy said. Hell, that's what he had been trying to do.

In the distance Kaplan heard sirens. He walked over and grabbed the old man and pulled him to his feet. "Come on, we're getting out of here."

"I'm not going anywhere," the old man protested.

"That wasn't a request. Stay here, you die." Kaplan stuck the gun in the old man's face. "Now let's go."

On his way to the door, pulling the old man along, Kaplan stopped and took one last look at the dead deputy. A dead soldier who, like himself, had spent most of his life serving his country. Protecting his country. And those in it.

The approaching sirens grew louder. Kaplan herded the old man with a renewed urgency across the street to the parking lot where he'd parked his Harley.

Nightfall came early tonight aided by the dark clouds masking the sky, remnants of the late afternoon thunderstorms.

Kaplan's riding jacket was draped over the backpack attached to the sissy bar. He slipped it on and removed the half-helmet strapped to his backpack. "Here." He held out the helmet to Tropical Shirt. "Put this on."

"I'm not going anywhere with someone I don't know and I'm sure as hell not getting on that." He pointed at Kaplan's motorcycle. "You're probably one of those Hell's Angels, aren't you?"

"Again, stay here and die." Kaplan started his Harley, swung his leg over, sat down, and pointed his finger at the old man. "Those men trying to kill you were pros and pros tend to have backup. So you can get on and I'll keep you alive, or else you can stay here and take your chances. But with or without you, I'm leaving now."

The old man hesitated and then, with an expression of resignation, slipped the helmet over his head and climbed on the back of the Harley.

Kaplan turned the bike onto Rebsamen Park Road to make his getaway toward downtown. A block down the street, a dark colored sedan pulled into the middle of the road and accelerated toward him. An arm extended from the passenger window and in the hand was a gun.

The muzzle flashed as the car sped toward them. Kaplan leaned the bike to one side and twisted the throttle. The rear tire lost traction and spun wildly against the asphalt while Kaplan guided it through a hundred and eighty degree turn leaving a plume of black smoke. He righted the bike, regained traction, and accelerated in the opposite direction. His passenger tightened his grip around Kaplan's waist.

"I don't know who you are," Kaplan yelled, "but someone is going to a lot of trouble to see you dead."

"I know. I know." The old man's voice filled with panic. "Can this thing go any faster?"

"I thought you didn't like motorcycles."

"I like bullets even less."

"This happen often? Being shot at I mean." Kaplan asked.

"Too many times."

Kaplan gave another twist of the throttle. In his mirror, he saw the headlights initially fall behind then start to catch up. Speed for speed Kaplan figured his bike would hold its own, even with the extra weight on the back. At this speed though, if the old man shifted his weight at the wrong time, Kaplan could lose control and they would both end up eating asphalt.

He headed west on Rebsamen Park Road and within seconds was paralleling railroad tracks to his right. An apartment complex blurred by on the left as the road snaked a slight curve to the right. That was when the yellow railroad crossing sign suddenly appeared. Railroad crossings were always a crapshoot. Some were smooth and he could barely tell when he crossed them while others so rough he'd almost lost control of his bike. He gripped the handlebars and maneuvered the bike's angle so he took the crossing perpendicular to the tracks.

As soon as he cleared the tracks, an unmarked traffic circle immediately followed. Kaplan braked hard, almost locking his rear tire. He yelled to the old man, "Let me do the work, keep your body inline with mine."

As he entered the traffic circle, Kaplan applied pressure to the left grip causing the bike to lean hard left while keeping both knees snug against the tank for stability before propelling out the other side of the circle. His pursuers would have to slow even more. Their car couldn't take the traffic circle at the same speed Kaplan had and this should give him a chance to put extra distance between them.

"You can lighten up on that grip now, old man," Kaplan said to Tropical Shirt.

A grassy field opened up on the right, a void of darkness beyond. He recognized the smell of a freshly mowed golf course.

The road was basically straight with gentle curves, which allowed Kaplan to accelerate to even faster speeds. His sense of direction told him he was heading west. Or northwest. He couldn't really be sure. In the humid night air he could smell the river nearby, he just didn't know how far away it was. Or where this road might lead.

On the right he passed a sign that read *Rebsamen Park Golf Course*. Then it was back to the lonely stretch of tree-lined dark road. The glare in his side mirror made him nervous. The headlights were gaining on him. He glanced down at his speedometer—90 M.P.H.

After two minutes, at a mile and a half a minute, he detected an illumination in the distance. The trees on the right disappeared and the distant lights became visible as he saw their reflection off the river's surface. Racing toward the lights, he passed two entrances to a pedestrian/bicycle pathway on his left. The pathway paralleled the road he was on and then rose up and over the road before ultimately crossing the river.

He realized his mistake too late.

The road ahead was blocked. The lights he'd seen earlier turned out to be the streetlights on the pathway that crossed the river. But he had already passed both entrances to the pathway. The sign ahead read *The Big Dam*. And there was no road across it.

A dead end.

Tropical Shirt tapped him on the shoulder. "Now what?"

He slowed the bike to a stop and looked up at the overhead pathway that crossed above the dam. He saw people walking and jogging and bicycling. The sign called it the Arkansas River Trail. "Up there." He turned the Harley around and pointed up at the cyclists on the elevated pathway. "That's where we're going."

"Then we better hurry," the old man pointed back down Rebsamen Park Road at the oncoming car. "Because they're about to cut us off."

CHAPTER 4

KAPLAN TWISTED THE THROTTLE AND accelerated straight at the oncoming car.

"Are you insane?" Tropical Shirt yelled.

"Shut up and hang on."

Kaplan gauged the rate of closure. By the time the two head-on vehicles reached each other their closure speed could easily reach 100, perhaps 120 M.P.H. No chance for him to take the closest access onto the Arkansas River Trail at this speed. To do that, he'd have to slow down to make the ninety-degree turn and by then the oncoming car would be on top of him. In order to get onto the Arkansas River Trail, he'd have to play chicken with the car's driver and swerve into the parking lot to his left at the last minute. Then, while the car was turning around, he'd have time to take a different access onto the Trail.

He was betting the driver of the car would want to play chicken too. He was also betting the driver would *not* be the first to flinch.

"They'll kill us."

"No kidding. I think that was their plan all along." Kaplan held steady and straight, head on with the oncoming car. "Or would you rather I stop and try to reason with them?"

As the gap between the Harley and the car closed, Kaplan

felt Tropical Shirt bury his head in his back.

"Holy Mary, Mother of Jesus, save me," the old man muttered.

Kaplan counted down the dwindling space between the bike and the car. At the last possible second, he feinted the Harley to his right then turned back hard left.

The ploy worked, the driver swerved to his left allowing Kaplan's Harley to zip past on the car's right and into the parking lot.

Kaplan kept his speed through the parking lot, slowing at the last moment and only enough to navigate the ninety-degree turn to the Trail. As he left the parking lot to cross the road, he noticed the car had not turned around. Instead, it was heading backwards in reverse. No problem. Kaplan drove his Harley onto the Arkansas River Trail and accelerated along the concrete pathway.

The car, now only forty feet below and to his right on the road parallel to the trail, screeched to a stop. The man from the passenger seat pulled himself half out of his window, sitting, feet inside, head and arms outside, butt on the door. He started firing.

The first two rounds missed.

Kaplan accelerated. He crossed a wooden bridge, which turned back to the concrete pathway. The driver put the car in forward and matched the Harley's speed. Still on Kaplan's right and still down on the street below. The third round from the man's gun struck the back of the Harley. He felt the thud reverberate through the bike's chassis.

"That was close," Tropical Shirt yelled.

Kaplan looked ahead. Two black and yellow striped posts blocked the ramp to four-wheeled vehicles. The sign stated in bold letters, *No Motor Vehicles Allowed*. He was about to make an exception to that ordinance. Beyond the posts, lights lined the ramp like a miniature runway leading across the skyline. In the distance, the lights lining the bridge curved to the right and went across the Arkansas River.

The gunman's fourth round struck the chrome on the right side of the Harley's front fork. A spark. A thud. A vibration. Kaplan centered the Harley between the posts and accelerated up the ramp.

The street, and most importantly the car, disappeared beneath the Trail's overpass as the Harley climbed higher above the ground.

By Kaplan's estimation, the above ground span of the Big Dam Bridge was the better part of a mile in length, at least four thousand feet or more. It looked to be eighty to ninety feet above the river, higher on one side of the dam than the other. The water wasn't visible in the darkness, just a black void beneath the bridge with the occasional reflection from the dam's lights.

There were several pedestrians and joggers on the bridge, all of whom jumped to the side as the motorcycle roared toward them. Kaplan scattered more than one group who were startled by the sound of his horn and the roar of the Harley's engine. The cyclists he had seen earlier must have seen him coming and had already pulled their bicycles to one side of the bridge. He knew from their sign language they were yelling obscenities at him. Those with cell phones had probably already called 9-1-1.

Just past the midway point, the bridge curved right, and then curved right again as it descended to ground level on the opposite riverbank. The Arkansas River Trail continued along the north side of the river too, paved, heading east with just enough curves to allow Kaplan to maintain a safe speed between thirty and forty. In a way, he was glad to slow down.

He was also glad no one was shooting at them.

For the moment.

He kept riding for several minutes on the Trail, past more annoyed joggers, walkers, and bicyclists, past another golf course until the cluster of lights in front of him became bright enough that Kaplan knew he was getting closer to the city's congestion.

From the lights across the river illuminating the night's sky, Kaplan saw a horseshoe like rock formation to his left. He slowed and looked for a road or path leading up the hill, which he found seconds later. Pavement turned to gravel and, after a series of s-turns, opened into a large space Kaplan figured must be used for parking.

Tall rocky cliffs encompassed roughly two-thirds of the area, which wrapped around them like a box canyon. With the shadows cast from the city lights across the river, the horseshoe cliffs looked like an old quarry from years past now turned into some kind of hiking or climbing area.

He pulled his Harley to one side and brought it to a stop. He killed the engine and extended the kickstand with his left boot heel.

This was as good a place as any to stop and have a heart-to-heart with Tropical Shirt.

CHAPTER 5

"WHY ARE WE STOPPING HERE?"

"Get off." Kaplan said.

"I beg your pardon."

"I said get off my bike."

"You're leaving me here?"

Kaplan shook his head. "No. I can't get off until you do."

"Oh." The old man slipped off the left side of the bike. "Yes, of course."

Kaplan pulled his keys from the ignition and unlocked his seat. He lifted it up, removed a sack from underneath, and then locked the seat back in place.

"What's that?" Tropical Shirt said as he removed his helmet and placed it on the sissy bar.

Kaplan reached into the sack and pulled out his Beretta Px4. "My guardian." It was a beefy handgun, not one for shooters with small hands or weak grips. He slipped it in a specially tailored pocket on the inside of his jacket. He grabbed two full magazines from the bag and stuffed each into pouches sewn into the jacket lining. He reached back into the leather bag and pulled out a smaller pistol, pulled up his pant leg and slipped it into another tailored pouch on his boot.

"You are a regular rolling arsenal."

"I believe in being prepared." The scene from the restaurant flashed through Kaplan's mind. "Which I wasn't back at the restaurant." He looked at the gray-haired man, "Now, what the hell happened back there?"

"I can't tell you. It's privileged information."

Kaplan stepped forward, grabbed the man's shirt, and pulled him close. With the light from the city, Kaplan could detect a trace of fear in the old man's eyes. "Privileged, my ass. I just saved your life. There are four dead men back at the restaurant, three bad guys and one good guy. There were at least three customers laying on the floor bleeding. No telling if they are dead or alive. And all of this is because of you. I know you're in the Witness Security program, which means you're more than likely a criminal who has testified or is about to testify in a federal trial. The three bad guys back at the restaurant sure looked an awful lot like mob guys to me. And it won't be long before the men in that car come looking for us on this side of the river."

Kaplan tightened his grip on the old man's shirt and lifted him to his toes. "No more jerking me around, old man. Start talking or so help me God—"

"Okay, okay."

Kaplan relaxed his grip and let go of the old man's shirt.

"To start with, it is not *old man*, it is Tony. Tony Napoli."

"New identity?"

"Of course. Fully backstopped by the U. S. Marshals Service. And, yes, I am supposed to testify but the trial is not for another two months. I have spent the last month bouncing from hotel to hotel, city to city, never the same place more than three or four days at a time. Much to my dismay, Little Rock was supposed to be my permanent relocation area. I just got here today. I was supposed to go house hunting with a realtor tomorrow."

"Was the deputy your case handler?"

"Yes," Tony said. "Inspector Mike Cox. He picked me up in Memphis this morning and drove me here. We spent all afternoon locked in a crappy hotel room signing paperwork, receiving, and reviewing my new identity documentation. When we were finished he gave me some cash and, because it was so late and we never had lunch, we decided to go out and grab a bite to eat."

"And yet somehow, on your very first day in a Marshals Service assigned relocation area, your cover gets blown? Doesn't that seem odd to you? Like someone stacked the deck?" Kaplan paused for effect. "And not in your favor."

"It does lend that appearance." Tony held out his hand. "You have a name?"

"Kaplan."

"First or last?"

"Doesn't matter." He pushed Tony's hand aside and looked down the hill from the direction they came and saw two small headlights glowing in the dark. Then he heard the hum of a small engine. "We got company, stay behind me."

As the four-wheeler approached, Kaplan decided against pulling his weapon just in case it was some sort of security patrol.

It wasn't.

The ATV stopped ten feet in front of him. The glow from the headlights revealed a camouflage paint scheme.

A strong Southern drawl shouted from behind the headlights. "Looky here, Bobby, we got ourselves some city slickers."

"Whoever they are, Glenn," a second voice said, "They ain't up to no good being here after dark."

"What da hell you boys doing out here anyway?" The voice was Glenn's.

"Minding our own business," Kaplan replied. "Now why don't you mind yours and leave."

"Maybe you are my business, boy. Maybe it's my business to keep city slickers like you out of our park."

"Know what I think?" Kaplan said. "I think you two are a couple of Arkansas peckerheads with nothing better to do on a Friday night than hang out here with each other." He heard Tony blowing his breath in disbelief at his words. "Maybe you two were coming up here to get drunk or smoke some weed. I don't really care. But, I do think it's in your best interest to get the hell out of here before you both get hurt."

"Did he just call us peckerwoods?"

"Sure did. We'll see who gets hurt, city boy. It's time someone taught you some manners."

"And I suppose that someone is you?"

"You blind *and* dumb. Damn straight, I'm 'bout to kick your ass."

Kaplan waited for the two men to appear in front of the headlights. And then he knew what he was up against, two knuckleheads looking for trouble.

Looks like they found it.

Glenn and Bobby looked like they stepped right out of the movie *Deliverance*. Bobby smiled. Most of his teeth were missing. That was the only thing scary about him. He wasn't tall and was skinny as a rail. He wore a camo shirt and jeans hung too low below his waist.

Glenn, the driver, was closer to Kaplan's height of six-one. That was where the similarity ended. He had a good hundred pounds on Kaplan, most of it in his gut. He had the Confederate flag tattooed on one arm and a swastika on the other. He wore camo pants held up by orange suspenders with a dirty white wife-beater underneath. His camo ball cap held back his long stringy hair and his face was covered in a shaggy red beard. His size would intimidate most people, but Kaplan wasn't most people. He knew Glenn would be slow and easy to handle, then Bobby would be free to do what he did best—run.

Despite the two men standing in front of him, Kaplan was more concerned with what he had just noticed in the distance.

"You don't want to do this," said Kaplan, keeping his eye on the horizon.

"Scared I'm fixin to whoop your ass?"

"You like hospital food?" said Kaplan.

"Why is that, asshole?" Glenn smacked his right fist into his left palm.

"Because that's all you're going to be eating for the next few days."

"Bobby, you keep an eye on the grandpa whilst I put a hurtin' on this wiseass."

Bobby moved first, which was the wrong thing for both of them.

As Bobby stepped toward Tony, Kaplan hooked his arm around Bobby's neck and used him as a weapon to knock Glenn back against the four-wheeler. He released his hold on Bobby, who was already in a slight daze from the headlock, spun around, and landed his elbow against Bobby's head. Consciousness left the man before he hit the gravel.

He should have run.

Now it came down to a matter of momentum. Momentum could hurdle one racecar past another on the track or turn a certain loss into a victory on the gridiron. In a fight, it could be an ally or an enemy. If you knew what you were doing, you could use it to your advantage. Glenn didn't look like he knew much about momentum.

Glenn pushed himself to his feet and charged at Kaplan head on. Kaplan sidestepped, slammed his elbow into the back of the man's neck, and followed up with a kick to the man's kidney. Glenn's momentum carried him past Kaplan and onto his hands and knees. Kaplan stepped forward and smashed a roundhouse kick to the man's jaw. The big man fell face first into the gravel. Next to him were two of his teeth.

"You two need to crawl back in the hole you came from." Kaplan muttered.

Kaplan glanced up at the sky and turned around. "Come on, Tony, we need to—"

Tony was gone.

CHAPTER 6

SENIOR INSPECTOR PETE MOSS JUST SHOT THE perpetrator.

It all started when the white male suspect walked out of the bank manager's office holding a hostage in front of him, his arm wrapped around the woman's throat, gun to her neck. The only part of the perp not shielded by the hostage was his head.

"Drop the gun. Drop the gun," Moss yelled.

The man moved his gun and pointed it toward Moss.

Moss was holding his Glock and reacted the way he'd been trained when a witness's life was threatened—with deadly force. Moss slowed his breathing and concentrated on the shot; nervousness under pressure would only get the hostage killed—and maybe him as well. He gently squeezed off a round striking the man in the neck. The man dropped his gun and tumbled to the ground. The hostage fled. He fired two more shots into the fallen man's chest. Then, for some reason, an extra shot to the man's crotch.

He couldn't help it.

The perp was wanted for murder, was considered armed and dangerous, and was a convicted sexual predator—so the crotch shot seemed a fitting act of revenge for one of the most heinous crimes.

That's when his instructor started yelling.

The *VRLE-30* firearms training simulator at *VRTraC* in Chicago—short for Virtual Reality Training Center, pronounced *virtrac*—was so realistic, so intense, Moss was caught up in the moment. The virtual reality training simulator had five screens and a 300-degree, fully immersive training platform, which tested the gamut of real-world skills. Initially, Moss thought it would be worthless training but was surprised at how quickly he forgot it was only a simulation.

"Excessive force, Moss."

"What do you think rape is?" Moss yelled back at the instructor. "Besides he was already dead."

"You could have lost your star on that one."

His instructor apparently was not amused and started quoting procedure and regulation.

Moss had been with the U. S. Marshals Service for almost twenty years and outranked his instructor. The guy was still wet behind the ears and had already earned a reputation for puffing his chest, strutting around like a peacock, and scolding senior deputies. The little jerk got off on his power trip. Moss let him get away with it, this time.

In Moss's opinion, the kind of sleaze bag in this scenario didn't deserve procedure, besides this was only training, not real life. He had grown tired of the government bullshit and just plain weary. He'd worked too many night shifts in his Marshals Service career. It seemed on every assignment, he drew the night shift. Even though this was training, working the evening shift sucked. And why couldn't the training be assigned during the day? He'd rather be at home, drinking a beer, and watching the Cubs on his brand new 60-inch HD television. Best seat in the stadium, with his own private restroom and kitchen.

Instant replays. No post-game traffic jams.

He was raised by a strict single mother on Chicago's Southside and, despite the odds, he was a Cubs fan. In fact, he couldn't remember a time when he wasn't a Cubs fan. Even his favorite president—Ronald Reagan, another unlikely choice given his background—had been an announcer for the Cubs, which was probably the main reason he was Moss's favorite. It didn't matter that the Cubs hadn't won a World Series since 1908. Despite their miserable season or the fact that, once again, they were ranked dead last in their division, the Cubs were *his* team.

"Are you ignoring me?"

Moss realized the instructor was still droning on about regulation. He shook his head. "No, please, dazzle me with some more of your brilliance."

The flush-faced man put his hands on his hips and stared at him.

Moss had been given this *refresher training* detail just two weeks after relocating to the Chicago field office from a seven-year WitSec stint at the Little Rock office. His selection to the Enforcement Division at the Chicago office was his chance to finally move back home and hopefully work fewer nights. He'd always heard his fellow deputies say *nights and weekends is where the action is*…and they could have them both.

Moss was a big man, four inches over six feet, and hadn't seen the scales under two seventy-five in ten years. In his mind he wasn't overweight even though the doctor said he could stand to lose fifty pounds. He was still solid as a rock. A left tackle in college, Moss never gave up his workout regimen. It was how he dealt with stress. That, and alcohol. Both kept his mild-mannered, matter-of-fact demeanor on an even keel. He only drank off-duty and never mixed the two, work and alcohol. It had helped him through two failed marriages and the tragic death of his mother several years ago when a busload of senior citizens on their way to a gambling casino in Mississippi crashed on the interstate. The bus driver fell asleep at the wheel, ran off the road and down an embankment killing exactly half of the forty-two passengers on board.

As a black man, it also helped him deal with the government's failed discrimination policies. Especially in his early years when there was a tremendous lack of diversity in the Marshals Service. Back then it was a white man's agency. He worked and fought hard to move up the ranks. On his own terms, by merit and skill, not the color of his skin.

Then he was assigned to the Little Rock field office. It was a step back in time. Like being thrown through a time warp into the racial-tension filled fifties and sixties. It seemed as if all his hard work had been for naught.

Until he was selected for the Chicago Enforcement position.

The overhead speaker interrupted his instructor's tirade. "Deputy Moss, you are requested to call in immediately."

Moss glanced at his watch. *What now? I've already missed an hour and a half of the game.* He looked at the young, arrogant instructor, turned, and walked off the simulator platform without saying another word.

He reached into the side pocket of his black cargo pants, pulled out his cell phone, and dialed the number. "Pete Moss."

He heard the man on the other end of the line snicker.

"Yeah, yeah. I've heard all the peat moss jokes. Calling in as requested."

The voice on the line cleared his throat. "Senior Inspector Moss, there has been an incident in Little Rock."

His heart skipped a beat. Both of his ex-wives still lived in Little Rock, not that he cared, he didn't, but he couldn't think of any WitSec business in Little Rock that he hadn't handed over to his replacement during the transition. Certainly nothing that would warrant an after-hours phone call.

"What kind of incident?"

"Are you familiar with WC 7922?"

"A little. Cox is assigned that case."

"Inspector Cox is dead, the witness has been breached, is now missing, and about forty eight hours from being considered a fugitive from justice."

"Cox? Dead? Mike Cox?" Moss was in disbelief.

"Senior Inspector Moss, this is official notification that you have been temporarily reassigned back to the Little Rock office."

CHAPTER 7

HE THOUGHT ABOUT LEAVING TONY ALONE IN the quarry. This wasn't Kaplan's fight, but he'd promised the Deputy U. S. Marshal he would keep Tony alive until he could deliver him to a WitSec safe site.

Alive.

No guarantees beyond that.

And he would deliver. A promise made was a promise kept.

Thirty yards away he could see Tony's khaki slacks and silver hair against the dark quarry walls. The idiot was trying to climb the nearly sheer face of the cliff. In loafers, no less. What the hell was he thinking? The man must be pushing seventy. He glanced back over his shoulder and calculated how much time he had left until the real threat arrived.

He would be cutting it close.

Kaplan ran the distance to the quarry wall. The old man had climbed about twelve feet up the cliff wall. Just out of Kaplan's jumping distance.

"Get down."

"No. You are going to get us both killed."

"What? By morons like those two? Not likely. Besides, they were nothing more than a couple of bullies acting tough and looking for somebody to push around. They were harmless.

Now get down."

"No." The old man kept climbing. "You go your way, I'll go mine."

"Last chance."

"Go away."

Kaplan took several steps back and calculated his next move. Tony was fifteen feet above the base of the cliff.

"Look, I don't want to hurt you, so get back down here."

"What are you going to do, shoot me?" Tony climbed another three feet up the cliff wall.

"Don't say I didn't give you fair warning." Kaplan reached down, picked up a fist-sized rock, and hurled it at Tony, striking him in the head. The old man hung motionless on the wall for a few seconds then fell toward the ground and landed on top of Kaplan.

It was a solid impact and knocked him to the ground. He rolled Tony off him, glanced at the sky, and jumped to his feet. He grabbed Tony's shirt by the collar and hauled him to his feet.

"Anything broken?" he asked.

Tony leaned over, cupped one hand over a knee and rubbed his head with the other. "Son of a bitch. You could have killed me."

"We need to leave," Kaplan commanded. "Now."

"I need a minute." Tony gasped for air. "To catch my breath."

"A minute from now we'll be dead."

"Wha—?

Kaplan pulled Tony upright and pointed at the rapidly approaching helicopter. Its searchlight scanned the riverbank but its trajectory was directly toward the quarry.

"Look." Kaplan pulled him toward the Harley. "This is a horseshoe canyon, if they get here first, they cut off our escape route. I promised Deputy Cox I'd keep you alive and deliver you to a WitSec safe site. I didn't promise what shape you'd be in when you arrived, now let's move it."

The spotlight beam moved up the hill and stopped on the redneck's four-wheeler. It scanned across their unconscious bodies where it seemed to pause, momentarily evaluating what they saw. Tony moved toward Kaplan's Harley with renewed urgency.

Kaplan jumped on the bike and started the engine with a roar. Tony was two seconds behind him. The spotlight found the Harley. Kaplan shifted it in gear and twisted the throttle, spraying loose gravel and dust as he accelerated toward the exit pathway.

Gunfire erupted from the copter. The ground around them was peppered with bullets. The pilot maneuvered the copter to cut off the bike's escape.

"Can you use a gun?" Kaplan yelled over the thumping noise of the copter blades.

"Of course."

Kaplan reached into his jacket and pulled out his weapon. He handed it to Tony butt first. "Aim for the spotlight."

The rotorcraft dipped as if trying to cut off their escape by using its blades to herd them back into the quarry. "What are you waiting for?" Kaplan yelled. "Shoot."

No telling where the first two rounds went, somewhere across the river no doubt. The third round hit something. Kaplan saw a spark fly from the copter and it pulled up leaving Kaplan a clear path down the gravel roadway.

He was a third of the way down when the gravel pathway

made a slight bend to the right, directly toward the hovering rotorcraft, which had backed out over the river. More gunfire strafed the ground around them. The spotlight followed his every turn, its blinding beam hampering his vision down the hillside.

Tony fired again and the copter's spotlight exploded in a fiery blaze. The hillside went dark except for the Harley's headlight. As the roadway curved to the left, gunfire erupted around them again.

Tony fired two more rounds and the gunfire went silent. The copter rotated right and then banked left and started losing altitude. It angled toward the hillside, threatening to cut off their escape.

Over the thumping sound of the blades slicing through the humid air, Kaplan heard a strange noise coming from the copter as it plummeted toward them. It sputtered and whined and made a sound like metal grinding metal.

The rotorcraft began to lose its tug-of-war with gravity. He needed to get off the hillside before the copter came down on top of them.

And he was certain it was coming down.

He flipped on his high beams. The gravel roadway ahead appeared straight and would soon transition to asphalt.

Kaplan twisted the throttle to the stop and gambled the road ahead was clear and straight. He was certain Tony was about to go into cardiac arrest as the Harley rocketed down the hillside road.

But, it worked.

Barely.

The explosion behind them created a plume of fire that roiled skyward into a glowing red mushroom cloud along the north bank of the Arkansas River. The concussion wave jolted the Harley and Kaplan eased off the throttle slowing the bike to a stop. Tiny metal fragments from the disintegrated rotorcraft rained down on them and blanketed the hillside behind them with flaming debris.

"That was close," Tony said.

"Too close," he said as he turned around and held out his hand. "Now give me my gun back."

Kaplan felt Tony jab the barrel into his ribs.

"Not yet," Tony said. "I'm setting some new ground rules."

Without hesitation and in one smooth motion, Kaplan grasped the barrel of his pistol with his right hand and smashed his left elbow into Tony's face knocking the old man off the bike and onto the ground.

He pushed down the kickstand, dismounted, and walked around the back of his bike. He looked down at Tony and said, "I'm getting tired of your foolishness." He ejected the magazine from his gun, put in a fresh one, and slipped it back in his jacket.

Tony was holding his nose, blood oozed through his fingers. "I think you broke it."

"Nope. Didn't hit you hard enough. Broke a few capillaries is all. Next time you won't be so lucky."

"What do we do now, smart guy?"

Kaplan dug around in his back pocket and pulled out a folded bandana. He threw it down at Tony. "Hold that against your nose," Kaplan pulled his cell phone from his jacket pocket, "while I make a phone call."

CHAPTER 8

IT WAS LIKE BEING HIT IN THE GUT WITH A
baseball bat.

"Are you kidding me?" Moss's even keeled demeanor
evaporated. "I just got to Chicago and now I'm being sent back
to Little Rock? Isn't there another inspector who can take this
case? Like, in Memphis. Or anywhere closer than Chicago."

There was an uncomfortable, long silence before the voice
spoke.

"Sir, the order came from HQ. I'm required to read it to you.
Due to Senior Inspector Peter Moss's familiarity with the Little Rock,
Arkansas area and the inner workings of the staff and functionality of
the Little Rock Office along with his many years of exemplary service
to the United States Marshals Service, Senior Inspector Moss has been
temporarily reassigned to Witness Security, assigned WC 7922, and is
hereby instructed to report to Little Rock immediately. The recovery of
this witness is considered a Marshals Service top priority. It is signed by
the Director. Do you understand these orders?"

He didn't seem to have a choice. The order came from DC.
He was still a few months from retirement eligibility with full
pension benefits. What was another two or three weeks back in
Little Rock going to hurt anyway?

"Senior Inspector Moss?" The man repeated. "Do you

understand these orders?"

"Yes, of course I understand the orders," mocked Moss. "What happened?"

"Take down, sir. A restaurant in Little Rock."

"Which one?"

The man on the line told him.

"Know it well. Any civilian casualties?"

"Five, sir. One dead, four injured, two critical."

"Responders?"

Moss could hear paper shuffling. "Little Rock PD, Arkansas State Police, FBI, and us."

"Who called the FBI?" Moss asked.

"Little Rock PD. They already have a man on the scene."

"Could this get any worse?"

The voice hesitated. "It is worse."

"Explain."

"According to eyewitnesses, *our* witness was last seen on the back of a motorcycle fleeing the scene—"

"And?"

"And a dark sedan was making chase, and shooting at them."

"Description? Plates?"

"According to LRPD, witnesses stated the vehicle appeared to be a late model Crown Vic. No one got the plates."

"What about the motorcycle?"

"Witness at the scene stated it was a dark color and rumbled like a Hog."

"A Hog?"

"A Harley Davidson, sir."

"I know what a Hog is," snapped Moss. "That narrows it down to half the motorcycles in the country. Anything else?"

"Yes, sir. Little Rock PD received several complaints of a

motorcycle fitting the same description on a pedestrian and bicycle pathway known as the Arkansas River Trail. And just now on the wire is a report to North Little Rock PD of an explosion along the north bank of the Arkansas River. The caller said an airplane crashed, but that has yet to be confirmed. Units are responding at this time. You think it's connected, sir?"

"Obviously the motorcycle went where the Crown Vic couldn't. Smart move." Moss thought about the witness. "And you can bet the explosion had something to do with…" Moss paused, "the witness. He's no doubt responsible for this. Who's working with me?"

"I'll have someone meet you at the airport in three hours.

"I want Deputy Jon Hepler."

"Sir, he's not WitSec."

"I don't give a damn. He might be a P.O.D. but I've known and worked with him for years." He made reference to *plain old deputy*. Not a derogatory term, since they were all officially considered Deputy U. S. Marshals; it was just an internal way of distinguishing between WitSec and non-WitSec deputies. "He's a good friend and I trust him with my life."

"But, sir—"

"No buts," Moss interrupted. "Call whoever the hell you have to, just have Hepler read in on this case by the time I get to Little Rock." Moss hung up before the man could respond.

† † †

The assassin was known only as Valkyrie.

Like the Norse mythological valkyries, the assassin sent those chosen to die on a one-way trip to the afterlife.

Others in the same line of business called themselves assets, but the term seemed so tired and overused, even though the job was the same. Valkyrie solved problems in a permanent way and preferred to call it by what it was—Valkyrie was an assassin.

And contract killing was a lucrative business.

One that had been around for ages.

There was always someone willing to pay to have another killed, thus there was never a shortage of hired killers. Most assassins took on more than one contract at a time. Valkyrie was different. A single contract, million-dollar minimum. Paid in advance. It weeded out window shoppers. Only the elite inside the world's inner circles had even heard of Valkyrie's existence and most of them thought the assassin was a rumor or urban legend of sorts. Business only came to Valkyrie through these inner circles, for it was only these elite that had the means to find and hire the best. Valkyrie used a form of subterfuge for assassinations—never be seen by the client... rarely by the victim.

This latest contract was triple the minimum, three million dollars, half already deposited in an offshore account.

Urgency and complexity determined the cost of each contract, and this contract was both urgent to the client and complex for Valkyrie.

Valkyrie's new client went by the code name Shepherd. The killer knew nothing about the man except that the name sounded like it came from the Cold War era. The assassin didn't care, it was all about money and Shepherd was paying well. To Valkyrie's surprise, Shepherd accepted the terms quickly. Clients normally tried to negotiate a lower fee. Three million was a lot of money, even for Valkyrie. The willingness of the client to pay such a high price caused Valkyrie to wonder if more money should have been put on the table.

Once a deal was struck the process was simple, Valkyrie made arrangements to receive an electronic briefing package via an anonymous email over a secured VPN. The virtual private network was more expensive than most but worth the extra money ten-fold. It routed through six thousand encrypted servers before landing in Valkyrie's inbox. The only thing Shepherd had to do was log on to a secure server with the username and password from the email and upload the file. It was as simple as that. After Valkyrie received the file, the URL for the website was removed and all traces vanished in virtual thin air.

Impervious from intercept.

Untraceable from either end.

Valkyrie sat in a leather recliner, laptop in place, and with the stroke of a few keys and a click on the trackpad, the file opened on the screen. Extensive and complete, no detail of the target's life had been omitted. Age, weight, height, aliases, passports, driver's licenses, friends, relatives, every location he'd ever lived, every job he'd ever had, past lovers—it was all there. Valkyrie was looking at the man's entire life under a microscope. There was nothing, it seemed, Shepherd didn't know about the target except one thing.

The most important thing.

His current whereabouts.

Valkyrie scoured the file learning as much as possible about the man. It would take several hours to digest this much information. Time Valkyrie didn't have. A person's past provided a wealth of information to the discerning eye. And Valkyrie could discern what others could not, more quickly than most. A gift that elevated the assassin to a level of prominence in a dog-eat-dog business.

The target presented a unique challenge for the assassin. He had traveled extensively over the past few years, most of it under an assumed identity. Valkyrie understood why. If the man wanted to stay alive, his true identity had to remain disguised. Which made Valkyrie's job more difficult. The assassin could see by the file the target had many enemies and most wanted him dead. He had survived several prior attempts on his life. This time he would not be so lucky.

The target was last seen in Little Rock, Arkansas not much more than an hour ago, which meant the trail was already growing cold. Valkyrie was an hour away by private jet plus thirty minutes to get to the airport plus another fifteen minutes to pick up a rental car. Essentially three hours behind the target. An almost insurmountable gap unless the target made a mistake which, based on his file, was unlikely to happen.

Valkyrie closed the laptop and slipped it inside a backpack. *Plenty of time to read more about the target on the flight.* Valkyrie placed a call to the airport, grabbed a go bag, and left the luxurious Denver flat for the Centennial Airport where the chartered Hawker 400 XP would be fueled and ready to go.

CHAPTER 9

KAPLAN ENDED THE CALL AND MOUNTED HIS
Harley. The raging fire on the hillside behind him had ignited a
brush fire. The breeze pushed it up and around the inside of
the horseshoe shaped quarry to the point where it would soon
threaten the grove of tall pine trees at the top of the cliffs.

First responders were on their way and within a short
time the area would be swarming with firefighters, police, and
emergency personnel searching for possible survivors.

"Tony," Kaplan shouted. In the distance he heard sirens.
The direction seemed to be just beyond the quarry. "We need to
leave now or we're as good as dead. It will take thirty minutes to
get where we need to go and we're not exactly inconspicuous."

Tony stood and slipped onto the rear saddle. Kaplan shifted
the bike into gear and sped off down the Arkansas River
Trail. He knew what was west of him on the Trail; he didn't
dare return the way he came. The directions he just received
indicated the Interstate was not very far north of the river. He
just needed to get there without the authorities spotting him.

He needed a place to hole up and hide while he sorted things
out. Like how to keep Tony alive until he delivered him to a
WitSec safe site. It seemed the promise he made to the dying
deputy was getting more and more difficult to keep. Several

people wanted the old man dead and didn't care if Kaplan was collateral damage.

He took the first road he came to and exited the Arkansas River Trail, which took him through the perimeter of a North Little Rock neighborhood. The road made a series of turns before it merged onto Fort Roots Drive. In the distance, a car rounded a curve with its blue lights flashing. To his left, above him on a hillside, were two sets of red flashing lights navigating through a series of switchbacks as they descended the hill toward the crash site.

Blue lights meant cops.

Not good.

Red lights meant emergency response vehicles like fire trucks and rescue units. Not good, but better.

Kaplan made a hard left and turned up Fort Roots Drive as he opted for the red lights. Rock walls lined both sides of the road as it ascended the steep grade. He accelerated toward the first switchback and passed a fire truck with its siren wailing. Forget pulling to the curb and yielding the right of way, he didn't have time. He needed to get as far away from the crash site as he could in as little time as possible. In the first switchback, he swerved to avoid a rescue unit that had cut the turn short and taken some of his lane.

After clearing the curve, Kaplan twisted the throttle and accelerated up the winding road again. The old man's grip tightened on his waist. Ahead he saw another set of flashing red lights rounding a switchback and head in his direction. Another rescue unit, judging by its size.

He glanced back down the hillside and saw a string of vehicles with blue lights racing toward the Arkansas River Trail and the wreckage of the helicopter.

All but one.

A single set of blue lights had turned onto Fort Roots Drive, apparently in pursuit of him. It was imperative he keep distance between the cop car and the Harley.

Fort Roots Drive snaked back and forth through several switchbacks until it reached the hilltop where it opened up onto a huge complex. He should have put two and two together earlier, however in all the excitement, he didn't. Until now. The complex buildings were unmistakably of U. S. Government origin. By the look of the structures—military. And that made sense. Fort Roots Drive. Fort Roots.

He passed through an abandoned security checkpoint, the kind with a horizontal retractable metal gate. Another fire truck thundered past him toward the exit. The guardhouse was empty, in fact, there was not a guard in sight anywhere. He wondered if the post was manned anymore or if the guards had left the gate open and scrambled in response to the explosion on the other side of the complex. He had no intention of sticking around long enough to find out.

He made a right turn at a red brick building positioned so close to the road it was almost in it. The road curved to the right in a long sweeping arc with traditional bland government buildings to his left side while a grassy meadow opened to the right. Even though he'd never been here before, it looked typically familiar. Most military installations had the same general look and feel about them. Architects and engineers did not need creativity to satisfy the government's regulations and requirements.

The road swept left then back to the right and that's when a mammoth-sized building appeared on the left. He realized what it was at the same time he saw the lighted sign, Eugene

Towbin Veterans Affairs Hospital.

He must have entered the hospital grounds through a rear entrance, which meant the main entrance was still in front of him. He hoped there wasn't another guard post. He might not be so lucky the second time.

He accelerated straight ahead and the complex changed appearance from a governmental architectural style to a private sector look. Commercial really. No guard post in sight.

In his mirror, flashing blue lights appeared in the distance. Now was not the time to get complacent and run the risk of getting caught. He blasted through two red lights and past a strip mall on his right. He didn't know where he was going just a general sense of which direction the interstate should be based on the instructions he received on the phone. The blue lights disappeared from his side mirrors. Ahead, traffic was heavier.

He couldn't run the third traffic signal because the intersection was too congested. However, he saw a sign directing him toward the interstate. He needed to turn left, which meant he had to wait for the turn signal. And that meant time sitting still in traffic. Time that would allow the police car to catch up to him.

He pulled into the left turn lane behind a Ford F-250 pulling a horse trailer. Cars were darting through the intersection from his right and his left on the crossing road. The street sign said MacArthur Drive. He counted the seconds, hoping he'd see the light turn green. Two cars pulled in behind him, a Toyota Camry and a Chevy Malibu, which was a bit of a relief because blue lights had already appeared behind him and were closing the gap.

The green turn arrow appeared about the time the North

Little Rock Police cruiser was still two hundred yards from the intersection. It stayed in the far right lane. Cars pulled clear of the lane to give the police car passage and, for a brief moment, Kaplan thought it might not be in pursuit of him.

He followed close behind the horse trailer and as far to the left as possible in attempt to use the Camry and Malibu as a screen from the patrol car. The police cruiser entered the intersection then stopped, blasted its siren, and turned hard left.

Now he knew he was a person of interest. What he didn't know was why. On second thought, he knew why and where to find the answer.

It was sitting right behind him.

CHAPTER 10

THE DEAD DEPUTY'S WORDS ROLLED AROUND in Kaplan's head.

You have to get him to a safe site.

Promise me you'll deliver him to WitSec.

Witness Security.

Of course this was all about Tony. Kaplan made a promise to his fellow Army Delta Force brother and U. S. Marshals Service deputy to keep Tony safe and he wasn't doing a good job of keeping it. What was it the man said?

I know all these cops…they're good ole boys. All they'll do is get him killed.

In the meantime, it looked like they might get Kaplan killed too. Unless he could lose them and lose them now.

"Hold on," Kaplan yelled back to Tony.

Tony's grip tightened.

Kaplan twisted the throttle and accelerated around the F-250 towing the horse trailer. Both oncoming lanes had traffic. He kept the Harley close to the trailer and Ford truck as he passed leaving only inches to spare. Oncoming cars swerved and honked.

The first car swerved to avoid Kaplan's motorcycle and sideswiped the car next to it. Then the driver overreacted and swerved back, crashing into the back of the Camry that was previously behind Kaplan. He glanced in his mirror and saw traffic in both directions grind to a halt leaving the patrol car stuck with nowhere to go.

He was momentarily free and clear, although he knew that wouldn't last long.

Police had radios. Kaplan knew two things about those radios.

First, they were buzzing with chatter.

Second, he was probably the topic of discussion.

Within thirty seconds Kaplan found what he was searching for. The interstate. He entered the left turn lane to the on-ramp and glanced a final time in his mirror for any signs of the police cruiser.

Nothing.

Kaplan breathed a sigh of relief for the first time since this ordeal started. He might stand a chance of getting the old man to safety after all.

He went under the overpass, turned left onto the on-ramp, accelerated, and merged with traffic. In order to blend in, he paced the Harley with the fastest traveling vehicles. He found three cars traveling west on Interstate 40 keeping their highway speeds between eighty and eighty-five. That worked for him. Now he just needed the next twenty minutes to be uneventful, which, based on the night's events thus far, was unlikely.

Keeping Tony out of sight was not an easy assignment. Especially on a motorcycle with the man clinging to his waist wearing a tropical print shirt. His Harley was not quiet and drew glances from almost every motorist he passed. He needed to ditch his bike and pick up a nondescript automobile and he had to do it quickly before the authorities widened their search area and search parameters. Authorities would eventually figure out his need to change vehicles if he was to stay off their radar. The longer it took him to do it, the odds increased he would get snared in their dragnet.

He had to get in front of this one and formulate a plan. Staying ahead of the authorities would be more difficult without the resources he'd become accustomed to having available on demand. This time he was on his own. No one had his back.

At least, not yet anyway.

Tony had apparently given up on trying to talk over the roar of the motorcycle engine. Or maybe he was formulating his own plan. At any rate, he couldn't be trusted.

Traffic was still heavy on the interstate at this hour. After all, it was a Friday night, which meant more than the usual number of residents were out doing whatever they do and going wherever they go on Friday nights. This worked in his favor.

Soon, he spotted a group of four motorcycles ahead riding together holding a speed of seventy-five.

Motorcycle riders tend to form up in groups when traveling on high-speed highways. It was a camaraderie and safety thing. Safety in numbers. A single motorcycle rider was almost invisible to most drivers. A group was not. Which was a good thing. Unless you're a wanted man. Or in his case, transporting a wanted man. Life was full of risks and this was a gamble he had to take.

Kaplan signaled the riders as he pulled alongside. A man in his sixties with a long gray beard blowing in the night air had been elected, or self-appointed, as ride leader. He gave Kaplan a thumbs-up and a head nod to fall in behind. His timing couldn't have been better because less than five minutes after he joined with the riders, the group passed an Arkansas State Police cruiser going the opposite direction. Unlikely that a group of five bikes would draw much more than a second glance. It worked. He had blended in with the riders.

Kaplan stayed with the group until the Arkansas 365 exit. He broke from the rest of the motorcycles, took the elevated off-ramp to the right, and turned left at the light. When he crossed back over the interstate he glanced up the highway and saw the four motorcycles pulling to the side of the road. Behind them, a pair of flashing blue lights.

Arkansas 365 branched to the right as Arkansas 100 began on the left. He checked his mirrors. Still clear. The group of motorcycles would know which exit he took so he had to assume that by now the trooper did as well. Or perhaps not. The group of riders wore vests that read *Knights of the Night*. Maybe they wouldn't be very cooperative with the trooper. It really didn't matter because Arkansas 365 went in two directions at the exit and it was Kaplan's intention to be out of sight before anyone could figure out which direction he went.

He followed the instructions he'd been given to the letter and, even though he'd been there before, he still almost missed the turn onto River Road. It seemed to pop up out of nowhere in the darkness. River Road turned into Plantation Drive, which ended with a tee at River Road Drive.

When the motorcycle slowed, Tony said, "What the hell happened here? Looks like a disaster zone."

"It was. Tornado ripped through here back in April. Took out most of the neighborhood."

"Fatalities?"

"Unfortunately Tony, yes."

"You from around here?"

"No. I told you before I was just passing through. Now shut up, you're asking too many questions."

When he'd seen the news about the disaster four months ago, Kaplan didn't know if his friend was alive or dead. He called but didn't initially get a response. It was a long twenty-four hours, waiting and not knowing. He knew coming here now was not the best idea, but he didn't have many options.

"Is this a safe house?"

"No. But it's safe enough for now." Tony was starting to grate on his nerves. Maybe he should just turn around and leave.

You have to get him to a safe site.

Promise me you'll deliver him to WitSec.

"Tony, either shut up or I'll leave you on the side of the road."

He turned left and seconds later pulled into a driveway he'd only ever been in once before. A man was standing in the dark outside his garage.

Kaplan pulled next to the man and stopped. He killed the engine, turned his head, and said to Tony, "Get off."

"You won't have to tell me twice," Tony said. The old man peeled off the rear saddle and collapsed to the ground.

"Is he okay?" The man asked.

"He's fine," said Kaplan. "Legs probably went numb on the ride out here." He turned to Tony and said, "Shake your legs and get up, old man."

"I've been watching the news," the man in the driveway said. "Is that you two?"

Kaplan nodded. "Mind if I park this thing in your bunker?" He made reference to a storage bunker behind and under the house. "I'll bring you up to date in a few minutes."

The house sat on the banks of the Arkansas River northwest of Little Rock and slightly south of the town of Mayflower. It was a good-sized brick home with a beautiful view of the rolling hills of North Central Arkansas on the horizon across the river. Heavy clouds from earlier thunderstorms had dissipated and revealed a modest orange moon in the serotinal sky. Amber moonlight danced across the flowing waters of the river casting an eerie glow across the terraced backyard. It was still hot and humid but a breeze blowing off the water made it feel cooler than the city.

It had been several years since Kaplan had visited. Not because they weren't good friends; rather that life just seemed to get in the way.

The bunker wasn't visible from street level. Even from the house it was imperceptible. The bunker was built under the first terraced drop in his friend's backyard. Looking back at the house from the river, Kaplan could see the bunker doors. Above the doors at house level sat a broken concrete bench. It was a good place for Kaplan's friend and his wife to sit and watch the river make its way toward the Mississippi…until the tornado uprooted a large tree and crashed it into the house, breaking the bench along the way.

He opened the doors, rolled his Harley inside, and stowed it to one side of the bunker. For the most part, his friend stored lawn equipment inside. Riding mower. Weed eater. All the required tools to maintain a yard half the size of a football field. Like most storage sheds, unused items found their way down there too. Junk mostly. Half a dozen lawn chairs, a moldy sink, several flowerpots and bags of potting soil, and a stack of lumber that had waited too many years to be used. A place where things were stored and forgotten.

He hurriedly unloaded his saddlebags into his backpack and gathered everything he thought he would need. He didn't know when he'd return to retrieve his bike although he sensed it wouldn't be anytime soon.

Ten minutes later Kaplan rejoined the two men, who were still standing in the driveway and made an attempt at introductions. "Jeff, Tony. Tony, Jeff."

"We have already introduced ourselves," said Tony.

Jeff nodded in agreement.

"How's Kam?" Kaplan said, referring to Jeff's wife.

"Curious, as I am."

"So you told her?"

"Not much I can keep from Kam. I told her as much as I know. Which is nothing more than whatever's been blasted across the news and your cryptic phone call. How about we go inside and you can explain what trouble you and your friend have gotten into."

Kaplan moved toward the door and said, "He is not my friend."

"Amen to that," Tony mumbled.

The three men went inside where Kaplan introduced Tony to Kam and noticed her reaction when she saw Tony's bloody face.

"Your nose has been bleeding," she said. "Are you okay?"

"I am now, thank you for asking," Tony replied in a sarcastic tone. He pointed at Kaplan. "And no thanks to him. He hit me with his elbow after he hit me in the head with a rock. He says he was trying to save my life but—"

"Shut up, Tony or I'll hit you again." It only took his glowering stare to stop the old man from running his mouth.

Kam walked toward the kitchen. "Anybody want something

to drink?"

Kaplan nodded, "Would you mind making some coffee? Might be a long night."

"You got it. How about some chips and homemade salsa? Jeff made it fresh today."

"That would be great," said Kaplan.

Kaplan recounted the night's events with numerous interruptions and embellishments from Tony.

After hearing the remarkable story, Jeff and Kam were quiet, almost as if shell-shocked. They sat next to each other on one of the two leather couches in the family room.

Finally Kam said, "Let me get this straight. After you evaded the car following you and rode into the quarry, a helicopter miraculously located your position and started shooting at you? Don't you find that odd?"

"Yes, as a matter of fact, I do," Kaplan said. "It was almost as if they knew we were there."

All three turned and looked at Tony.

He raised both hands palm up. "What?"

"Oh, so now you don't have a thing to say? Your Italian tongue tied?" Kaplan said. "I think you have some explaining to do."

CHAPTER 11

MOSS CLIMBED DOWN THE AIR STAIR OF THE Beechcraft King Air turboprop. The flight from Chicago was mostly smooth until they got closer to Little Rock and the pilots flew through some of the left over clouds from the day's thunderstorms.

He carried with him one bag and a briefcase, more than enough to get him by for a few days—which was all the time he planned on spending investigating this case.

Deputy U.S. Marshal Jon Hepler was waiting for him inside the fixed base operator. Hepler was a few inches shorter than Moss, had thinning blond hair, and a snappy, albeit juvenile, sense of humor. He usually wore long sleeves to cover the tattoos on his forearms, a permanent reminder of his days as a police officer in a small Florida town. Tonight however, he wore short sleeves and his tattoos were visible.

On his left arm, just above his wrist was the popular police 1* shield. A play on words—one asterisk—one ass to risk. Above that were an eagle and a tattered American flag along with a depiction of his brother's dog tags. His brother, Moss remembered, was a casualty of the war in Afghanistan. On the inside of his right forearm, St. Michael, the patron saint for peace, held another 1* shield. Hepler said he put it on his right arm because that was his gun hand. As superstitious as Moss thought it was, Hepler put it there to make him faster and more accurate so that he could defeat any foe.

He had his star on his belt and his gun mounted on his hip.

Moss had known Hepler since his first day in Little Rock seven years ago. And they became good friends right away. He wasn't referred to as Jon, but rather JP.

When Moss lived in Little Rock, he and Hepler, also a Chicago Cubs fan, frequented a downtown sports bar on a regular basis, especially during baseball season.

Hepler grinned when he saw Moss, "You missed a good game tonight, Dirt Man. Cubs rallied in the ninth to take it to extra innings." Hepler had called him Dirt Man since day one. A dig on his name Pete Moss—*Peat Moss*.

"Asshole," Moss said. They shook hands and bumped shoulders. "The pilots couldn't find the game on the radio. ATC gave us a few updates along the way but I never heard the final score."

"Six to five. Cubbies in the eleventh."

"Sounds like I missed a good one."

"You did. It was a regular barnburner there at the end." Hepler's expression turned serious. "Weren't gone from Little Rock very long, were you, Pete?" He teased. "What? Three weeks, tops?"

"Barely two and here I am, back in this redneck hell hole again." Moss pushed his overnight bag strap over his shoulder. "Let's get moving, you can brief me on the drive in."

"By the way, prick, thanks a lot for ruining a perfectly good night's sleep."

"What?"

"Requesting me on this job at the last minute. Hell, if you

wanted to talk, you could've called."

"And have you miss out on all the fun?"

"I don't know whether to thank you or shoot your ass."

"It was the least I could do for an old friend."

"Next time, don't do me any favors."

The sedan Hepler was driving was a dark green Crown Vic. It was one from the motor pool and Moss had driven it on numerous occasions. An older model worn out from years of driving on the dilapidated roads of Arkansas. Although scheduled to rotate out of the fleet at the end of the year and be exchanged for a new model, Moss doubted it would get replaced for another couple of years due to all the budget woes in Congress. Hepler pulled out of the parking area and headed toward the restaurant.

"Any new developments?" Moss asked.

"What's the last thing you heard?"

"Let me think." Moss ran his hand across his bald head. "Last thing I was briefed was that a motorcycle fitting the description of the getaway vehicle crossed The Big Dam on the Arkansas River Trail, pissed off some joggers and cyclists, and an airplane crashed at Emerald Park Quarry."

"Not an airplane. A helicopter."

"A helicopter? Was it LRPD?"

"Nope," Hepler said. "No one knows exactly who it belongs to and there was no rotorcraft activity at the airport all night. ATC said it popped up on radar, moved across the river, and then disappeared. Nothing at the scene to identify it either. No 'N' number. No serial numbers on the aircraft, the avionics, or the engine parts recovered so far. No one has reported a missing aircraft. Nothing. A total mystery ship."

"Could it have been one of those low-level, hush-hush

military exercises?"

"I thought the same thing myself," Hepler said. "Called Little Rock Air Force Base and they said nothing was flying."

"Body count."

"Two. But they're pretty much toast. The M.E. said identification could take a while. He guessed weeks unless he got lucky or someone came forward."

"You think it was part of the hit? It might belong to whoever was out to get the witness?"

"Could be, I guess. I don't rightly know," Hepler said. "Too many loose ends at this point to tell who's who."

Moss thought about that statement for a second and then asked, "Anything on the motorcycle?"

"North Little Rock PD reported a motorcycle on Fort Roots Drive moments after the helicopter crash as did three emergency response vehicles. One NLRPD patrol car pursued but got locked up behind a traffic accident at MacArthur and Pershing and the bike got away. State Police pulled over a group of motorcycles on I-40 north of State Road 365. They indicated a bike fitting the description with two riders pulled in with them for a few miles and then disappeared. State Police thinks he probably took the 365 exit. Nothing after that."

"365, huh?" Moss ran through several possible escape routes in his head. "If that was him then he did one of three things. One, he joined State Road 100 and came back toward town."

"Why would he do that?" Hepler asked. "He had to know LRPD had already cast a net around the city."

"I agree. Too risky. Which also rules out east on 365. That would take him back to town as well. He had to take 365 west toward Mayflower. Keeps him on the back roads and away from high visibility areas."

"A possibility. He might even be trying to get to Conway by staying on the vehicle portion of the Arkansas River Trail," Hepler added. "He could follow it through Mayflower and come into Conway from the west."

"Then what?" Moss said. "He has to know by now there is a *BOLO* out to all the surrounding municipalities. He also has to figure there will be an eye in the sky soon looking for a motorcycle. It would stand out on the dark back roads. No, he took 365 for a reason and we need to figure out what it is."

"You're giving this guy an awful lot of credit."

Moss thought about that statement for a few seconds and then said, "Something tells me he's not your run of the mill getaway driver."

† † †

The dark green Crown Vic turned onto Rebsamen Park Road and was stopped at a roadblock. Two officers manned the barricade, one asked for the two deputies' identification. Moss handed his creds to Hepler who passed them out the window.

"Marshals Service," the officer said. "They're expecting you."

"They?" Moss spoke past Hepler to the officer. "Who are they?"

"LRPD homicide, FBI," the officer passed the credentials back through the window. "And one of yours."

Moss and Hepler looked at each other. "One of ours?" Moss asked.

"Yeah, U.S. Marshals Service." The officer stepped away

from the Crown Vic and signaled his partner to remove the barricade from the road. "Ask her yourself." He waved them through.

Little Rock police had cordoned off Rebsamen Park Road from Old Cantrell Road to Riverdale Road. The FBI ordered every establishment within that stretch closed. LRPD was instructed to have all the cars in the parking lots cleared out. Patrons of the restaurant were interviewed, statements taken, and subsequently sent home. The only vehicles remaining in the parking lot belonged to law enforcement, injured patrons taken to the hospital, or dead bodies.

As Hepler parked the Crown Vic, Moss observed the group standing in front of the restaurant, LRPD homicide and FBI he recognized, he had worked with both before on several occasions over the past few years.

The two deputies got out of the sedan and walked toward the crowd.

A woman pushed her way to the front and walked briskly toward them. She had the body of a runway model, long legs and zero body fat. Her long red hair hung loose around her shoulders and blew in the breeze. She had the cougar sex appeal of a woman in her forties, but a strictly business look on her fair skinned face that could keep a man at bay. A woman tired of the government's *boys club* attitude. A woman who didn't want to be here. She wore a black jacket with the Marshals Service logo and a matching black cap. She looked straight at Moss when she talked.

"I'm looking for Senior Inspector Moss."

"Looks like you've found him," Moss said. "But I think you already knew that."

She held up her creds, "April Moore."

Moss looked at her credentials, United States Marshals Service, Witness Security. "Why the hell wasn't I informed about you, Inspector Moore? This is highly irregular."

"I don't know," Moore said. "I was informed about you."

"So it seems. This is a problem. It is outside of WitSec security protocol and until I have proper authorization, you're out."

"I understand your dilemma, Senior Inspector," said Moore. "And like you, I'm following last minute orders as well."

"Which office?" Hepler interjected. "Who gave you the orders?"

Moore looked at Hepler and then at Moss. "I was assigned from the Atlanta office by Regional Chief Inspector Michael Johnson."

"Yeah?" Moss said. "How's ole Mike doing these days? Still running marathons?" It was a trick question. Johnson never used the name Mike and had undergone bypass surgery six months ago.

"I wouldn't know," she said. "Never met the man."

"How could that be? You just said he ordered you here."

She stepped closer to Moss. Her green eyes glinted under the streetlights. Her voice lowered, a sultry sound. "Inspector, two weeks ago I was a P.O.D. at the Des Moines office when I was selected on an Atlanta WitSec bid. My first day was yesterday. Tonight I was ordered here...to work with you. I don't know why, I didn't ask. I just did what I was told. The message was the Service wanted two inspectors on this investigation. I was told you used to work here and were reassigned from Chicago. I was also told you know the area, the ropes, and that you were easy to work with."

"Ha," Hepler laughed. "Dirt Man is the biggest S.O.B I

know."

"Dirt Man?" Moore asked.

"Inside joke." Moss checked his watch.

"It's late, I'll have to wait until morning to get authorization. So, for now, you can ride along." Moss looked around. It was a scene packed with an assortment of law enforcement officers. "How long have you been here, Inspector Moore?"

"Long enough to know the FBI is giving LRPD traffic management. Crowd control, that sort of thing. Strictly support." Moore paused and then said, "Inspector Moss, I was sent over here to be part of the investigation, not sit on the sidelines and watch. You're not going to pull any of that good ole boy crap on me, are you? What you know, I want to know. No holding back. You keep me in the loop at all times. I was ordered here as your partner. Where you go, I go. Is that going to be a problem?"

He'd had to fight the good ole boy system inside the Marshals Service for years and knew exactly how she felt. The last thing he wanted was to be identified as one of them. "It's only a problem if you insist on following me into the bathroom."

CHAPTER 12

"WHAT ARE YOU TALKING ABOUT?" TONY ASKED.

"Dammit, Tony." Kaplan raised his voice. "How did they know where we were? Are you wearing a tracker or something?"

"No. Nothing. I swear." Tony's voice sounded rattled.

Kaplan pointed at Tony's pants. "Empty your pockets. Put everything right here." He tapped the top of the coffee table in front of the leather couch with his finger.

Tony fished around in his front pockets and pulled out 73¢ in change and a money clip full of bills. The money clip was tarnished sterling silver with a turquoise stone mounted on top. Kind of a Southwestern look. Not what he would have expected of the Italian, but it looked expensive, and considering what he was learning about Tony, it probably was.

"Wallet."

Tony pulled a lizard skin wallet from his back pocket and placed it on the table.

"Pull off your belt," Kaplan said. "I want to look at it too."

Tony raised his shirt to unclasp his belt and that's when Kaplan saw the phone. It was the latest model iPhone from Apple. Cell phones were easy to track, iPhones especially, with their built-in GPS that can't easily be powered down or turned off by non-geeks. "How long have you had this phone?"

Kaplan asked.

"Got it today," Tony replied. "I don't even know how to use it. I got it the same time I got my new credit cards, passport, and driver's license. Cox had all my documentation ready when he picked me up this morning at the Memphis airport."

Kaplan picked up Tony's belt from the table, inspected it, and then handed it back. "You can put this back on." He pulled out the bills, several hundreds, fifties, twenties, a ten, a five, and two ones totaling $1437. All looked clean. He held up the money clip, flipped it over a few times, and then dropped it on top of the pile of bills. He pushed the pile toward Tony. "You can have this back too."

"What are you doing?" Jeff asked. "Checking for bugs?"

"Bugs are generally considered listening devices. What I'm looking for are any tracking devices Tony might be carrying."

"How do you know what you're doing?" Jeff asked.

"What do you mean?"

"I mean, all you have ever told me was you worked for the government…but this is a lot like that spy stuff I see on TV or read in thrillers. What is it you do for a living…truthfully?"

Kaplan stopped what he was doing and looked at Jeff. He had known Jeff longer than anyone else left alive. They grew up next door to each other and spent most of their childhood together. In high school Kaplan moved to another part of town, but they kept in touch. Until college. Then the communication between the two came to an abrupt end. He went one way and Jeff went another. Jeff met Kam, they married, and he got a job while she was a stay at home mom with their two sons. Their lives were busy doing all the things families do. Church. Little league. School activities.

Kaplan's life took a different path. He dropped out of

college when his parents died in a car wreck, enlisted in the military where, after two and a half years, he was selected for the Army Special Forces. Even though he was told his most powerful weapon was his mind, he was trained to kill. He had stayed on the United States government payroll ever since he retired from Special Forces.

After being in his friend's home, he realized Jeff had all those things Kaplan had longed for in life. He came close twice, but the important women in his life had a way of dying or disappearing.

His first relationship ended tragically when his girlfriend of many years betrayed him. Not infidelity—worse. Her troubles were seeded much deeper than that. She had gotten mixed up with the wrong people and tried to kill a man from her past. In the end, the life that was lost was hers.

The demise of his second relationship still remained a mystery to him. He was involved with a fellow CIA operative, his partner, when she, for reasons he never understood, left and was never heard from again. Not by him, anyway. The Director of Central Intelligence initially refused to divulge her whereabouts or the reason she left the agency until she disappeared. Then it seemed the DCI took a renewed interest in covertly locating her. Kaplan had been searching for her ever since with no luck until he finally got a lead on a man who might know her whereabouts, a man who lived in El Paso, Texas. The man Kaplan was going to see when this ordeal with Tony began.

Jobs and relationships always had dangerous consequences.

What Jeff had—a wife, good job, and children—were as far out of reach for him as the North Pole. Hell, what was he thinking? He might eventually get to the North Pole but he would never have the life Jeff had.

Thirty years had passed before he and Jeff reconnected through Facebook. They enjoyed a brief visit once before when Kaplan was traveling through. They talked about the days as kids when they rode their bicycles to the ballpark, high school girls they dated, and adolescent mischief they found themselves in on more than one occasion. More about their childhood than what happened during the thirty years they had not seen each other. They needed more time to catch up but tonight wasn't going to be that night.

Kaplan reached down and pulled his knife from his boot. With the flick of his thumb the blade snapped open.

"Guess it's one of those jobs you can't talk about, huh?" Jeff said.

"It is," Kaplan said. He laid Tony's documents side by side on the table. He picked one up and held it in front of a light.

"Gregg?" Kam asked from behind the island that separated the kitchen from the family room. "Are your job and what happened in Little Rock connected?"

He shook his head. "Not at all, this is about Tony. I was just a bystander who was too stupid to mind his own business. It's a coincidence I was even there." He looked at Jeff, "By the way, you recommended the restaurant."

"Sorry I did," Jeff said. "You should have called ahead and Kam could have fixed her famous risotto with spicy sausage. Sounds to me like you were just in the wrong place at the wrong time."

"I was planning on calling after I ate something and checked into a hotel. Neither of which, obviously, I was able to do." Kaplan smiled. "But hey, I did call, just under different circumstances than I had planned."

"Since you have involved us, Gregg, you need to let us know who you work for. I'm guessing CIA. Am I right?" Kam asked. "That's how you know all this stuff?"

Kaplan smiled. "That's what I like about you, Kam. Always straight to the point."

"I found the direct approach saves time," she said. "Especially when dealing with men. Subtlety is an art form not yet evolved in most males."

Kaplan stopped what he was doing, looked over his shoulder at Kam, and smiled. He turned back to the table and sliced a section from the spine of the passport. "Yes, Kam, I work for the CIA. My director won't be very happy that I got involved in another federal agency's business either. In fact, there is nothing about this the agency *will* like."

Tony laughed. "You're a spook," he bellowed. "I knew it had to be something like that. All the guns. The way you handled those two punks in the quarry. You're a machine, a cold hearted killing machine."

"In case you have forgotten, that *machine*, as you call him, just saved your hide," Jeff said to Tony. "He can't be too cold hearted or he would have left you out there to die."

"No, Tony's right," Kaplan paused. "I'm not the kid you knew growing up. I have changed. The job has a way of sucking out your soul and leaving only a shell that takes orders. The training teaches you skills...but there is a price to pay." He turned to Jeff. "If I could do it over, I would have found a woman like you did and settled down, but I'm afraid those days are gone forever."

He held the passport closer. "Kam, do you have any tweezers? And perhaps a razor knife?"

She walked to the bathroom and then returned to the

kitchen with tweezers in her hand. He could hear her pushing small objects from side to side. It seemed everyone had a drawer in the kitchen where everything ended up. A catchall storage drawer. He heard the drawer close.

She walked around the island. "Here you go." She placed the razor knife and tweezers on the table in front of him.

"Thanks." He picked up the tweezers and slipped them inside the slit he'd made in the passport. He gave a gentle tug and pulled out a thin, flat object the length of a grain of rice.

"What is it?" Tony asked.

"RFID chip," Jeff said. "I've used them to track inventory, but nothing like that one."

"He's right," Kaplan wedged the thin razor knife blade beneath the magnetic strip on the back of Tony's driver's license and pried it from the card. Behind the strip was a miniaturized secret compartment containing another RFID chip. This one was larger. "All passports have an RFID chip embedded in them, just like your credit cards, ID cards," he held up the driver's license, "and these."

Kaplan placed the RFID chips on the table. "This one," he pointed to the one he removed from the passport, "is not very powerful. Range is not much more than a few feet, depending on the surrounding conditions. This one," he held up the driver's license, "is much different. It has a signal range of up to 200 miles, accurate up to 150. And it is always active. It's a top-secret product of the Department of Defense. Only a limited number of people in the intelligence industry even know this one exists. It was in your driver's license because someone figured you'd carry it with you at all times. That way they can always track you."

"What about the phone?" Jeff asked.

"I guarantee someone is tracking it right now."

"Who would be tracking me?" Tony asked.

"Not regular cops or they'd already be here. Perhaps the Marshals Service but I doubt it...too risky. Maybe another Federal agency. My money is on some sort of private intelligence firm, one with plenty of resources and connections with the Feds. This is why they were on to you so fast. You were supposed to be a quick takedown."

Jeff interrupted, "Or lead them to something...or someone."

"When you say *feds*," Tony said. "Do you mean FBI or CIA or NSA? Or someone else?"

Kaplan looked at Tony while he pondered the man's query. "Yes." He paused. "In reality though, we can rule out CIA immediately because this is domestic and the CIA technically has no jurisdiction. Besides, this isn't the kind of thing the CIA would concern itself with. Nor the NSA for that matter either. The FBI, on the other hand—"

"You need to disable them, Gregg," Kam's tone sounded urgent. "Before they track him here."

Kaplan checked his internal clock. It had been too long since he and Tony had pulled into Jeff's driveway. He looked at Jeff and then at Kam. "I'm sorry, Kam. It's too late."

CHAPTER 13

INSPECTOR MOORE WAS RIGHT, MOSS COULDN'T keep her out of the investigation if the U.S. Marshals Service had ordered her in. And raising a stink about it up the food chain wouldn't exactly be his best move, especially in the middle of the night and in what he considered the twilight of his mediocre career. Furthermore, he understood her attitude; he'd experienced much the same thing. It didn't matter whether you were black or female; it was always an uphill battle for a minority in a white man's world.

Moss gazed into Moore's eyes, "Inspector Moore, I don't have a problem with you personally on my investigation. This isn't about you. It's about how your assignment was handled. That's where my problem lies. I was taken off guard, that's all. What I'm saying is the lack of proper WitSec protocol is not only irregular, it's a blatant violation of Marshals Service protocol."

"I understand," she said. "Like you, I just go where I'm ordered whether I like it or not. And I was fully briefed on WC 7922 before I left Atlanta."

"I've never heard of a case where the Inspector in charge wasn't given advanced authorization pertaining to the arrival of an outside Inspector. And you should have an authorization as well," Moss added.

"I do have one," Moore stated emphatically. She reached into her back pocket, pulled out a folded letter, and handed it to Moss. "I'm sorry, I should have given this to you first. But, you can't hold me at fault that you didn't get notified."

He unfolded the letter and read it. It looked official. And it was signed Michael Johnson, Regional Chief Inspector in Atlanta, Georgia.

Moore's voice held some sort of compassion when she spoke. Almost as if she knew he didn't want to be here either. Maybe the same thing had happened to her. Maybe she had plans that were shattered when she was given last minute orders to report to Little Rock.

"No, I don't suppose I can. Des Moines, huh? How'd you like it there?"

"Hated it. Nothing to see, nothing to do. I like mountains."

"Where'd you grow up?"

"Salt Lake City."

"They have nice mountains," Moss said. "And a big lake."

"A smelly lake most of the time," she added.

"It's a beautiful area. I've handled a couple of relos there."

"So, you're a Mormon?" Hepler asked.

"LDS," she corrected. "And yes."

"LDS?" asked Hepler.

"Latter Day Saints. PC for Mormon."

"Oh for crying out loud," Hepler ranted. "Why does everything these days have to always be politically correct? What the hell is wrong with the word Mormon?"

Moss looked at Hepler and shook his head. Then he looked at Moore. "Forgive my partner. Sometimes he engages his mouth before he engages his brain." He turned back to

Hepler. "Can we do the walk through now, JP, or do you have something else stupid you want to say?"

LRPD had cordoned off the restaurant and only allowed them to enter after they, once again, showed their creds. To the right lay three bodies on a raised section of the floor. One in front of the bar draped over a wooden railing and two behind the bar. Blood from the man on the railing had cascaded from the elevated floor to the main floor and dried into dark, carmine colored puddles. Another man lay on the floor to the left. He was dressed in a coat and tie. A halo of dried blood surrounded his head.

Inspector Michael Cox.

Beyond Cox was another body covered by a sheet. A courtesy extended for the only bystander casualty. The wounded had been rushed to the nearest hospital. Lab techs were using gel lifter to collect fingerprints from dried blood that could be used to help identify people at the scene during the shootout. Investigators had already taken statements from the staff and patrons. The blood soaked floor, littered with broken glass, splintered wood, broken chairs, and demolished tabletops, revealed a grisly scene. Plastic yellow tents marked dozens of shell casings. The room still held the lingering smell of gunfire mixed with spicy Cajun cooking even though it had been hours since the shooting. It also reeked of death.

"Why are these bodies still here?" Moss demanded.

"HQ wanted you to see the scene intact," said Hepler. "Told me to keep the M.E. on hold until you released the bodies."

"Why the hell would they do that? It isn't even my call. Release them now."

"Don't look now," Hepler interrupted. "But here comes a hundred and fifty pound hemorrhoid."

A man hurried toward them with short strides and rapid steps. Having dealt with the man in the past, Moss knew what was coming next. The man was a victim of Napoleonic complex. A man with an ax to grind with everyone it seemed. He was five-five on a good day, with a slim build and a head that seemed too large for his diminutive stature. He had the typical G-Man look right down to his black slacks, white dress shirt, dark tie, and a satin black jacket with the letters FBI stamped on the back.

His thick brown hair was longer than a typical flattop and held in place by gel or mousse or maybe even glue. Who knew for sure? His haircut rose over two inches above his scalp. A lame attempt to look taller. He had a reporter's notepad in one hand and an old gold pen in the other.

"Senior Inspector Pete Moss," the man said.

"Special Agent Richard Small," Moss replied.

Moss looked at Moore and asked, "Have you met the country's shortest G-Man?"

"As a matter of fact, Special Agent Small and I have met."

"The U. S. Marshals Service is out of this investigation. Your witness has escaped and is considered a fugitive. He's a wanted man. You stay out of the FBI's way and what's left of your career won't get derailed." His condescending tone was not lost on Moss.

Moss stepped close to the man and stared down at him. "Don't be a dick, Dick." Moss paused for effect. "This witness is still in the program, it isn't your jurisdiction, and you're out of line mentioning it. And even if he was considered a fugitive, it's still Marshals Service jurisdiction, not FBI. Did you even bother to read the eyewitness reports?"

The man waited a few moments and then replied, "First of

all, it's Special Agent Richard Small, not Dick. And yes, I did. If he wasn't trying to escape, then why didn't he stick around and wait until the cops got here?"

"Would you?" Moss paused until Small was about to respond then cut off the Special Agent's response. "Somehow his identity was breached and someone tried to kill him. If anything, the FBI should consider my witness a potential hostage and give this case top priority and cooperate with other agencies to ensure he is found safe. Let me make myself clear...Special Agent Small, it is WitSec's job to figure out how this happened and to find my witness. Not yours."

"The death of a United States Marshal *is* FBI jurisdiction."

"Then do your job." Moss pointed to the three dead men still lying on the elevated floor. "And while you are solving the murder of our Deputy U. S. Marshal, find out why those goons tried to assassinate my witness."

Small's face turned red. Either from anger or embarrassment. Or a combination of both. Moss didn't care. The man was intolerable to work with and over the years had amassed volumes of complaints against him from other agents, agencies, and civilians. But he always seemed to weasel his way out of the mess. Scuttlebutt was he had dirt on someone at the top, just enough to keep him out of trouble but not enough to get him assigned to a major field office like Chicago or Atlanta.

Small looked down and, as he turned to walk away, gave Moss a sideways glance with his close-set beady eyes and furrowed brow. Special Agent Small could be a problem.

Hepler walked Moss and Moore through the action timeline of the bloody scene as pieced together from eyewitnesses while the medical examiner's team removed the bodies. There were the usual discrepancies between reports; no two untrained eyewitnesses saw the same scenario exactly the same way. The biggest question left unanswered was the mystery man. The man in the jeans, boots, and a long sleeve black t-shirt. According to eyewitnesses, he jumped in and helped the deputy fend off and kill the assailants. Then, he and the old man in the khaki slacks and blue tropical print shirt disappeared out the front door. Most of the eyewitnesses only heard the motorcycle's engine roaring as it sped off, but two patrons had followed them out the front exit and witnessed the motorcycle being chased by the dark sedan. At the sound of gunfire, though, both men ducked back inside the restaurant.

"Any chance one of them got the plates?" Moss said.

"Both of the guys gave some numbers they *thought* were the right ones for the motorcycle," Hepler said. "But when LRPD ran them it came up a dead end. The only thing the two of them agreed on was that it was a Virginia tag."

After gathering all the pertinent information, Moss told Moore to leave her vehicle in the parking lot while Hepler drove them to the site of the helicopter crash. Once there, they had to show their creds and have them scrutinized by the cops on the scene, this time by NLRPD, North Little Rock Police Department. The Arkansas River separated the two cities, and their jurisdictions.

They were directed to an area designated by NLRPD for investigative parking separating them from the traffic pattern of emergency response vehicles attending to the crash site itself.

As they climbed out of the car Moore said, "I think I recognize your friend standing over there talking to some witnesses."

"How the hell did Special Agent Small beat us here?" Moss said.

CHAPTER 14

BEFORE HE AND TONY LEFT HIS FRIEND'S home, Kaplan needed to prepare the scene. He disabled Tony's brand new iPhone, placed it, the RFIDs, and all the documentation the U. S. Marshals Service had issued Tony in Jeff and Kam's hideaway bedroom at the top of the stairs.

Kam panicked when Kaplan said it was too late to stop the RFIDs from being tracked to her home. She pulled out a small hammer from the same drawer where she kept the razor knife and frantically raised it above her head to smash the electronic devices. Jeff rushed over and caught her arm before she could strike the blow. She indicated the last thing she wanted was to have their lives threatened once again. This time it would not be a tornado.

"What are you doing?" Her voice full of panic.

"I have an idea, Kam," Jeff said. "Just hear me out. Gregg, what do you think if we use these devices to trick whoever is tracking Tony? I could drive to the dump across town and toss them in."

Kam nodded her head in agreement.

"We're not dealing with amateurs, they already know the address. I'm sorry. It is too late for that."

Kaplan assured them someone *would* show up at the

residence and it was best for everyone if no one was home when they did.

Kaplan explained why and instructed Jeff and Kam that they had five minutes to gather any of their necessities, get in their Lexus, and head out of town. This was a longer amount of time than when the tornado struck and destroyed their neighborhood. Since that tragedy, they had prepared an escape bag in case they had another tornado strike.

Kam ran and recovered the emergency bag in their bedroom. When she came back in the room she had trouble controlling her breathing. "Honestly, in my worst nightmare I never thought we would ever need this bag and certainly not for this." Her voice trembled and cracked. Jeff walked over and put his arms around his wife in an effort to offer comfort.

"Leave the food on the table," Kaplan told them. Then he walked to the back door, opened it, and stepped outside. He turned around and smashed his elbow into the glass, shattering it, and sending glass shards onto the floor.

"What the hell did you do that for?" Jeff gave him a puzzled and angry look.

"Corroboration. I need it to look like someone broke in. It will confirm your cover story."

"What cover story?" Kam asked.

Kaplan walked back inside, his shoes crunching over broken glass. "When you get on the other side of Little Rock, use your security system app to activate your alarm. Then turn off your cell phones and don't turn them back on until you get to Florida."

"Florida? What?" Kam sounded bewildered.

Kaplan took a quick look at a map, gave Jeff specific route instructions, and told him to drive all night until they reached their new beach house in Sandestin, Florida on the Gulf of Mexico.

Before they went their separate ways, Kaplan pulled out a stack of hundred dollar bills and handed them to Jeff. "When you get to Florida pay only with cash, and when the authorities knock on the door, which they eventually will, just tell them you've been there a few days. Whatever they tell you about Little Rock and your house, have your story ironed out and act totally surprised. Same thing with the alarm company. Romantic getaway, no phones."

Kaplan, with Tony in the passenger seat, drove Jeff's black Jeep north on Arkansas State Road 386. Its full tank of gas allowed them to put much needed distance between them and Little Rock without having to stop and risk exposure. Kaplan's plan was to drive to Conway, take US 64 east to US 67, and stay on 67 until Poplar Bluff, Missouri. He'd worry about mapping out the rest later.

Kaplan and Tony rode in silence for a long time, which was a welcome relief. The first time Tony spoke was east of Conway.

"If they could track me, why didn't they just send another helicopter after me like at the quarry?" Tony asked.

"Two reasons I can think of," Kaplan answered. "First, I doubt they had another helicopter available and second, if they did, it would draw too much attention to launch another one. The first copter going up in a blaze was seen for miles and 9-1-1 calls alerted authorities. By then the authorities were on heightened alert. As soon as they put another copter in the air, everyone would be all over it. Air traffic controllers would be tracking it with radar, local cops would be chasing it with their own aircraft."

"Wasn't it kind of risky to route your friends back through Little Rock?"

"Not really. Not if they obey traffic laws. Unless these guys have instant access to government databases, it will take some time before they can gather any vehicle information. By then Jeff and Kam will be safe in their Florida beach house. The cops won't know anything about them for a while either."

"Why not?"

"Because nothing has happened to point them at Jeff and Kam." Kaplan turned his head and looked at Tony. "Yet."

"I don't get it."

"No, I guess you wouldn't. Whoever is tracking you will show up at Jeff's house sooner or later, and when they do, the whole neighborhood will be dialing 9-1-1."

"You think?"

"I guarantee it. That's why I wanted Jeff to activate his alarm system when I told him to, it will send the cops to his house to investigate *before* whoever is tracking you shows up. It will take some time for the Sheriff's Department to figure out where Jeff and Kam are, and, in the meantime, law enforcement presence will keep the bad guys away." Kaplan adjusted himself in his seat and settled in for the long drive. "You should get some shut eye. You'll get a turn to drive in a few hours."

"I don't have a license," he said. "Remember, you destroyed it."

"You're a funny man, Tony," said Kaplan. "Somebody is trying to track you down and kill you and you're worried about a stupid driver's license. Hell, if we get pulled over, a driver's license will be the least of our worries."

Tony reclined his seat and rolled to his right side leaving his back facing Kaplan.

He had promised WitSec Inspector Mike Cox that he would keep Tony safe. What had he gotten himself into? He was putting his life on the line for an old man he knew nothing about. In a few hours, he would demand full disclosure from Tony. The old man owed him that much. Besides, there might be another piece to this puzzle wrapped inside that information.

A piece that might keep him from getting killed.

"Where were you headed when all this started?" Tony asked while still reclined and facing the window.

"West."

"To see a woman?

The statement took Kaplan by surprise.

"What makes you think that?"

"Things you said back at the restaurant." Tony replied. "You told Inspector Cox you were just passing through and you didn't have time to babysit. I figured your urgency was because of a woman. It usually is, you know."

Kaplan looked over at the old man, curled on his right side, "Indirectly, I guess it is."

Tony turned over and pulled his seat upright. "That's kind of vague, don't you think?"

"Yes it is, because it's none of your damn business."

"What's the harm in sharing?"

"For crying out loud, if it will shut you up," Kaplan said. "I am searching for a woman and there is a man in Texas who can help me locate her. I was going to see him."

"Why don't you just call him? That's a long way to drive only to find out he isn't there?"

"Then I'll wait for him."

"What if he does not know where she is? It could be a wasted trip."

Kaplan didn't answer right away. "It doesn't work that way, Tony. It's complicated."

Tony must have taken the hint because he reclined his seat and turned toward the window again. "Women are always complicated," he said. "Sooner or later you will tell me. Everyone always does."

But Kaplan didn't hear him. A disturbing thought shot through his mind and ricocheted like a bullet in the brain. His insides tightened and cramped. A sickening feeling overwhelmed him. His body flushed. Anger filled his veins. Anger toward himself. How could he have been so sloppy? It was Tradecraft 101 and he blew it. In his hurry to get his friends clear of the house and on their way to Florida, he forgot to cover his own ass. He forgot to remove his Virginia license plate from his Harley. And there was no going back to get it.

CHAPTER 15

AS THE THREE DEPUTY U. S. MARSHALS WALKED toward the accident scene Moss noticed Special Agent Small talking with two men who looked like *Mutt and Jeff*. A tall man was grossly overweight and the short man was too thin. The only physical similarity was they both looked like they had been on the losing end of an ass-kicking contest. Their faces were bruised and bloodied. Their clothes, dirty and torn. The big guy had a busted lip and bloody gums. He held out his hand showing Special Agent Small two bloody teeth.

North Little Rock Police Department had cordoned off the area with yellow tape. An officer with the Arkansas State Police informed Moss that several troopers would remain on site to protect the scene until the National Transportation Safety Board arrived to investigate the crash.

Moss asked the trooper, "Have those two," he pointed to the men Small was talking to, "been interviewed yet? Other than by Special Agent Small."

"I believe so," the officer said. He pointed to a man in jeans and a tan sports coat. "When I arrived, they were talking to 'im. Detective with NLRPD."

"Thanks."

Moore and Hepler walked over to the man.

"Excuse me, detective." He held up his ID card. "Pete Moss, U. S. Marshals Service." He pointed to Moore and then Hepler. "This is Inspector Moore and Deputy Hepler." They each held up their creds. "May we ask you a few questions?"

"Four Feds," the detective said. "Three U.S. Marshals and FBI. This must be big."

Moss ignored the detective's sarcasm. "Have you interviewed the two men Special Agent Small is talking to now?"

"I have."

Moss waited for the detective to continue, but he didn't. Not on his own accord.

"Did they say what happened?"

"Neither one of them saw the crash. They said they were both unconscious at the time. The big guy said when he regained consciousness fire was all around him. Said he thought he had died and gone to hell."

"Did the blast knock them unconscious?"

"Nope. He said some guy on a motorcycle attacked them and knocked them both out. When he came to the guy was gone. Took the old man with him. Claimed the attack was unprovoked. Said they saw someone up here and came to see if they needed help."

"Did you get a description of the guy? And the old man?"

The detective opened his notepad. "They thought the old man was around seventy. Gray hair, khaki pants, and a dark shirt with flowers on it...like a Hawaiian shirt or something. Or to quote the big guy exactly, he was dressed in a *flowery fag shirt*."

"And the other guy?"

"Said he was big. And strong. Muscular type. Said he had thick dark hair and a heavy five o'clock shadow. He was wearing blue jeans, a black shirt, and leather jacket. The little guy said the man's hands moved lightning fast. Said he'd never seen anyone move that fast before. Big guy said basically the same thing. Said they got off their ATV to help and the guy went crazy and attacked them. He said it was unprovoked."

"You mentioned that already. Doesn't pass the smell test, though. These clowns don't strike me as the good Samaritan types."

"I didn't think so either. . .and they both have prior misdemeanors. I figured they started something and the guy finished it."

"Does he know which way they went?" Moore asked.

"No idea." The detective pointed to the top of the hillside. "The little guy did say when he came to he thought he heard a motorcycle up on Fort Roots Road heading toward the VA hospital but wasn't sure because of all the sirens. One of our responding patrol cars went in that direction and saw a motorcycle with a passenger on the back. He tried to pursue but got stuck behind a traffic accident. No way of knowing if it was the same men or not."

"Thank you, Detective." Moss motioned for Moore and Hepler to follow as he walked away.

"What do you think, Pete?" Hepler asked. "You think it's our witness?"

"Of course it's our witness. I'm too old to believe in coincidences like this one. You already briefed me on the reports. Like I said in the car, this tough guy and the old man took 365 and headed toward Mayflower or Conway. It's the only logical explanation."

Hepler's cell phone rang; he raised a finger and walked off. Moss noticed Special Agent Small answer his phone as well. Then the detective's phone rang. The Arkansas State Police officer started talking into the microphone strapped under his chin.

Hepler returned with an anxious look on his face. Several of the other LEOs were heading for their vehicles.

"What the hell is going on?" Moss asked.

"There's been a break-in at a home on the Arkansas River." Hepler replied. "River Road Drive. Just south of Mayflower."

"And?"

"And they found several high-tech RFID tracking devices in the home."

"Come on, JP, getting information from you is like pulling teeth. What else you got?"

"A cell phone and driver's license belonging to our witness's alias, Anthony Napoli."

CHAPTER 16

THE DARK OF NIGHT ENVELOPED THE BACK roads of Arkansas.

The Jeep's headlights illuminated only the area directly in front of the vehicle and Kaplan could see nothing on either side but darkness. This time of night the road was practically void of traffic.

It was farm country and farmers had to get up at the crack of dawn to work their fields. Which meant they were probably asleep right now. This was the Mississippi delta—flat, muddy, and fertile. Most farmers grew beans or cotton or rice. Several variables factored in on crop selection. He had no clue what they were. Nor did he care. He was convinced of one thing though, the mosquito should be considered the state bird. They were enormous and could suck your blood like a vampire.

Lack of traffic made the drive easier. Unfortunately a lone car on a highway in the wee hours of the morning was anything but inconspicuous to an eye in the sky or a LEO out on patrol.

US 64 joined US 67 at a small town called Beebe. Kaplan made the left turn. He planned to stay on 67 until Poplar Bluff, Missouri then he would look at a map. The streets in Beebe were deserted and everything was locked up tight, even the gas stations. It was a good thing Jeff's Jeep had plenty of gas because he wasn't sure when he'd see any signs of life again. A few minutes later, any trace of Beebe had disappeared into an abyss of darkness behind him.

He could see nothing on either side of the four-lane highway from the peripheral shine of his high beams except fields and the occasional tree. In his rearview mirror, a single set of headlights about two miles behind him.

When the pothole appeared in his headlights, it was too late to avoid hitting it. The impact jolted the Jeep to one side. Tony jerked upright in his seat.

"What the hell was that?"

"Just a hole in the road, nothing to get worked up about."

"I thought someone had rammed the car." Tony yawned and then said, "You and Jeff good friends?"

"We were once best friends. Why do you ask?"

"Just wanted to know if I could trust him to keep his mouth shut is all."

"He won't say anything. I've known him since childhood. We grew up next door to each other."

"You said you lost touch for a long time. People change. How do you know he won't go to the authorities?"

"Look, Tony, I don't have a problem with Jeff...it's you I'm not sure about."

He glanced at Tony and then back to the dark highway. "It's time to have a come to Jesus talk, Tony. Who the hell is trying to kill you?"

He could feel the old man's stare. He glanced at Tony. The old man lowered his head and tightened his lips as if struggling to come up with a response

"I already told you I'm not at liberty to discuss it," Tony quickly changed the subject. "I don't know anything about you. Even your friend didn't know about your profession. You claim you work for the CIA, yet you have never shown me any credentials. You might have saved my life back in Little Rock but how do I know it wasn't a setup? How do I know you're not one of them. You could be kidnapping me for all I know. You could have lied to your friends. This whole thing could be a ruse."

Kaplan was tired and fed up with Tony's incessant complaining. He sat in silence, not sure if he wanted to respond. Finally he said, "You're absolutely right, it could be a ruse. Of course, if I were one of the bad guys, you'd already be dead. I've had plenty of opportunities to kill you. Even thought about it a couple of times because you're such a pain in the ass, got a U.S. Marshal killed, and endangered the lives of my friends. Yet here you sit, alive and still running your mouth. It's because I gave my word to a dying U.S. Marshal and you know something else, Tony, I don't want to be here. I would rather be headed in the opposite direction. But I made a promise to Inspector Cox to deliver you to a WitSec safe site, and I only know the location of one. So unless you have a death wish, I suggest you start telling me who or what I'm up against."

Tony fidgeted. His defensive body language told Kaplan he wasn't going to give anything up.

"I'll make you a deal," Tony finally said after a few moments of silence. "Prove you are who you say you are and I'll tell you what you want to know."

Kaplan glanced at the old man and then returned his attention to the road. He reached down with his left hand, lifted his pant leg, and pulled something out of his left boot, switched on the overhead light, and handed it to the old man.

After a few seconds Kaplan asked, "Satisfied?"

The old man studied it, handed it back, and said, "Can I trust you?"

"You already have. With your life."

"By the way, I did not endanger your friends. You did. As soon as you took us to their house." Tony had a smug look on his face. "Now, what is it you want to know?"

Kaplan didn't get the chance to ask. The headlights he'd seen earlier in his rear view mirror had closed the gap and were now less than two car lengths behind him. He couldn't tell much about the car on the dark, deserted road. Just two bright lights shining in the rear window.

Kaplan checked his speed; he'd set the cruise control on the speed limit, so if it was a cop, he wasn't going to get pulled for speeding. His internal clock and familiarity with police procedures ruled out any chance law enforcement could be on to them this soon. The car stayed in the same spot behind him for several minutes, then pulled to the left, and accelerated.

Kaplan's initial thought was relief as he figured the car just wanted to pass him. Hopefully the 55 MPH speed limit was too slow for the driver.

The car pulled to the side of the Jeep and matched his speed. Instinctively, Kaplan's tactical training kicked in and he disengaged the cruise control. There was a flash and the left back window shattered. He depressed the brakes quickly and firmly. The car flew past and he got a good look at it as the Jeep's headlights lit up the car's side. A dark Crown Victoria. Just like the one that followed them from the restaurant and he evaded at the Big Dam Bridge.

He maneuvered the Jeep behind the Crown Vic. Once again, a shooter leaned out of the window and began firing at them.

"They're shooting at us," Tony yelled.

"Got any more helpful news?"

He swerved left and right in an attempt to throw off the shooter's aim.

A bullet hit the windshield. A spider web shaped crack appeared at the base of the windshield halfway between Kaplan and Tony. The bullet lodged in the back seat behind him.

"Are they the same ones from the restaurant?" Tony asked.

"Pretty good bet." Kaplan swerved left and right behind the Crown Vic. "Duck below the dash."

"Right." The old man did as instructed.

He accelerated and rammed the Crown Vic from behind. The car began to fishtail but quickly regained control.

Tony groaned as he bounced back and forth from the impact.

Part of Kaplan's tradecraft training had included a defensive driving course he'd taken at FLETC, the Federal Law Enforcement Training Center in Brunswick, Georgia on the property that was once Naval Air Station Glynco. FLETC's mission was to train personnel who protect our homeland. The course was not limited to defensive driving, there were several offensive maneuvers taught as well, including PIT— Precision Immobilization Technique. Its sole purpose was to force a fleeing car to abruptly turn sideways resulting in a loss of control.

It wasn't simply ramming the rear end of a fleeing vehicle but rather the systematic placement of his fender against the rear fender and applying a turning force causing a loss of traction to the rear tires of the fleeing vehicle.

Getting his vehicle in position for the PIT was the difficult part. Whenever he went left, the Crown Vic went left. Right, the Crown Vic went right.

Their highway speeds were frequently in excess of eighty miles per hour. The use of a PIT at this speed could end with a catastrophic result, however at the moment, it was his best option.

The vehicles jockeyed for position for nearly a full minute before the driver of the Crown Vic failed to correctly predict Kaplan's next move.

He placed the left front fender of the Jeep against the Crown Vic's right rear fender and applied the turning force.

The Crown Vic's tires lost traction. Its rear end fishtailed to the left. The driver over reacted when he tried to correct for the loss of control and the Crown Vic jerked hard to the left and flipped. Kaplan swerved and braked hard to keep from becoming entangled with the out of control car.

The Crown Vic rolled side-to-side several times, went airborne end-to-end, and landed in the wide grass median where it came to rest upside down.

Kaplan braked to a stop in the middle of the road. Tony rose from the floorboard, made a cross on his chest and said, "Are they dead?"

He pushed Tony's head below the dash, drew his weapon, and said, "Stay put. I'll check."

CHAPTER 17

HIS GUT INSTINCT WAS RIGHT. MOSS KNEW the home had to be near Arkansas 365 somewhere north of Little Rock. He and Hepler had already discussed possible escape routes for the motorcycle and determined the most logical route.

Moore plugged the address into her Android phone and provided him with directions to the house. A Faulkner County deputy manned the first roadblock at the entrance to The River Plantation subdivision on River Road. The deputy let them pass after making sure they had proper credentials to enter. Two ninety-degree turns later, River Road became Plantation Drive, which came to a dead end T-section with River Road Drive.

Before Moss reached the T-section Moore said, "Turn left."

He pointed in the direction of the mass of swirling lights. "I think I got it from here, Inspector Moore."

To the left and a few houses down on the right were several more cars; all but one was a Faulkner County Sheriff's vehicle. The other, Arkansas State Police.

Moss turned onto River Road Drive and pulled next to the law enforcement vehicles. He parked and the three deputies walked toward the house where once again a LEO stopped them. "Sorry, nobody allowed beyond this point."

They pulled out their badges and flashed them to the officer as Hepler stated, "U. S. Marshals." The officer stepped to the side letting them pass. Moss stopped at the end of the driveway with Moore and Hepler to survey the scene.

All the surrounding neighbors' houses were lit up. Nobody was sleeping tonight. This part of the subdivision was spared the destruction of the tornado that destroyed many of the homes just a few months ago. The street was lined with curious neighbors, most in pajamas or bathrobes. One man had a toddler on his shoulders. Moss saw silhouettes of people across the street looking out of their homes through parted curtains. At least they had enough sense to stay inside.

A young Faulkner County deputy assigned to crowd control tried without success to get the onlookers to return to the safety of their homes. The onlookers who had just survived an EF 4 tornado a few months earlier were not easily persuaded to return to their homes until they knew what was going on in their neighborhood. Moss didn't blame them.

The front of the two-story brick home did not reveal any obvious clues of a crime scene. The front door and windows were all intact. Several Faulkner County deputies were looking around inside with flashlights. Their beams swept through the interior of the dark home. Barricades connected yellow *Crime Scene* tape to cordon off the entire front yard and restrict access to the home.

Moore and Hepler followed Moss up the driveway. An overweight man with a badge and a gun strapped to his belt, put his hand out, turned and spat, then wiped his chin with the back of his hand. He blocked Moss halfway down the driveway.

"Stop right there," the man commanded. "This is a crime

scene just what the hell do you think you're doing in *this* neighborhood?"

"In this neighborhood." Moss clenched his fists at the implication. It was clear by the tone in the lawman's voice. "You mean what is a black man doing in a white neighborhood, don't you?"

Moore quickly stepped in front of Moss. "This is Senior Inspector Moss and Deputy Hepler." She pointed at Moss and then Hepler. She held up her creds. "And I'm Inspector Moore, United States Marshals Service."

Moss knew what Moore was doing. Her beauty and authoritative style were hard to resist even for the redneck cop. Moss appreciated it and applauded her efforts because right now he was resisting the urge to break the man's neck.

The big cop lowered his massive arms as he looked at Moore and smiled. His height, short thick neck, and giant gut made him look like a sumo wrestler with a badge.

"And you are?" Moore asked.

"Doug Hollister, Sheriff of Faulkner County." He turned to walk away. "And I don't need none of you uppity Feds poking around in my investigation. I'm already busy as a one-legged man in an ass-kicking contest." He should have kept his mouth shut. Moss was done listening to this ignorant cop.

He stepped around Moore. "Listen up, Bubba."

The big man whipped around. Moss could see the anger in his bulging eyes. Hollister had his hand resting on his revolver and Moss expected to see steam shoot from his ears any second. Moss stepped forward until they were nearly eye-to-eye, nose-to-nose. Inches apart. Like two menacing bulls scraping the earth with their hooves right before they charged.

"I don't give a rat's ass who you want or don't want involved in this investigation," Moss said. "This incident is connected to a crime that occurred in Little Rock tonight, which makes it part of a federal investigation and that, Sheriff, leaves you out in the cold."

"And if I refuse to yield jurisdiction?"

"For starters, I'll have your fat redneck ass arrested for interfering with a federal officer in the performance of his duties. And by the time the prosecutors finish with you, there will be a couple of dozen other federal charges tacked on as well."

Moss could see the man puffing out his chest.

"Is that right, mister big shot?" Hollister said. "On whose authority?"

"Mine," a voice said from behind Moss. The man walked in short rapid strides up to the sheriff.

"And just who the hell are you, little man?" Hollister emphasized *little* with his southern drawl.

"Special Agent Richard Small, Federal Bureau of Investigation."

Of all the people to come to Moss's defense, it had to be this little prick. Moss had to admit, though, Small's timing was impeccable.

"Now Sheriff," Moss said. "How about you remove your hand from your weapon and then take the time to give us a full briefing."

Hollister rubbed his chin. He looked at Moss and then back to Small. "Reckon I don't have much choice in the matter, now do I?" He looked directly at Small. "I'll tell *you* what I know so far."

Before the sheriff could speak, a flatbed truck filled with portable construction lights pulled up. "Where do you want these, Sheriff?" A deputy called out above the noise.

"Set a couple of 'em up in the front yard and put the rest round back."

The man replied. "Yes suh, Sheriff."

"What's with the lights?" Moss asked.

"Power to the house was disabled somehow," Hollister replied. "Don't know if it was a short circuit or what, but until we get an electrician out here, we won't have power."

"What happened, Sheriff?" Small asked. He opened his notepad and pulled his gold pen from his pocket.

"The neighbors heard the alarm and called 9-1-1," the sheriff explained. "Almost everyone we talked to said the alarm lasted about fifteen minutes and then stopped. The alarm company called when they weren't able to reach the owners, by then we had already sent a unit to investigate."

Hollister continued, "Looks like the owners weren't home. We're trying to locate them now. No cars in the garage. Forced entry through the back door. My deputies found a room upstairs with a concealed entrance. Inside were a cell phone, driver's license, credit cards, and several RFIDs sitting on a table."

"Sheriff," a deputy interrupted. "You really need to see what we found."

"What now?" Said the Sheriff.

Hollister, Moss, Moore, Hepler, and Small followed the deputy around to the back yard. He walked down a sloping terrace toward the river and pointed to the open doors of a bunker built into the ground beneath the house. "In there," he said.

Moss walked in with the rest of the group. Several flashlights illuminated the small space. It looked like any storage shed filled with lawn equipment and unwanted items stored and forgotten. Except the storage shed was actually a bunker built in the ground and there was one item that stood out. A black Harley-Davidson motorcycle.

"Looks like the motorcycle we been looking for." Hollister seemed happy his men made the discovery.

The deputy knelt down next to the Harley and put his hand on the engine. "Still warm." Then he ran his finger over a dent on the fender. "Looks like someone took a shot at him too."

Moss knew this was his first break. The pieces were about to fall together. He looked down and noted the Virginia tag on the back of the Harley. Just like the eyewitness report. "JP, run the plates."

Hepler walked outside the bunker with phone in hand. Less than two minutes later, he returned. "Good news and bad news, Pete."

"Pete Moss?" The sheriff guffawed. "Is that seriously your name?"

Moss ignored the man, "Always the good news first."

"Plate is registered to a Gregg Kaplan of Tysons Corner, Virginia."

"Good. What do you have on Mr. Gregg Kaplan?"

"That's the bad news," Hepler said. "We're locked out. I called it in to HQ and there is a codeword access, top-tier SCI clearance on Mr. Kaplan. Above Marshals and the FBI."

CHAPTER 18

KAPLAN POSITIONED THE JEEP WITH ITS headlights shining on the mangled hulk of the car. It was definitely a Crown Vic and had all the visual traits of a G-car, although it wasn't. The plates weren't government plates; they were Tennessee plates. Perhaps the car came from Memphis or Nashville. Maybe Knoxville.

Nevertheless, it meant the shooters were in Little Rock before he arrived, and likely before Tony. There could have even been a tail on Cox and Tony as soon as they left the Memphis airport. Another indication of a leak in the U. S. Marshals Service. The gunmen were already there waiting. Waiting for a chance to take Tony down. Kaplan was positive he was looking at the same car that chased after them from the restaurant in Little Rock.

Kaplan could see no movement in the car. He checked the chamber of his Beretta and ensured there was a round in it before he got out of the Jeep. "Stay down," he ordered through the shot out car window. "Don't be stupid and give them a chance to finish what they started."

"Okay," Tony said.

"And if you try to run this time, I'll shoot you myself." Kaplan's furrowed brow deepened.

Tony nervously bobbed his head up and down.

Kaplan knew he didn't have long. On this lonely stretch of highway, it could be thirty minutes before another car came along or it could be five. There was no way of knowing and he wanted to be long gone before another vehicle showed up and called 9-1-1. Because at this hour of the morning, Jeff's Jeep at the scene would make an impression in someone's mind.

An eyewitness.

With a description.

He ran in serpentine fashion toward the overturned car, the barrel of his gun leading the way. The radiator was cracked, steam hissed from behind the grill. The roof was partially crushed, more on the passenger's side than the driver's, leaving very little headroom for occupants. The driver was suspended upside down, arms dangling beside his head, held in place only by his fastened seatbelt. The airbag had deployed and fully deflated by the time Kaplan arrived. The door was caved inward, trapping the man's left leg between the door and the seat. Both feet were turned sideways and both legs were broken below the knee. His left shoulder was separated and his left arm snapped halfway between the shoulder and elbow. He had cuts and gashes. Both his face and the deflated airbag were smeared with blood. His eyes were open and he gasped for air. Kaplan stuck his head inside the collapsed window frame; the man's neck was broken. He would die before help arrived.

Kaplan looked across the cabin; the passenger side was empty. He checked the back seat, nothing. But he had anticipated that. When the car flipped, he had seen the faint image of the man thrown from his perch on the door. He stepped away from the car and looked around on the median. In the grass near the opposite lanes of traffic was the shadow of a body. The shooter ejected from the car after impact was laying in the median.

Kaplan stood over the man's body. He pointed his gun at the man and then lowered it. The shooter was obviously dead. His arms and legs twisted around his body like a contortionist. Being ejected from a car and hitting the ground at eighty miles per hour had a tendency to do that.

Kaplan checked his internal clock; he had been here two and half minutes. It wasn't safe to remain any longer. He reached down and checked the man's pockets. No ID. He returned to the dying man still hanging upside down in the car. No more gasping sounds. He checked the man's pulse, already dead. Kaplan checked his pockets. No ID either. He spent a few seconds searching the area for the men's weapons but found nothing. There was no telling how far or which direction the guns landed.

Time to go.

He ran back to the car, put it in gear, and pulled away from the crash. Five minutes later he passed a car going the opposite direction and knew responders would soon be dispatched to the accident. It was a head start, but not a comfortable one. And his lead was getting shorter.

He drove in silence for several minutes. Finally he turned to Tony and asked, "Who the hell is trying to kill you?"

"The list is long," Tony confessed.

"Who are they?"

"There are a lot of them, Mr. Kaplan. Can we just leave it at that."

"No, we can't. Those guys from the car," Kaplan said. "They aren't like the men from the restaurant. Those men were Italian, like you. The men in that car were Caucasian. American. And they looked a lot like feds...or former military."

"Sicilian."

"What?"

"I am Sicilian. The men in the restaurant were Italian. My family comes from a small island off the northern coast of Sicily called Lipari. Therefore I am Sicilian, not Italian. There's a big difference."

"Not to me there isn't. And not to most people, either. It's one and the same."

"Well, most people are wrong."

"Is this a mafia thing?"

Tony laughed. "You have watched too many *Godfather* movies. It is not like that at all. Maybe it once was, but not any more. It's a lot more sophisticated now. Not as many turf wars. Mostly it is an enterprise. Big business."

"So you *were* in organized crime?"

Tony paused and then said, "I am a broker."

CHAPTER 19

AS THE JEEP PASSED THE *SEARCY CITY LIMIT* sign, Kaplan saw three police cars, a rescue vehicle, and a fire truck pass him going in the opposite direction.

Fast.

Lights flashing.

Sirens blaring.

At this time of the morning, knowing what he knew, their destination was a no-brainer.

"What kind of broker?" Kaplan asked Tony.

"You misunderstand," he said. "I broker anything."

As they entered the town of Searcy, streetlights lined the highway. While he talked, Tony was doing that thing again with his hands. Thumb touching his first two fingers. Palm up. Wrist bouncing. He recognized it as a typical Italian gesture. Or Sicilian, in Tony's case. "What do you broker?"

"It depends on what my client needs. I once had a client in Argentina who wanted women so I connected him with someone who dealt in human trafficking. It's rather appalling I know, but they both paid very well. You see, all I do is make the introduction, after that, I have nothing further to do with it. I brokered for a man in Mexico who wanted guns. I don't know what he did with them. In my line of business, you don't ask questions. I've brokered prescription drugs to a South American drug lord, false passports to a man in the Cayman Islands, and recruited accident victims with Medicare information for several health care companies in South Florida." He held up his fingers and made air quotes when he said *health care*.

Kaplan glanced at Tony, then back to the highway. "You realize the people you deal with are heavy hitters. They don't take kindly to anyone ratting them out."

"*Omerta.*"

"What?"

"*Omerta.* It's a code of silence against giving evidence to the cops. For ratting them out I'm a *pezzo di merda.*"

"What does that mean?"

"Pezzo di merda. Like you would call someone a *piece of shit* in English. If I'm caught they will stuff a bird in my mouth and then a bullet to the head."

"Because you sang like a canary." Kaplan smiled.

"Exactly."

He thought about what Tony said. If the old man was providing testimony against the types of criminals he mentioned, it was incredible he was still alive. He was up against some very powerful underworld players with connections that ran far and wide and a lot of money to spend to silence the old man. Corrupt money to protect their businesses. Kaplan was starting to understand why Inspector Michael Cox wanted him to deliver Tony only to a WitSec safe site.

He took an exit on the northeast side of Searcy.

"Why are we stopping?" Tony asked. He leaned over and looked at the gas gauge. "We have plenty of gas."

"We need new clothes." Kaplan pointed to the Walmart sign. "Open twenty-fours hours."

Kaplan parked the Jeep beyond a vehicle farthest from the entrance. He rolled down the three good windows and scraped the broken glass from the fourth onto the floorboard. On the off chance someone walked by he didn't want extra attention drawn to the vehicle. Cracked windshields happen all the time. And a car with its windows down in August isn't going to raise anyone's eyebrows. Odds were no one would come out here anyway, so it was strictly a precautionary move.

Fifteen minutes later with a road atlas, two shirts, and a pair of dark slacks in a bag, all paid for with cash, he and Tony got back into the Jeep. They changed in the car. Kaplan remained in his jeans but scrapped the black long-sleeve t-shirt for a tan *Dickies* work shirt. Tony changed into dark brown slacks and a shirt that was a color Kaplan had trouble describing. Not purple or red or even wine. Plum, maybe. But, the combination suited Tony.

He pulled out of the Walmart parking lot and stopped behind an all-night pancake house. He tossed the old clothes in a dumpster and pulled out on East Race Avenue. He didn't take the on ramp to the highway; instead he drove under the highway and pulled into a Waffle House. "I need something to eat. I was too busy saving your ass in Little Rock." He parked on the side of the building away from all the windows. No sense advertising which vehicle he was driving.

Kaplan and Tony walked in and sat down in the booth nearest the entrance.

The diner smelled of burnt coffee. Booths wrapped around two sides of the diner and a row of stools lined the counter. It was empty except for the man behind the counter who looked too old to be working the graveyard shift in an all-night diner. An apron covered his dingy t-shirt. His hair was thin. And greasy. Almost as greasy as the griddle behind him.

"What'll it be?" The man asked.

"Got any fresh coffee?" Kaplan asked.

"You ordering food?"

"Yes."

"Then I'll put on a fresh pot now. It'll only take three or four minutes." While he spoke he ripped open a bag, dumped the grinds in a hopper and shoved it in a machine. With the push of a button, fresh coffee started dripping into a carafe. "What'll it be?"

Kaplan said, "Three eggs scrambled, bacon, hash browns, and biscuits and gravy."

"And you?" He looked at Tony.

"I'll have the same."

"Coming right up."

The man turned around and tossed a glop of lard on the griddle and worked it with a spatula into a fine glaze on the cook top. Within minutes Kaplan heard bacon sizzling and smelled freshly brewed coffee. His stomach growled. He was hungrier than he realized. The plate of food arrived and he shoveled it down. His last meal had been over twelve hours ago in Knoxville, Tennessee.

As Tony was finishing his meal, Kaplan noticed a pickup truck pull into the parking space in front of their window. The truck was covered in a camouflage wrap with a gun rack in the rear window. Two young men jumped out laughing. Beer cans tumbled from the cab onto the parking lot. They laughed louder. Easily amused. Both were about the same size, one had short dark hair tucked beneath a tan cap with a Ducks Unlimited logo, the other had short red hair and a John Deere cap. They looked like high school seniors who probably worked on their fathers' farms by day and went looking for trouble by night. And it was a Friday night.

Technically, Saturday morning, a time when young people across the nation would unwind from the week by drinking enough to act stupid.

Both boys wore jeans with dirty work boots. The guy in the John Deere cap wore a shirt that said something about rice and grain. Ducks Unlimited wore a t-shirt with PETA scribed across the front in big bold letters, which seemed odd until Kaplan read the subscript—People Eating Tasty Animals.

Through the window PETA pointed at Kaplan with both index fingers in a drum roll fashion.

The cook turned around when he heard the door open. His face fell. "Look boys, I don't want any trouble tonight. Go on and get out of here before I have to call the cops on you two again."

"Call the cops then," John Deere said. "No one will answer. They got called out to a fiery car crash out on South 67. All of them."

Kaplan's gut clenched. *Fiery.* When he left the smashed up Crown Vic, there was no fire. Or any signs one might ignite. He looked at Tony and said, "Let's get out of here."

"I'm not finished yet," Tony said.

PETA squeezed into the booth and sat next to Tony. "You heard him. Let the man finish."

John Deere sat down next to Kaplan.

PETA said, "We're hungry. Why don't you buy us breakfast too?" More laughter.

Kaplan said nothing.

Tony turned his attention back to his plate. "You boys are making a big mistake," he said.

"How's that old man?" PETA stared at Kaplan.

"You should leave while you can," Tony said and took a bite of his biscuit.

"What if I say we're staying?" John Deere said.

Kaplan picked up his half-empty coffee cup and swirled the dark liquid inside until it almost lipped over the edge of the cup. "He's right. You should leave now."

John Deere pulled a knife from his pocket and clicked it open.

Tony gave John Deere a nervous glance and said, "You really shouldn't have done that."

Before John Deere could respond, Kaplan's elbow smashed into his face with a mighty upward force. The cartilage in the kid's nose gave way and his head snapped back. Kaplan seized him by the nape of the neck and slammed his forehead into the table. Coffee splashed from the cups. Silverware rattled on the tabletop. Kaplan pushed the unconscious kid to the floor.

Kaplan quickly scooted out of the booth. PETA was already standing two feet away pointing a handgun at Kaplan's head. His hand shook.

"Johnny?" PETA nudged his unconscious friend with his boot.

"He can't hear you," Kaplan said. "Get in your truck and leave or you'll join your friend."

"You forget who's holding the gun."

Kaplan's left hand moved with swift accuracy as he turned sideways and deflected the gun to his right, PETA's left. The gun fired. The bullet hit the base of the counter and lodged in the wood molding. In one smooth motion, Kaplan's right hand grabbed the barrel and twisted PETA's wrist inward, past the breaking point, which sent PETA to his knees. Kaplan kept twisting until the gun came free from the kid's hands and was now in Kaplan's hand and pointed at PETA's head. "Looks like I am."

"Son of a bitch, you broke my wrist."

The cook's mouth dropped open. "How'd you do that?"

"Practice." Kaplan thrust his knee upward in PETA's face. The kid fell over, nose bleeding and unconscious.

Kaplan fished three twenties out of his pocket and tossed them on the counter. "For the meals and inconvenience. Also, coffee and aspirin. They'll need both when they come to."

Kaplan turned around and Tony was standing next to him. "I warned them," the old man said.

"Kids these days just don't listen."

CHAPTER 20

KAPLAN AND TONY HURRIED ACROSS THE
Waffle House parking lot toward the Jeep parked out of view
from the diner's windows.

"Here," Kaplan said. He tossed the Jeep's keys to Tony.
"You're driving."

Tony caught them in midair, "I can't drive like you. I don't
think this is a good idea."

"None of this is a good idea. Now get in and drive."

Kaplan got in, adjusted the seat, and settled in to a
comfortable position. He estimated it would take a little over
two and a half hours to get to Poplar Bluff. He pulled out the
road atlas he bought at Walmart, reached into his backpack,
and pulled out his mini-Mag penlight.

While Tony drove, Kaplan studied the map. "As a precaution,
I think we should alter our route. If we're being tracked, and
I'm pretty sure we are by now, especially when word gets out
about what just happened back there, we should veer away
from a straight-line path to our destination. It will add a few
extra hours driving time but it will muddle their guess of our
intentions."

"A few hours? You think that's a good idea? I thought time
was of the essence."

Kaplan ignored the question. "In Paducah, we'll turn south toward Nashville. We should get another car and dump this one. We can do both in Nashville. They'll be looking for the Jeep by now."

Kaplan reached his right hand to the base of his seat, felt around, and found the correct button. The seat's motor hummed as his seat back reclined. Yesterday hadn't turned out at all like he'd expected. Or had planned. It had been almost twenty-four hours since he left Virginia and now he was on his way back. His original itinerary called for a good night's sleep in Little Rock, an early wake-up call, and then another long day's ride to El Paso.

The man he'd met last year in Yemen lived in El Paso. He held the key to the whereabouts of the woman for whom Kaplan was searching. The man, according to his handler, was the only one who knew her current location. A location he might be reluctant to reveal at first, but Kaplan was certain he could persuade him.

His thoughts returned to his own carelessness. How could he have made such a stupid mistake? A rookie mistake. Tradecraft training taught him to identify and resolve multiple complex scenarios simultaneously. Now his failure to pay attention to detail made his current situation even more complicated. When law enforcement showed up at his friend's home and found Kaplan's motorcycle and ran his license plate through motor vehicles databases, alarm bells would go off at the CIA. He would be back on the grid and the agency would have to officially deny he was in an operational status inside the United States. No one at Langley would be happy.

His friends' lives might be in jeopardy. The only thing working in their favor was that they bought the vacation beach

house in Sandestin two weeks ago and, with any luck, the
banking and property databases hadn't been updated yet.

† † †

Valkyrie hung up the phone.

Shepherd had informed the assassin about the break-in
at the home on the Arkansas River. No one was home and
all of the old man's WitSec identity documentation had been
discovered inside the home along with several RFID tracking
devices. How Shepherd obtained that information Valkyrie
did not know. Nor care. What Valkyrie did want to know was
whether Shepherd had someone else working the same job.

Shepherd said the target would move east. The old man and
his companion would keep to the back roads, stay out of sight,
and change vehicles often.

East.

But to where?

† † †

While Hepler and Moore made phone calls, Moss and
Special Agent Small walked through the house with Sheriff
Hollister. It seemed that whoever broke into the home hadn't
stayed long. Barely long enough to regroup and formulate a
plan. Perhaps they even tried to map out an escape route. It
appeared they did have time enough to find something to eat
in the house and make a pot of coffee.

Moss knew the witness's background. The Department of
Justice's contract with the witness was to provide testimony
against several crime families. And in so doing, he would

incriminate many other underworld figures as well…in the United States and abroad. Any number of whom had the resources to hire an assassin. These were ruthless people driven by power and greed.

According to his file, the witness's location had been compromised twice before, and both times for the same reason—his refusal to follow WitSec security measures. The witness's involvement in several philatelic organizations was an activity WitSec repeatedly instructed him to abandon for his own safety. A passionate hobby he couldn't seem to give up. He continued to purchase rare stamps to add to his collection. Moss wouldn't be surprised if the cause of this breach weren't for the same reason.

It was his job to locate WC 7922, aka Anthony Napoli, before the bad guys did. At this point, Moss had to assume this Kaplan fellow was keeping the witness alive for a reason. For what, he did not know.

After a thorough search of the home, no evidence of blood was found except a trace amount on a sink in a half bath behind the family room. Not enough to amount to more than a small cut or bloody nose. Even though samples were taken for DNA testing, by the time those results came in it wouldn't matter, this would all be over.

Before he and Small started the walk-through, Moss gave Moore and Hepler specific instructions. Moore was to call U. S. Marshals Service headquarters to see if they had the clout necessary to get information on Gregg Kaplan. If not, since the Marshals Service was Department of Justice, maybe somebody there knew somebody up the food chain who could pull a few strings. He tasked Hepler with coordinating a review of all traffic cams in Little Rock that might have picked up the dark sedan pursuing the motorcycle. Once he had investigators looking at video, Hepler was to ensure an APB was issued for Gregg Kaplan. Moss wanted the all points bulletin to include Arkansas and any state that shared a common state line with Arkansas.

One thing was certain; Gregg Kaplan was a person of interest. His motorcycle was there. But where was he now? And was the witness still with him? What about the homeowners? Where were they? It was beginning to seem probable that the owners weren't home when Kaplan and the witness arrived.

"Inspector Moss?" Moore's voice called to him from the back door.

Moss walked down the stairs. "Find out anything?" He walked toward her and she met him in the middle of the family room.

Hepler came through the door at the same time. Moss and Moore turned toward him.

Moss turned back to Moore, "Well, what did you find out?"

"Not good," she said. "Not only is the Marshals Service locked out of Mr. Kaplan's file, all of Justice is as well. His info is locked up tighter than Fort Knox."

Moss turned to Hepler. "Get anything useful from the traffic cams?"

"Nada," Hepler said. "The car wasn't seen on any traffic cams that we could find. And if Justice can't get his file—"

"He's NSA or CIA." Moss interrupted.

"My money says he's a spook," Hepler said.

Moss rolled his eyes. "Come on, JP. You think everyone's a spook. I need something now, his trail is growing cold and I don't intend to end my career with a failed assignment. Find out what vehicles the owners have and let's start looking for them. I want to know about anything that seems out of the ordinary. I'll determine whether it's relevant or not."

Hepler raised his finger. "There was one thing, Dirt Man. Maybe it's related." He fished a piece of paper from his back pocket. "There was a fatal one-car accident a couple of hours up the road from here. Two people killed. One died in his seat belt and the other was ejected from the vehicle. A black Crown Vic. No IDs either. The car caught fire and burned. Arkansas State Police and Searcy Police responded. Two weapons were found in the grass median."

"Maybe one day you can explain this *Dirt Man* thing," Moore said. "When did the accident occur?"

"Little over an hour ago." He looked at his watch. "Probably closer to two by now."

"Timing is right," Moore said.

"Yes it is," Moss said. It was a lead. And a direction. Not much, but something worth checking out. If it was the same Crown Vic from earlier, then they knew something he didn't. Perhaps they were following the witness. Or knew where he was going. "Run the prints on the weapons and see if we get any hits.

"Also," Moss continued. "Hitch a ride back to your car with Special Agent Small. I need someone in the office to coordinate this operation. Contact Arkansas Motor Vehicles and issue BOLOs on all vehicles registered to this address." Moss turned his attention to the red-haired woman. "Inspector Moore, looks like you and I are going to the booming metropolis of Searcy, Arkansas."

She smiled. "Wouldn't want it any other way."

CHAPTER 21

KAPLAN SET HIS INTERNAL TIMER FOR TWO hours. That would put him just this side of Paducah, Kentucky. He'd told Tony the planned route and instructed him to stop on this side of Paducah for gas so there would be no need to stop in town. Not as many closed circuit cameras outside the city either. Street level surveillance was a growing trend nationwide, even in the smaller communities, despite the outcry from concerned citizen groups about Big Brother and invasions of privacy.

Kaplan also knew that regardless of the fact Homeland Security had claimed not to use license plate tracking information gathered by private intelligence companies, agencies like the NSA and the CIA still did. With the current sophistication of this tracking data, a license plate could be tracked in real-time across town or across the country. Privacy advocates had been worried about cell phones being traced when the rapidly expanding, more intrusive threat to privacy was license plate tracking with traffic cams.

His fleeting anger toward his amateurish mistake had dissipated. Dwelling on it served him no purpose and would only keep him from focusing on his mission. He closed his eyes and let the drone of the highway carry him into slumber.

He awoke suddenly and knew something wasn't right. The drone of the highway was gone and the Jeep was parked in front of a gas pump. Tony was nowhere in sight.

Kaplan reached into his backpack and pulled out a baseball cap. He tugged it low on his forehead and got out of the Jeep. There was one other car at the pumps. A young woman with long dark hair was pumping gas into a shiny black GMC Terrain.

As he approached the entrance to the all-night Mini-Mart, he scanned the open interior through the plate glass windows that lined the front of the building. No sign of Tony. He tilted his chin down and used the brim of his cap to shield his face from the Mini-Mart's cameras. A man of Indian heritage sat inside a glass booth.

Kaplan walked up to the glass booth avoiding eye contact with the attendant, "Bathroom?"

"Straight back and to the left," the man said.

Kaplan took two steps when Tony came around the corner. "What the hell do you think you're doing?"

"I'm seventy, I needed to stop. My bladder is not as young as it used to be. We are about forty-five miles from Paducah and we were down to a quarter of a tank, so I filled up."

"Wake me next time," Kaplan walked toward the back of the store. "My turn."

When Kaplan returned to the Jeep, Tony was standing in front with the hood open.

"Mr. Kaplan, we have a problem," he said. "Car won't start."

Kaplan leaned over and reconnected a loose cable. "No, I guess it wouldn't."

"Did you do that?"

Kaplan ignored him. "I'll drive." He held out his open palm.

Tony handed him the keys.

They both got in and Kaplan started the Jeep.

"I was not going to leave you if that's what you were thinking," said Tony.

"Nope, I'm guessing you weren't."

Kaplan drove in silence toward Paducah in the pre-dawn light. It wouldn't be long before the sun would be glaring in his face, always an issue when traveling east in the early morning unless the sky is covered with clouds. He glanced at Tony; the old man's eyelids were already sagging. His head bobbed a couple of times, each time he opened his eyes, then gravity would pull them shut again.

Kaplan broke the tranquility. "Tell me more about this broker thing," he said.

Startled from slumber, Tony jumped in his seat. "What?"

"How did you get started as a broker?"

Tony looked at him while he rubbed the sleep from his eyes. "Long story."

"We seem to have plenty of time."

Tony took a couple of deep breaths. "It started many years ago when I was living in Miami."

"How long ago?" Kaplan interrupted. "Give me a framework in time."

"Thirty years, at least." Tony readjusted himself in the seat. "It began rather innocent actually. A car in South Beach hit my roommate while he was crossing the street. In the crosswalk too, mind you. Ended up with a broken arm, lots of bruises, nothing very serious but it put him out of work and he got fired from his job. I told him he should sue the driver for medical expenses and lost wages." Tony paused. "To make a long story short, turned out the driver was the teenage son of a very wealthy and prominent Miami plastic surgeon. The father offered my roommate thirty grand to shut up and go away. Thirty grand was a lot of money back then—"

"It's a lot of money now."

"Right. Anyway, a light bulb went off in my head. It got me to thinking there was potentially a lot of money to be made. I just had to find the right people. Come to find out, there were literally thousands of people who would take a bump from a slow moving car for fifty percent of the take."

"Kind of like an ambulance chaser."

"Except I was not a lawyer...more like an unofficial mediator. I'd go straight to the drivers and try to arrange a settlement to keep it out of the legal system. The odds were good. Most of the time it worked, sometimes it didn't and I'd find a cheap lawyer and have him file a lawsuit. First year I pulled in over a hundred G's—and that was my take."

"That's a lot of con money."

Tony laughed. "Turned out to be a drop in the bucket, as one would say."

In the distance, Kaplan could see the glow of city lights reflecting off the clouds above. "What do you mean?"

"After doing a little research about corporation formation at the Miami-Dade Public Library, I got more creative and devised a plan. A long-term plan. Pure genius, if I do say so myself. A venture sure to net hundreds of millions of dollars a year. Billions over a lifetime. But it took considerable startup capital to fund the kind of corporate network needed to make it work and I couldn't exactly waltz into a bank and ask for a loan."

"So you went to someone with a lot of money."

"Yes. And there was only one man I knew at the time

with that kind of dough. In my mind it was going to be a match made in heaven, but as it turned out, even heaven had archangels. He put his son in charge of my venture. Big mistake. And the son was not a patient man. He never understood the business model. He expected immediate grandiose results as opposed to the slower safer model I devised. His impatience caused mistakes in the field and, being the idiot that he was, he only knew of one way to address those mistakes and that was to make an example of anyone who made a mistake. But when too many people started coming up missing or dead, the authorities were pressured to investigate."

"Who was he?" Kaplan asked.

Tony shook his head. "A bigger dumbass I have never met. Anyway, I had the son, with his father's money of course, set up a multi-level corporate structure under one ultimate corporate umbrella. After that, it was just a matter of recruiting."

"Recruiting what?"

"In the beginning, mostly people to participate in the medical scam. It was the keys to success...make or break to the plan. Ground floor, if you will."

"You mean finding people to jump in front of cars?"

"No, no. That was chump change. The money... the king's ransom was in billing. That's when I became a broker. When the corporation needed doctors, I went out and found doctors who needed patients to bill. When the billing company needed insurance information, I found thousands of people willing to sell their health insurance information for a few bucks. Whether it was private health insurance or not, didn't matter. The big bucks came later with Medicare and Medicaid, almost no oversight. In the beginning we staged accidents. Very elementary scams that I soon figured out weren't even necessary. Our corporate structure cross-billed and the insurance money poured in. One-car accidents could reap thousands from medical payments billed to auto insurance, doctors' billing to health insurance, lab bills...labs that the corporation owned, by the way. It was all just a paper shuffle. Our doctors prescribed medications so everything looked legit and soon we ended up with a stockpile of prescription meds. High dollar meds too. Before I knew it, I was brokering meds all over the world at black market prices."

"Sounds like the kind of crap that still goes on today."

"In a way, it does. Except now I think they are all in cahoots with each other...doctors, health insurance companies, and drug companies that is. It's still all about billing."

"And no one ever got caught?"

"Sure they did. There were casualties. Those were factored into my model. Publicly, the corporate level would be appalled, clean house, and in some instances even prosecute. But, the higher the Feds looked in the corporate structure, the cleaner it was. Some facilities were even shut down...guess who owned the replacement? New corporation name but owned by the same conglomerate at the top. What I had to contend with and hated was repeatedly explaining to the son that this was part of the process...not killing off every mistake. But he still—"

"Hold that thought," Kaplan interrupted as they reached the outskirts of Paducah and he saw a cop car parked on the side of the road with his radar speed gun mounted in the windshield. He looked in his rear view mirror and saw the patrol car pull out and fall in behind him. He glanced at the speedometer, he wasn't speeding so what was the cop's interest in tailing him? Could the authorities have already put out a BOLO on the Jeep? "Looks like we got company."

"Were you speeding?"

"Nope. But it won't be a good thing if he runs these plates." Kaplan spotted an all night diner a block ahead on the right. "I'm not going to wait around and give him the chance."

Kaplan flipped on his right turn signal and tapped the brakes. As soon as he did, the rack of blue lights lit up.

"Now what are you going to do?" Tony said. "You can't very well beat up a cop."

Kaplan braked and pulled to the curb. He was struggling to formulate a viable plan but coming up short.

The police car's siren came on and Kaplan heard the *Interceptor* engine kick into high gear as the patrol car made a u-turn and sped off in the opposite direction.

"That was close," Tony said.

"Too close... we need to dump this car now. We can't wait till Nashville."

"Getting paranoid?"

"As much time as has passed and the fact that we're still in the same vehicle? You bet. We've been pushing our luck for a while and now that it's daylight..." Kaplan turned into the parking lot. "...staying in this car any longer is just plain stupid."

He pulled up to the front door of the diner and got out of the car. Next to the entrance he bought a copy of *The Paducah Sun* from a newspaper machine. They walked inside, sat down in a booth, and ordered coffee. He flipped to the classified section and pulled it out, and then he handed the rest of the paper to Tony. "See if there is any news about Little Rock while I find us a car."

Within minutes he found what he was searching for, a cheap older model non-descript sedan that might make it a few hundred miles down the interstate. The clock above the diner's grill read 6:30 a.m. It was early, perhaps too early to make the call, but he did it anyway.

After several minutes of talking, he turned off his phone. "Anything in the paper?"

"No. Maybe we will learn something tomorrow."

"Tomorrow we'll be far gone from here and you'll be safe and sound in WitSec's custody."

Kaplan chugged the rest of his coffee. "Drink up," he said to Tony. "We need to get moving."

Five minutes later he had located the address given to him over the phone, made a quick drive by, and parked the Jeep a couple blocks away. After stuffing the Jeep's tag in his backpack and leaving the keys in the ignition, he and Tony walked toward the address. Other than a stray cat followed by a litter of kittens, he and Tony were alone on the streets of the dilapidated neighborhood.

"Kind of a rough part of town," said Tony.

"Looks that way. Guess I'll owe Jeff a new car."

"You might owe him more than a car."

Kaplan narrowed his eyes and stared at Tony, then looked ahead at the road and wondered if Jeff's home would be okay. "You might be right."

The car turned out to be a 1991 Mercury Sable station wagon and not a sedan as advertised in the paper. It was parked in the weeds on the front yard. Actually the weeds were starting to grow around the car. Two ruts marked its path in and out of the yard.

The Mercury Sable and its Ford counterpart Taurus were two of the most popular model cars in the late eighties and early nineties. Especially the Taurus. 1991 was about the time its popularity began to wane. The car's original color was wine, now it was faded and bleached by the sun. Several oxidation spots blotched the roof, hood, and trunk.

The owner met them at the front door. He was barefoot. His jeans were torn and his undershirt dingy. He smelled like he was on a two-day drinking binge, which could explain the man's foul mood at that hour of the morning. A cigarette dangled from his lips with an extra long ash just waiting for gravity to pull it free. He claimed the oil had recently been changed and the air conditioner didn't work. When he moved his mouth to speak the ash fell to his front porch.

He held out a key to Kaplan, "Here. Drive it around the block."

Kaplan took the key, "That won't be necessary."

Kaplan walked over to the vehicle and reached through the front grill under the hood. A second later the hood popped loose. He raised it and made a cursory check of belts and hoses. He slipped into the driver's seat, inserted the key, and started the engine. A puff of gray smoke billowed from the rusted tailpipe. The cloth seats were ripped and stained and the interior reeked of smoke and booze, which wouldn't matter anyway since, with no air conditioner, he'd have to drive with the windows down.

He put his left foot on the brake and pressed hard. With his right foot he pressed the accelerator revving the engine past a fast idle. He worked the gear selector from drive to reverse and back several times. Remarkably, the transmission never slipped.

A few minutes later he walked back to the front porch where Tony stood waiting.

"You are not seriously going to buy that clunker, are you?" Tony said to Kaplan.

The man on the porch frowned at Tony's remark.

Kaplan reached into his pocket and pulled out a stack of bills. He counted out four, one hundred dollar bills and held them out. "It'll get us where we're going."

"Where's that?" The man asked.

"St. Louis."

The man took the bills, nodded, and stuffed them in his front pocket. Then he walked back inside his shanty of a home.

No bill of sale. No title. Nothing. In this neighborhood, the money for the car was nothing more than booze and drug money.

They were two blocks away when Kaplan stopped and attached the license plate from the Jeep to the Sable. Two minutes later, he drove up the on-ramp to I-24 southbound toward Nashville.

"I can not believe you paid four hundred dollars for this junk heap," Tony said.

"It's all about hours," Kaplan replied.

"Hours?"

"It will be several hours before anyone can tie us to this car. By then, we'll be in a different state and a different car."

CHAPTER 22

MOSS ARRIVED AT THE SCENE OF THE ACCIDENT just after the sun broke the horizon in the eastern sky. Inspector April Moore slept almost the entire time they were on the road from Mayflower, Arkansas to Searcy, Arkansas. He drove the distance in just under two hours, which included a stop in Conway for food, gas, and restrooms, the only time Moore was awake for more than fifteen minutes.

It had been a long night. In reality, it had been a long twenty-four hours. Yesterday at this time he was just getting out of bed at his home in Chicago. What he wouldn't give to be back there now. Instead he had been working an evening shift in firearms training only to be interrupted and reassigned to WitSec. And to make matters worse, the assignment landed him back in the town he had just moved from, Little Rock. A town he'd grown to loathe during his WitSec tenure at the Little Rock Field Office.

A long day and a long night and now, as the sun cleared the tree line, he was staring at a charred Crown Vic upside down in the grassy median. The grass in a three-foot perimeter around the car was scorched. The twisted wreck's original paint melted off by the fiery crash.

He turned and poked the woman in the arm. "Moore, wake

up. Get ready for some crash-burn physics."

She roused in her seat and he could see her absorbing the scene in her mind.

"Looks toasted," she said. "Burned hot enough to take off the paint."

"Yep." Moss surveyed the scene. The lanes closest to the median were closed in both directions. Arkansas State Police were funneling all the morning travelers into one lane causing a minor backup of traffic. Gawkers made it worse. There were two fire trucks, two rescue units, state, county, and Searcy police cars, and a newer model black Ford panel van with *WHITE COUNTY CORONER* stamped on the side in bold, white letters. Two men in coveralls were loading a body bag through the rear door.

He was following the trail of his witness and the man accompanying him. A man who he now knew was Gregg Kaplan. A man who had connections of his own high in the ranks of the federal government. This search continued to get more complicated. The trail had been easy enough to follow, though; Kaplan left a string of bodies behind him like breadcrumbs. Whether deliberate or unintentional, it had kept the mystery man from falling out of sight altogether. At first he thought Kaplan was a fugitive and might be connected to Tony, but now he knew the man was not. But who was this mystery man? More importantly, why was he with Tony?

Moss signaled Moore. "Come on. Let's check it out," he said. He rolled himself out of his seat and into the morning air. It was warm and damp and he knew it would be another Southern scorcher with afternoon thunderstorms firing up shortly after lunch. There was no breeze. The air had a lingering stench of burnt vehicle mixed with recently sprayed chemicals on a nearby field by a crop duster. Moss looked around, on his side of the road was a field of soybeans—waist high and leafy. Across the highway, corn, which seemed to have just tasseled. The saddest thing of all was that he had been in the South so long, he actually knew what these crops looked like.

The Searcy Police chief held up his hand signaling Moss to stop as he approached. Moss pulled out his creds and held them up for the officer to see. Moore did the same. "Figured the feds would show up sooner or later. Didn't expect the Marshals though."

"What made you think the feds would show up?" Moore asked.

The chief looked at Moss then turned to Moore. "Crown Vic, no IDs, and those." The chief pointed to two handguns lying in the grass. Both Glocks and both with sound suppressors.

The chief gave Moss and Moore a full briefing on the one-car accident. He explained the skid marks on the asphalt indicated the car swerved and lost control. Since no large animal tracks could be found as a source of the swerve, he had initially attributed the crash to be caused by the driver falling asleep at the wheel.

"I'm not buying it," Moss said. "Something's not adding up. But what?"

"You think it's connected to the incident in Little Rock, don't you?" The chief asked. "Is that why y'all are here?"

Moss gave him a quizzical look.

"The shootout at the restaurant was all over the late news last night and the scanner at the station has been buzzing all morning."

Moss paused. "Hard to say. At this time, the only similarity is the type of vehicle and even that would be speculation at this point. A lot of people own Crown Vics. It's a popular car. I'm sure there are a few folks around here with sound suppressed handguns too. What do you think, Chief?"

"I reckon there's a handful, but these two ain't from around these parts. Plates were hard to trace but finally we found out they belong to some corporation in Memphis. Seems it don't exist either. Not at the registered physical address anyhow. Nothing there but a vacant lot."

"Anything suspicious on the car?" Moore asked. "Like dents or paint transfer."

"Think someone ran them off the road?"

"Just a thought," she said.

"Nothing on the car we could find. That's why I'm ruling it a one-car accident. My men have been up and down the highway. Searched the medians. There is no evidence of other vehicle involvement." The police chief looked at Moss. "I'll make sure you get a copy of my report if you want it."

"Thanks. That would be great." Moss paused and looked at Moore then back to the chief. "I think Inspector Moore and I will run into town and get something to eat. Any suggestions?"

The chief looked at Moss and snapped his fingers. "That reminds me. You might want to talk to the cook at the Waffle House?"

"What for?" Moore asked.

"He had some excitement early this morning, not long after we arrived here at this scene. I haven't had time to check it out but maybe the ruckus is connected to your incident in Little Rock somehow."

"What happened at the Waffle House?" Moss asked. "And how might it be connected?"

"It seems a couple of our younger trouble makers got

their asses handed to them." The chief explained. "By a man traveling with an older gentleman. Seems they picked on the wrong guy this time. He put 'em both in the hospital. Broken noses, concussions, and one with a broken wrist. They're still at White County Medical Center. I got an officer holding them until I can get there and question them."

Moss glanced at Moore then back at the chief. "We would like to talk with them too," he said.

Thirty minutes later both young men were sitting at a table in the hospital in front of Moss and Moore. With the exception of the cast on one man's right arm, they looked the same. Both had swollen blood-crusted noses and black eyes.

Moore started the questioning. "We need descriptions of the men you got into a fight with at the diner last night. Was the older man wearing khaki pants and a dark blue shirt and the younger man in jeans and a black shirt?"

The men didn't respond. Neither one wanted to talk.

Moss stood and leaned his body over the man with the cast. He placed his palms flat on the table revealing his massive arms and large hands. "For starters, how does assault with a deadly weapon sound?" Moss pressed down on the man's arm and pinned the cast to the tabletop. He rapped on the cast with his knuckles. The man winced. "Now listen up. I'm a big man who hasn't eaten in a very long time, which means my blood sugar is low. And when my blood sugar gets low, my patience evaporates and I get mean. You either answer Inspector Moore's questions or I'll ask her to leave the room. Now, you wouldn't want that to happen, would you?"

The young man began to squirm in his chair. "Okay," the man tried to pull his arm away from Moss. "The old man was wearing brown pants and purple shirt."

"And the younger man?" Moore asked.

"Jeans and a tan shirt, I think."

Moss held up his phone. On it was a photo of the witness. "Recognize him?"

"Could be the old guy, I guess. I'm not sure."

Moss handed the phone to the other man.

"Looks familiar. I think so. It all happened so fast."

Moss flipped to a photo of Kaplan. It was the photo from Kaplan's driver's license. Hours earlier, Hepler had copied it and sent it to his phone. "What about this guy? Was he one of them?"

The man with the cast looked startled and then angry. "That's him. That's the asshole who did this to us. I'll never forget his face."

Moss showed it to the other man. "Yeah. It's him all right."

Moss felt the vibration from his cell phone and the screen changed to incoming call—Hepler. He signaled to Moore, "Take over. It's JP."

He stepped into the hallway and answered, "Talk to me."

"You're not going to believe what showed up this morning in Paducah, Kentucky," Hepler said. "Came across the wire about ten minutes ago."

"JP, I've been up all night and haven't eaten. I'm not in the mood."

"Low blood sugar kick in, dirt man?"

"JP, I need information. Now."

"Okay sourpuss, here goes…Paducah PD responded to the *BOLO* on the black Jeep. They found one parked in a run down neighborhood with the keys dangling from the ignition. Tag was missing but I ran the VIN and, lo and behold, it is registered to the same address in Mayflower where our witness was."

"No kidding?"

"Yep," Hepler said. "And I took the liberty of shifting the search parameters to the east, north, and south of Paducah. I can't imagine he'd double back to the west knowing the world is looking for him."

"Good thinking," Moss said. "As a minimum, he's two hours ahead of us. Moore and I will leave and head to Paducah."

Moss noticed Moore coming from the hospital room with her cell phone held to her ear. She gave him thumbs up.

"Anything else I can do for you, Dirt Man?" Hepler asked.

"As a matter of fact, there is," Moss said. "Couple of things actually. First, call Paducah PD and have them canvas the town for any cars for sale by owner. The newspaper is probably a good place to start. Maybe we'll get lucky. He wouldn't have dumped the Jeep without lining up another vehicle and it isn't very likely he would stick around Paducah. He knows he left a trail, he won't stop running."

"Okay, what else?"

Moss walked out of earshot of Moore.

"Sniff around and see what you can come up with on Inspector April Moore. I can't put my finger on it, but I have a strange feeling about her." Moss paused. Moore was off the phone and staring at him. "And do it discreetly," he whispered into the phone.

"You got it, Dirt Man."

He hung up and walked over to Moore, "Jeep turned up in Paducah."

"Where's that?"

"Kentucky," he said. He motioned to the hospital room

where the two young men were, the police guard still outside the door. "Did you get anything else from them?"

"Not really. Guy with cast was whining about missing work. Said his father was going to *hit the roof*. His exact words."

"Wah. From what I've seen of this Kaplan fellow, those two are lucky they aren't in a coma."

"Or the morgue."

Moss smiled, "Or the morgue."

CHAPTER 23

HEAT FROM THE EARLY MORNING SUN radiated through the driver's side window as he drove toward Nashville. The man who sold him the car was right, the air conditioner didn't work and even with the fan speed set to high, Kaplan could feel beads of sweat rolling down the back of his neck. Moisture under his arms formed dark circles on his shirt. Rolling down the window didn't help much either, as the August morning air was already hot and humid. It was only a two-hour drive to Nashville, but in this heat, it would be a brutal two hours. Morning clouds already showed roiling signs of vertical development, a forewarning of another thunderstorm-riddled day in the humid South.

Tony had been asleep, or pretended to be, since ten minutes outside of Paducah. He claimed to be almost seventy, but he moved like a much younger man. Kaplan wasn't sure how much he could trust this stranger he was trying to protect and regretted getting involved. But, he gave his word to the dying WitSec deputy, a former Delta Force soldier just like himself. And he wasn't one to go back on his word. He had only done it once. Never again. Besides, it was the right thing to do, stepping in like he did. He looked at the sleeping man. There were too many things about Tony that weren't adding up.

Something else bothered him too. Over the past few years he'd become quite proficient at staying out of sight and off the grid, so how was it that so much misfortune had followed them? He had removed all the tracking devices from Tony's possessions and left them in Mayflower. Unless the old man had a device implanted under his skin. As unlikely as it was, it would explain his current situation. Was Tony really the problem?

Or was it him?

Bad luck and trouble *had* plagued him for the past few years. Ever since the incident on St. Patrick's Day in Savannah, Georgia, his life had seemed to take one bad turn after another.

He could only remember one other time when his life went into such a tumultuous downward spiral. It was his second year of college when his parents were t-boned by a loaded eighteen-wheeler. They were killed instantly, or at least that was what the police told him. That was when he dropped out of college and joined the Army. His tour in the military was good for him. The discipline and regimented schedule were things he needed at the time. He always knew when and where he was supposed to be—twenty-four hours a day. And Special Forces helped him vent his anger. Come to grips with the sudden loss of his parents. His life turned around, and so did his luck.

Tony's constant interruptions annoyed Kaplan so he was glad to have some quiet time to reflect on his current situation.

Immediately after entering Tennessee, Tony sat upright and pointed at a road sign for an upcoming rest area. "I need to make a pit stop."

Kaplan smiled. He could stand to stretch his legs. And the sign also indicated a welcome center; one he hoped included air conditioning.

Kaplan took the rest area exit and chose a parking spot across from the main entrance. The welcome center was indeed air-conditioned and he savored the cool, crisp air in the main lobby. His eyes followed Tony as the old man swiftly moved toward the men's room. Several wooden rocking chairs and a kiosk full of road maps and tourist information filled the lobby. Kaplan monitored the rest room door carefully. Tony didn't seem to get it that Kaplan was his only chance of survival.

While he waited, Kaplan used a second burn phone to locate a replacement vehicle in Nashville. It would be expensive, very expensive, but he had more than enough cash in his backpack to cover the cost and a lot more. He placed the phone call and made the necessary arrangements.

After five minutes of waiting, Kaplan was growing concerned. He'd seen several men go in and out and still no Tony. He gave the old man another two minutes then went inside the men's room. Tony was standing at a sink washing his hands. "What took so long?"

"I told you," Tony said. "I had to go."

"And we need to leave now. We have to meet a man about a car in a couple of hours." He handed the keys to Tony. "I'll give you directions."

An hour later the faded Mercury Sable turned onto Gallatin Pike in East Nashville. Kaplan knew from past experience that Nashville had the highest crime rate per capita than any other city in the country and East Nashville was the worst part of town. The area where he directed Tony was seedy and run down and criminal elements roamed the streets.

It was a perfect place to dump the Sable.

† † †

Angelo DeLuca caught a lucky break.

After his men failed in Little Rock, he thought all was lost. Three men dead and nothing to account for it.

Until now.

The text message on Bruno's phone simply read: I-24 red Mercury Sable wagon.

The rest was up to him to figure out.

His luck was about to change.

He spotted the Sable fifteen minutes ago on Interstate 24 and was now two hundred yards behind it on Gallatin Pike in East Nashville. And the old man was driving.

An earlier communiqué specified Nashville as part of the planned escape route. That's what DeLuca was counting on. Where he'd made plans to spring his trap. His orders were simple by definition but difficult in execution, intercept the Sable and extract the old man. The fate of his companion was irrelevant, but the old man was to remain unharmed. His was a different destiny.

It was up to the remaining four, himself included, to complete the task that the first three had failed to finish. The fiasco in Little Rock had been a setup. Someone else knew it was going down. And that someone had a different plan in mind for the old man. A plan that involved hit men waiting outside the restaurant in Little Rock to take the old man down. DeLuca had to assume they hadn't given up and were still in pursuit.

Also in pursuit of the snitch would be the U. S. Marshals Service. The old man was too important to the Marshals Service and the Department of Justice to let get away. His testimony would bring down dozens of top criminal figures, from drug lords to human traffickers, from arms dealers to health care defrauders.

And the man at the top, DeLuca's boss.

His job was to make sure the old man never made it to the witness stand.

† † †

Using his cell phone's GPS, Kaplan directed Tony two blocks down a side street where he told him to pull to the curb. The street was littered with trash. Abandoned cars were turned into permanent lawn ornaments, a few with concrete blocks under bare wheels. Two out of every three of the cookie-cutter style houses was abandoned. Windows and doors boarded, graffiti painted on the outside. In Nashville, this part of town was known as an epicenter of criminal activity. There were crack houses, whorehouses, and meth labs.

The thick humid air had a putrid stench about it—a combination of rotting garbage, urine, and feces.

"Leave the keys in the ignition and let's go," Kaplan said.

"We are getting out of the car *here*? Is it safe?"

"No."

"Then why—"

Before Tony could finish, Kaplan was out of the Sable, retrieved his backpack from the back seat and had walked around to Tony's door. "Get out," said Kaplan. He gripped the Sicilian's arm and turned back in the direction of Gallatin Pike.

Pulling to the curb behind the Sable was a black Chevrolet Impala. A hundred feet behind it, three gangbangers policing their turf walking down the middle of the road toward them.

Two big men unfolded out of the Impala's seats. Italians. Just like the ones from the Little Rock restaurant. They either had a fetish for black or they had a funeral dress code in the mafia. They made no attempt to conceal their weapons, just jammed them in their front waistband in proud display. One meant for intimidation.

If the Italians in Little Rock had names like Vito, Nico, and Sal, these big guys had names like Gianni and Tito. Gianni was Kaplan's size. Tito, much larger. He was the enforcer. His sheer size was more intimidating than the weapon stuffed in his waistband. Which is why Kaplan chose the fictitious name, Tito, meaning *giant*. Yet Kaplan knew something they didn't, there were three East Nashville gangbangers fifty feet behind Gianni and Tito and closing. And right now, they were his only allies.

Two carried metal pipes, the other a baseball bat.

Tito said, "You have two choices. You can get in the car peacefully."

"Or?" Kaplan said. Forty feet and closing.

"Or I shoot you and stuff you in the trunk."

"What are you doing?" Tony whispered. "These guys aren't close enough for you to do... that thing you do."

Thirty feet.

Kaplan said, "Why don't you make me an offer I can't refuse?"

Gianni pulled his pistol from his waistband. He was a Southpaw. A lefty. "Real funny, tough guy. I don't know who you are, but you just made the wrong choice."

Twenty feet.

"Oh I see, you're going to kill us. But that was really the plan all along, wasn't it? Shoot us in cold blood. Leave us dead in the middle of the street."

Tito pulled his gun. "Not him, we want him alive." He used his barrel to point at Tony and then back at Kaplan. "You though, are expendable. A dead man if you don't do what I say."

Ten feet.

Gianni heard them first. He spun, gun leading the way. One of the metal pipes smashed his wrist. His gun fired, the bullet ricocheted off the asphalt. Gianni screamed. His wrist was bent downward, all of the small bones in his mangled hand probably shattered by the impact. Bloody grooves swelled on his hand from the threads on the end of the pipe.

Tito sidestepped the swing of the baseball bat as if he felt it coming from behind. He turned, gun in hand, and fired. The shot hit the man with the baseball bat in the chest. He fell to the pavement and never moved again.

Using his right hand, Gianni pulled a switchblade from his back pocket and buried the blade into his attacker's thigh. The man yelled and dropped the metal pipe. He grasped his leg with both hands.

Tito raised his gun toward the third attacker but was too slow. The metal pipe struck the barrel and knocked it from Tito's oversized mitt. The attacker swung again and Tito caught the pipe mid-swing with a single hand and tossed it on the ground.

What was left was a brawl; a one-armed man versus a one-legged man and two large men with nothing but fists, and Kaplan wasn't hanging around to see the outcome. He grabbed Tony's arm and pointed toward Gallatin Pike.

"Let's get the hell out of here."

Tony didn't argue. They both turned and ran from the scene of the brawl.

CHAPTER 24

DELUCA FACED A CONUNDRUM.

Lose two more men or lose the old man.

Sitting next to him in the driver's seat of the champagne silver Buick LaCrosse was the last of his men. The last and the most trusted. Bruno had been DeLuca's second-hand man for nearly five years. Bruno had been in and out of the family since he was a teenager and would turn forty in less than a month.

Bruno said, "Boss, we need to help."

DeLuca watched the old man and his companion run down the Gallatin Pike sidewalk. He looked back at his men and a pit rose in his stomach. It was too late.

"Boss?"

He knew Bruno was loyal and would never question his decisions. On more than one occasion, they had been forced to abandon their men and watch them die. When several more gangbangers ran from houses toward the fight, he knew this was another one of those times. His men were lost. They were tough strong fighters, but in the end, they would lose.

He lowered his head and shook it in disbelief. Five men down. His boss would not be happy.

DeLuca looked up and saw a taxi pull to the curb. The old man and his companion piled into the back. His impetus was the old man. It had been his objective from the beginning. He pointed ahead. "Follow the cab and don't lose it or we will meet the same fate."

† † †

Kaplan gave the taxi driver the address, which was actually more than a quarter mile from his true destination. He didn't want the actual address to show up in the taxi company's records. If he were alone, he would have picked a place even farther away, but he didn't think the old man could walk a long distance. Certainly not in the short amount of time required. Tony was getting to be more of a burden. He had to risk the drop off point being closer than his comfort level. Even the brightest trackers drawing a radius would have trouble pin pointing his destination. When they did pick up his trail again, he would have put more time between him and his pursuers. Time equaled distance. And distance equaled a better chance of survival.

He and Tony walked up to the massive wrought iron gate of the high-end residential community on the outskirts of Nashville. The gated community was equipped with an elaborate security setup with temporary pass codes for guests. According to the man Kaplan spoke with on the phone, the temporary one-time codes were good for only six hours or until activated, whichever was less, then the system deleted the codes rendering them useless for repeat use.

Kaplan entered the code and the gate slid open.

Five driveways on the left sat a 2003 silver Mercedes SL55 AMG coupe. They walked up the long circular driveway to a home Kaplan guessed was at least six thousand square feet situated on three acres, give or take. There was a two-car garage at the main house and a three-car garage beneath a carriage house. Both buildings had matching mountain stone facades typical of this area.

Kaplan rang the doorbell. The door opened before the chime finished. A tall man with reddish gray hair stood in the doorway wearing an expensive tailor made suit.

He said, "Here to look at the car?"

Kaplan nodded.

The man looked at his watch. "I almost gave up on you, we need to make this quick, I have to be at my lawyer's office in thirty minutes. To expedite this transaction I have a certified copy from a mechanic on the condition of the car."

Kaplan and Tony followed the man to the Mercedes. He crawled in the front seat and started the engine. It sounded like a cat purring. No vibrations, no rattles, and the air conditioner worked. A far cry from the old Sable he'd just dumped in East Nashville. The interior was in pristine condition. As was everything else visible to Kaplan's discerning eye.

"You mentioned a cash deal on the phone?"

Kaplan reached into his backpack and pulled out two stacks of one hundred dollar bills. The stacks were banded in ten thousand dollar bundles. He placed one banded bundle on the hood and counted out forty single bills. "Fourteen," Kaplan said.

"Since it's a cash deal, I'll go as low as sixteen-five."

Kaplan placed another ten bills on the pile. "Fifteen."

Tony leaned over and whispered to Kaplan, "How much money you got in that backpack anyway?"

"Enough."

The man stepped back and rubbed his chin. "The cash is tempting but that's lower than I'm willing to settle."

"Final offer."

"I don't know," the man said. "I just—"

Kaplan scooped up the bills and looked at Tony. "Let's go."

"Wait," the man said. "All right, I'll take it if you agree we put down on the sales receipt and title you only paid five grand for the car." The man stuck his hand out.

"That's weird." Kaplan said. "Normally it's the buyer who is trying to duck the taxes."

"No, that is not it at all. This is my soon to be ex's favorite car. Part of the divorce settlement is that I sell it and she gets the proceeds. She will be madder than a hornet I sold it for so cheap."

Kaplan held onto the money. "Sign the title first."

The man reached into the glove box and retrieved the title, pulled a pen from his shirt pocket, and let it hover over the document. "How should I fill this out?"

"Just fill out your part and sign it, I'll take care of the rest later."

The man stared at Kaplan for several seconds then glanced at Tony. "Sure, no problem." He signed the title and held it out for Kaplan.

Kaplan swapped the cash for the title and two sets of keys.

"It even has a full tank," the man said.

"Much obliged." Kaplan shook the man's hand. He looked at Tony. "Get in."

"Where you from?" the man asked.

"Birmingham," Kaplan replied.

CHAPTER 25

MOSS LEANED ACROSS THE FENDER AND
slipped his pen through the bullet hole in the windshield.

After the Paducah Police Department located the Jeep,
the street was closed to everyone other than residents and
officers proceeded to interview neighbors in order to locate
any witnesses. The police weren't getting much cooperation
from the locals. The Jeep was treated as a crime scene, as per
Hepler's instructions, and was cordoned off with yellow crime
scene tape and orange traffic cones.

A detective was half in and half out of the back seat
fishing around in the rear back cushion. He wore jeans, a black
Paducah Police t-shirt, standard issue black tactical sport boots,
and rubber gloves. His bag was lying on the street with its top
pulled apart. He held a pair of eight-inch extractor tweezers.

"Looking for the slug?" Moss said.

"Yeah," the detective mumbled. "Pulled one out of the
door but I can't seem to locate this one. But it has to be here."

"Maybe it went through to the trunk."

The detective leaned back and gave Moss an annoyed look.
"I do this for a living, that was the first place I checked. It
didn't pass through. It's in here somewhere. I'll find it...sooner
or later."

Moore walked up and stood next to Moss. "Detective," she said. "I have a knife if you want to cut the seat open."

"Thanks anyway," he said. "But I got this. One of you could hand me my penlight if you wouldn't mind. It's in my bag, side pouch."

Moss looked in the man's bag and pulled out the light. "Here you go."

The man held up his hand without looking and Moss placed the light in his palm.

"Thanks," he said.

"Anything you can tell me about the slug from the door?" Moore asked.

"Definitely a forty-five."

Moss and Moore looked at each other and smiled.

"Got a dent on the left front fender with paint transfer," she said to Moss. "Could be from a PIT."

"A PIT, huh? Maybe Mr. Kaplan is smarter than we gave him credit for. Now we have a good idea it wasn't a one-car accident in Searcy."

"Got it," the detective said. The slug clinked inside a glass container. He crawled out of the back seat and held the two glass containers side by side. "Both forty-fives. Striations look identical so I'm pretty sure they came from the same weapon, but I won't know for certain till I get it to the lab. My initial guess is they came from a suppressed Glock."

"How could you tell that just from looking?" Moore asked.

"Ballistics is my thing, ma'am. With a clean slug, I can place the exact weapon manufacturer ninety percent of the time," the officer said. He held out one of the glass containers. "And this is a clean slug."

"Excellent. Run ballistics and send the results to the Searcy,

Arkansas police chief. Two suppressed Glocks, both forty-fives, were found at the scene of an accident a few hours ago. I'll bet your slugs match one of them."

"Sure thing." The detective placed a chain of custody seal over the containers' lids, scribbled something on the top, and placed them in his evidence bag.

Moss signaled Moore with a head nod and they walked toward his Crown Vic. "So what do you think? Is Mr. Kaplan deliberately leaving a trail?"

"Perhaps he's just careless," she replied.

"Good guy or bad guy?"

"Bad guy," she said with no hesitation. "He's running with your witness. He knows the law. If he were a good guy, he'd hole up in a police station somewhere and wait for us to come to him."

"That's where we disagree, Ms. Moore." Moss paused, more for effect. "You're right about one thing, though. If he is who we think he is, then he does know the law. He knows the Marshals Service is looking for its witness. But he is also dealing with somebody who is trying to kill the witness. Why else would he leave the Jeep where we could find it? He's leaving a trail for us to follow. And right now, a trail only law enforcement has access to. He's deliberately getting local police departments involved."

"Plausible, I guess," she said. "But I'm not convinced. You're making a lot of assumptions, which surprises me. You don't strike me as the type to give anyone the benefit of the doubt."

What she didn't know was that Gregg Kaplan was handling the situation the same way Moss would have and now he felt he was starting to gain some insight into the mysterious man and his thinking.

He took a deliberate glance at his watch. "Think I'll check in with JP." He pulled out his cell phone and placed the call. She leaned against the Crown Vic and listened.

"Expand your search radius to two hundred miles," Moss said. While he listened he looked at Moore and rolled his eyes. "Anything out of the ordinary?"

"This might interest you," Hepler said on the phone. "Seems there was a turf war in East Nashville between a couple of Italians and several members of a gang. One gangbanger dead, one stabbed in the leg. Didn't fair too well for the Italians either. Both are in critical condition at a nearby hospital. Identities unknown."

"How is this helping me?" Moss said. He noticed Moore had walked away from the Crown Vic and was talking on her phone.

"The car they found was registered in Paducah."

"Inconclusive. I need more."

"All right. How about this, Dirt Man? The plate belongs to the Jeep taken from Mayflower."

He looked back at the Jeep and smiled. "Now you got my attention."

He finished getting the update from Hepler and then lowered his voice. "What about the other matter?"

Hepler said, "Officially the creds check out."

"Officially?" Moss asked. "What the hell does that mean?"

"The credentials are registered and issued to April Moore. But I couldn't find anyone who has ever met this person."

Moss saw Moore hang up her phone as a Paducah detective approached. "Gotta go," he said to Hepler and hung up.

"Excuse me, Inspector," the detective said. "But we got a

lead on a possible getaway car."

"An older model Mercury Sable?"

The detective's face showed his bewilderment. "How'd you know?"

"Sources."

"The man who sold it said the two men were in a big hurry. Physical descriptions match the ones you gave us. He heard them say they were on their way to St. Louis."

"Thanks, Detective. I guess we'll check it out," Moss said. He turned to Moore. "Let's go."

They walked to the Crown Vic and climbed in.

"How long will it take us to get to St. Louis?"

"Don't know, don't care."

"What do you mean you don't care?" Moore asked.

"We're not going to St. Louis."

"Then where *are* we going?"

He looked at her. "Nashville."

CHAPTER 26

THE SILVER MERCEDES ZIPPED ALONG
Interstate 81 east of Knoxville, Tennessee with the cruise
control set at 73 MPH, a speed Kaplan figured would not draw
any unwanted attention from law enforcement. Almost three
hours had passed since driving out of Nashville and he was
starting to feel his luck change. He pushed back in the soft
leather seat and relaxed his grip on the steering wheel.

Tony had been asleep in the passenger seat for most of the
drive, his head resting against the window and his hot breath
blowing steam on the glass with every exhale. It seemed the
old man had reached the point of exhaustion and couldn't stay
awake any longer. At least he wasn't snoring.

After buying the Mercedes, he tossed his last burn phone
in a nearby dumpster before he drove onto the interstate. All
three burn phones trashed and now he was in need of another
one.

Tony grunted then sat up straight. "Where are we?"

"Three hours east of Nashville."

"Well, I need to go again and I'm hungry," Tony said. "And
I want to take care of them in that order."

"Tony, you're like taking care of a baby. All you do is whine,
pee, and eat." Kaplan pointed to a road sign. "How about

Dandridge?" The sign indicated the exit was three miles ahead. Perfect. Tony could take care of business and Kaplan could get another burn phone. Then he would find some place for them to eat. Fast food. He wanted to get back on the road and put more distance between him and whoever was after Tony.

The situation in East Nashville was perplexing. The men didn't want to kill Tony. Whoever Tony had double-crossed wanted him alive for a reason. Perhaps to watch him suffer before they put a bullet in his head. Or maybe Tony possessed something or knew something that they wanted...or needed.

"Sounds good," Tony finally said.

"Who were those guys back in Nashville?"

Tony hesitated. "How should I know?"

"They were under orders *not* to kill you. Their orders were to capture you alive. So I'll ask again, who were those guys?"

Tony said nothing. He just stared at Kaplan.

Kaplan raised his voice. "This isn't funny. I need to know what I'm up against. *Who* I'm up against. Or else we're both as good as dead." Kaplan knew that was a lie, but Tony didn't. He was perfectly capable of keeping them both alive. He had the skills; he just needed information. Forewarned is forearmed. The only way he was going to get Tony to talk was to scare the hell out of him.

Tony sat still and said nothing.

"Dammit, Tony. I've killed people who were less trouble than you." He let his foot off the accelerator and the Mercedes slowed as he navigated his way down the Dandridge exit. He snatched Tony by the collar. "Talk or your ass goes out on the street."

"All right, just take your hands off me." He loosened his grip on Tony. "They work for the Scalini family."

"Scalini? As in Martin Scalini, the New York crime boss? And the son, that was Max, right? I thought you said this wasn't a mafia thing."

"No. I said you've watched too many *Godfather* movies. I also said I was a broker and a recruiter. You once called me a criminal, when in reality everyone I deal with is the criminal. I connect criminal with criminal and take a fee for the introduction. What they do next is their own business. I am not the hardened criminal you think I am but I know things. A lot of things about a lot of people. And they are criminals, big ones and little ones. That is why I am in WitSec. I primarily brokered for the Scalini family. A man I connected Scalini with killed his son, so now the old man wants me dead."

"Those men didn't seem interested in killing you. Seems to me they wanted you alive."

"I am positive they do want me alive. Scalini would have ordered that. I have known Martin a long time, death is preferable to what he has in store for me."

"Torture?"

Tony didn't answer his question. "In exchange for my testimony, the Department of Justice put me in the Witness Security program."

"Who killed Scalini's son?"

"You don't want to know."

"I asked a question, that generally means I want to know the answer."

"Let's just say their resources are better than Scalini's."

Kaplan turned right after the exit and pointed to a fast food chain establishment. "Get it and go."

"I'd rather have a sit down meal," Tony said.

"Tell you what," Kaplan motioned to the hamburger joint.

"We eat this one on the road and keep moving. If we make it to our destination before nightfall then we'll talk about a sit-down meal."

Tony stared at him for a few seconds and nodded. "Deputy Cox was a lot more accommodating than you."

"Yeah? How did that turn out? Deputy Cox is dead. We keep moving whether you like it or not."

After they got their food and returned to the car, Kaplan drove around until he found a store that sold prepaid cell phones. He bought two. He'd learned over the years he could never have enough burn phones. They had a lot more uses other than telecommunications. On many occasions when he knew his phone was being tracked, he'd used it to misdirect his pursuers.

Within minutes after getting back on Interstate 81, Kaplan opened a burn phone and placed a call.

The man who answered said two words. "Code in."

They were well-known words to Kaplan, requiring voice authentication to get through to his handler. Kaplan coded in and was directed to another man.

"Damn, Gregg," his handler said. "What part of *stay off the grid* didn't you understand?"

"I was put in a compromising situation."

"Compromising enough to derail your career?"

Kaplan looked at Tony. "No, not sure if it was."

"We started getting hits on your motor vehicle records last night. First from the FBI and then later from the U. S. Marshals Service." The man paused. "What kind of shit storm did you start in Arkansas?"

Kaplan briefed his handler while Tony pretended not to listen.

"I can't believe you got mixed up in Marshals Service business. They won't like this upstairs."

"Well don't tell them then." Kaplan took a deep breath. "I'm already in enough trouble with the upstairs office. No one needs to see or hear my name for a while."

"Might be too late for that. What's your next move?"

"Tomorrow I'll drop the old man off at the SSOC, then I'll be back on assignment...and out of sight."

"Quit calling me old man," Tony interrupted.

"I'll keep this quiet as long as I can," his handler continued. "But remember, you did this voluntarily. I won't go down with you, so if they ask—"

"I know the routine." Kaplan terminated the call.

"I have a question," Tony said.

"In a minute." Kaplan raised his index finger to signal Tony to wait while he placed another call.

The voice on the other end was a familiar one. "The B & B," the voice said.

"Dick, it's Kaplan." He paused long enough for the man to recognize his name. "I need to make reservations for two. Tonight. No call in. No verification. No guest register. Will that be a problem?"

Dick hesitated. Kaplan knew he had put him in a precarious position. They had been in the same business for years. Kaplan trusted him and needed his help. The man and his wife ran an off-the-books CIA safe house in Lexington, Virginia.

It was as close as he dared get Tony to the SSOC, the U. S. Marshals Service Safe Site and Orientation Center, without first contacting someone from WitSec and arranging for a transfer. Any effort to take him all the way to the SSOC without a U.S. Marshals Service escort would likely be an attempt in futility.

The SSOC was located on the Virginia side of the DC suburbs. He'd been there once before, under special circumstances. When he did, he was required to go with a Marshals Service escort in a Marshals Service vehicle. Eighteen months ago when Kaplan flipped a Russian agent, the CIA insisted, with uncompromising arm-twisting, that Kaplan would not leave the Russian's side until the man was safely locked inside the SSOC. A rare exception was made allowing an outsider to know the location of the SSOC. Somebody at the top of the food chain with the CIA had pulled a favor from somebody in the Marshals Service to break protocol. Kaplan would have liked to have been a fly on the wall during that conversation.

The location was a carefully guarded secret. Even from the witness.

Especially from the witness.

"We have rooms available," the man finally said. "What time shall we anticipate your arrival?"

"Late arrival."

"Excellent. Susan and I look forward to catching up."

Kaplan hung up and noticed Tony still staring at him.

"Where are we going?"

Kaplan didn't answer right away. He didn't want to answer at all. Finally he said, "Tonight we'll stay in Lexington, Virginia. Tomorrow you will no longer be a pain in my ass. I plan on handing you over to the U. S. Marshals Service."

CHAPTER 27

ALWAYS ONE STEP BEHIND WAS HOW MOSS felt about tracking his witness and Gregg Kaplan. By the time he and Moore arrived in East Nashville, two tow trucks were ready to haul the Sable and Impala to the impound yard. The only evidence there had been a crime were bloodstains on the asphalt. With assistance from the Marshals Service at the Nashville Field Office, Nashville PD had wrapped the crime scene up in less than three hours.

One Italian man and three gangbangers were under detention by armed guards at Nashville General Hospital. None were talking. The badly beaten black men remained conscious. The Italian was in a coma and his prognosis was bleak. If he did survive, he would likely remain in a vegetative state.

One gangbanger and one Italian were in the morgue. They weren't talking either.

The investigation was at a standstill.

Moss had nothing more than a hunch where Kaplan was taking his witness and he wasn't going to share it with Moore. Not yet anyway. Not until she earned his trust.

He pulled out his phone, put it in speaker mode, and called Hepler.

"You're on speaker, JP, catch us up," he said.

Hepler said, "Checked the local papers for cars for sale by owners and there are dozens. I enlisted help and we made it through the entire list with no luck." Hepler cleared his throat then continued, "Checked out Craigslist as well. Same thing, nothing."

"He could have paid someone to buy the car for him since he knows we'd get a description of him," Moore said.

Both men went silent. Moss hadn't thought of that angle although it was conceivable. Then again, it shot a hole in his theory that Kaplan was leaving a trail for him to follow. A big hole. Not something he was willing to admit. Not right now. He *wanted* to believe Kaplan was leading him somewhere in particular. Somewhere he could arrange a secure delivery of the witness to the Marshals Service. And then it hit him with full force clarity—he knew where Kaplan was going. He was going home.

"We need to find out what he's driving now," Moss said. "JP, check out that auto trading web site and see if anyone is selling a higher end vehicle nearby while Moore checks out the local cab companies." He looked at her. "See if there were any fares originating from East Nashville during the time frame of the incident. If there were, match descriptions and get the cabbie here. I want to talk to him personally."

"Okay, I'm on it," she said.

Moss took his phone out of speakerphone mode. "JP, let me run something by you." He walked out of earshot of Moore. "I think I know where Kaplan is going."

"Oh yeah? You get a crystal ball and not tell me? What are you thinking?"

"Where did you say Kaplan lives?"

"Let's see." Moss heard tapping on a keyboard. Hepler

continued, "Tysons Corner, Virginia."

"And what might be of interest to the Marshals Service not terribly far from Kaplan's home?"

Hepler was silent for several seconds.

"Perhaps say, in Alexandria," Moss added.

"Oh my God. The SSOC?"

"That's what I'm thinking," Moss said. "And he's smart enough to pull it off."

Angelo DeLuca kept the Buick between three quarters of a mile to a mile behind the Mercedes allowing cars to pull in and out between them. He needed to remain within surveillance range without being detected. There were very few Mercedes of this model on the road, which made it easy to keep his target vehicle in sight. DeLuca's car, on the other hand, was nondescript and blended in with the other vehicles on the road. It was chosen because the color and make were forgettable.

DeLuca had dreaded the phone call to his boss, Martin Scalini, who had a reputation for not tolerating failure. As a matter of fact, that's how DeLuca moved into his current job, disposing his predecessor when the man botched a job for Scalini. That's why he relied so much on Bruno Ratti.

Bruno the Rat, a name coined by Scalini, was known for his cunning and ruthlessness. The name was fitting too, not that he would ever rat on the family, but the Italian name Ratti meant slyness. And Bruno lived up to his name in every way.

Scalini had reason to be upset; DeLuca had been entrusted with a crew of men and instructed to capture the Sicilian alive and preferably unharmed. If he had listened to Bruno and waited until the old man came out of the restaurant in Little Rock, containment would have been much easier and the doomed melee might have been avoided. Bruno was right. Despite the fact Bruno had left the employ of the Scalini family twice before and then returned, DeLuca still made the right choice in keeping him by his side. Bruno, he knew, could be trusted.

After the short pit stop in Dandridge, Tennessee for food, the Sicilian and his companion made two more stops, an electronics store and a gas station. He and Bruno had no opportunity to make their move at either location. That was three hours ago and now, the sky ahead was darkening as thunderstorms loomed above the Appalachian Mountains in the western Virginia sky. Sunset was still three hours away and he hoped he'd get another chance to move on the old man before dark.

† † †

Moss felt the vibration of his cell phone in his pocket. It was Hepler. An hour ago, Moss and Moore interviewed the taxi driver who picked up the witness and Kaplan. The descriptions matched. The drop off address was a shopping strip mall in an affluent part of the greater Nashville area. He'd relayed the information to Hepler and instructed him to refine his search to vehicles for sale within a three-mile radius of the strip mall. Hopefully this was good news.

Moss answered, "Talk to me, JP."

"Good news and bad news. Four vehicles inside the call zone. One was sold yesterday and one is still for sale. We can rule those two out. That's the good news."

"There are still two unaccounted for, JP. What's the bad news?" Moore's phone rang. She answered it and walked off.

"That was the bad news. No one is answering at either of the numbers so the status of those vehicles is still unknown."

"What kind of vehicles are they?"

"Let's see," Hepler paused. "A silver 2003 Mercedes SL55 AMG and a black 2007 Toyota Tundra. I tracked the addresses for both numbers, each one is about a half a mile from the taxi drop off point only in opposite directions."

Moss looked in Moore's direction and noticed her expression change to stern. She spoke harshly to someone and hung up. She walked back toward him. "That's a tough call," Moss continued to Hepler. "I could see Mr. Kaplan choosing either one. Let's put out—"

"Hold on, Dirt Man," Hepler interrupted. "We just got in touch with the Tundra owner. It has not sold yet."

"Keep trying the Mercedes owner and in the meantime issue a BOLO on it." Moss looked at Moore. "Let me know the minute you have something." He hung up before Hepler could respond.

"What's up? You don't look happy."

"I'm not," she said. "I've been recalled. Can you take me to the Nashville airport?"

"I guess so. Where are you going?"

"Back to Atlanta."

They drove in silence the thirty minutes it took to get to the Nashville airport. He contemplated telling her of his speculation about where he thought Kaplan was taking his witness, however after she mentioned she was leaving, he was glad he had kept it to himself. He pulled the Crown Vic to the curb in the departure area of the airline she mentioned.

She opened her door. "I hope you find your witness," she said. "And I still don't think you should go easy on Mr. Kaplan. He is aiding and abetting in my opinion. If it were up to me, I'd throw the book at him."

"Yes, Inspector Moore, I am aware of your feelings," he said. "I'll keep that in mind when I catch him. And I *will* catch him."

"Good luck," she said. Then she got out and closed the door.

"You too," he yelled through the open window.

His phone vibrated. Hepler.

"Moss," he answered.

"Confirmation from the Mercedes owner. He sold the car for cash this morning to a man fitting Kaplan's description who was accompanied by a man fitting the witness's description."

"Good work. Send local PD over with pictures to verify the identities."

"Already in the works."

"I just dropped Ms. Moore off at the airport, Atlanta yanked her back, or so she said."

"Still don't trust her do you?"

"Nope. I say good riddance." Moss rubbernecked looking for traffic before pulling away from the curb. "I'm going to get some go-go juice and hit the road."

"Where to now, Dirt Man?"

"The SSOC."

CHAPTER 28

U. S. MARSHALS SERVICE WITNESS SECURITY
Inspector April Moore walked away from Senior Inspector
Pete Moss's car and into the Nashville terminal. She waited
five minutes after he pulled away from the curb then walked
back outside and hailed a taxi. She had lied to the man since
the moment they met. And now, for some odd reason, Moss's
hard-line attitude toward Gregg Kaplan had changed. He
seemed to have made some sort of connection with him,
totally opposite the personality profile she received on Moss.
He had the reputation of never giving anybody the benefit of
the doubt when working a case.

Moss's rugged handsome looks were sexually appealing to
her. She had even toyed with the idea of trying to seduce this
big strong man, but now he was a liability.

Moss had without a doubt figured out where Kaplan was
going. Kaplan wasn't taking a straight route; instead making a
veiled attempt in misdirection. Moss was also right about the
man leaving clues only law enforcement could find, one of his
more enlightened moments over the past twelve hours or so.
She wasn't going to waste any more time riding in a car with
Moss, always several hours behind Kaplan and the witness. She
needed to get in front of them. She needed to be there, waiting

for them when they arrived.

She instructed the taxi driver to take her to the General Aviation fixed base operator where her Hawker 400 XP business jet was waiting to take her to Washington National Airport in Washington DC.

She had already figured out where Mr. Kaplan was taking the Marshals Service witness. He was headed to the Safe Site and Orientation Center outside of DC. And with his credentials, he would likely be able to place the witness in the top-secret facility where no one would have access to him. Not even her. She climbed the air stair into the Hawker where she noticed a manila envelope sitting on the table addressed to her. She suspected it might reveal the secret location of the facility the Marshals Service called the SSOC. It was addressed simply, VALKYRIE.

The assassin studied the location and formulated her plan based on the information Shepherd had provided.

She smiled.

It could work.

She decided to modify her assignment to confuse the authorities and throw them off her trail. Valkyrie had originally hoped Moss would lead her to the target and make this easy, but things had a way of not working out. After this was over, whether she was identified or not, it wouldn't matter. The money was enough to keep her off the grid for years.

This time Shepherd would get more than he paid for. When the witness showed up with Mr. Kaplan, she would kill them both.

† † †

The roads leading into Lexington were still wet even though it was no longer raining. He glanced at Tony and noticed the old man's head was bobbing up and down. The lack of stimulation had dulled the old man's mental alertness. He couldn't be tired; hell, he'd slept most of the time they were on the road. And when he wasn't sleeping, he was running his mouth.

Kaplan nudged him on the shoulder, "Tony, we're here."

Tony lifted his glasses and rubbed his eyes. "Lexington?"

"Yes. You want to eat first?"

"Sit down restaurant, right? No more fast food. That stuff is clogging my arteries."

"That's funny. First you were concerned about driving without a license, now it's clogged arteries. Why don't you just worry about staying alive?"

Tony ignored his comment. "Where are we staying?"

"At The B and B."

"I love B and Bs. They always have a wonderful hot breakfast."

"No. *The B and B*. It's an unofficial CIA safe house. Once we go in, we're locked in until morning...or at least you are anyway. In all honestly, I shouldn't even be taking you out to eat. But, I figure we have a few hours to play with before anyone could close the gap. By then, you'll be tucked away safe and sound."

"How safe is it?"

"It's called a *safe house* for a reason, Tony, what do you think? Two ex-spooks run it as a courtesy to active and former operatives who need to duck out of sight for a day or so."

"Let's eat now."

"Figured you say that. Italian okay?"

"Southern Italian or Northern Italian?"

"I don't know, Tony. It's not like you really have a choice."

"I'm a harsh critic when it comes to Italian cuisine."

"You won't be disappointed." Kaplan turned and looked at the old man. "You eat anything other than Italian?"

"I like all kinds of foods. I love to eat and I love to cook. I'm especially fond of French Creole cooking, especially Caribbean style. Ever had any?"

"Oh yeah." Kaplan felt a genuine smile for the first time since this ordeal started. That was it, an epiphany. Food. Their love for the same type of food was the common denominator that put Tony and him in the same place at the same time. Because French Creole and New Orleans style Cajun food weren't that far apart. "I love it. I think the best food I have ever eaten was in Guadeloupe."

"I think I know that place, but my favorite spot is in Martinique. It is a quaint little joint…actually it's a dump, but the food is awesome."

"Well, tonight you're in for an Italian treat. The owner is a friend."

Kaplan pulled the Mercedes into a side lot of *Francesco's Little Italy*. It was a square building with white washed concrete walls and an old-fashioned neon sign flashing by the roadside. He backed into a parking space. "Let's go."

Tony got out and proceeded toward the main entrance.

"Tony," Kaplan shouted over the traffic noise. "This way, side entrance."

"What is this?" Tony was bouncing his upright palm again, fingers touching thumb. "Are we eating in the kitchen or something?"

"Tony I am trying to be nice, which isn't easy with you, so don't say another word." Kaplan rapped on the side door.

The door opened and a medium-sized man with graying

dark hair and dark eyes stood in the doorway. His eyes lit up. "Signor Kaplan. Buon giorno. It has been long time." His Italian accent thick. He gave Kaplan a hug. "Please come in. Come in."

"Francesco, this is Tony." Kaplan winked. "I told Tony you serve the best Italian food he will ever eat. Is the booth available?"

"For you, is always open." He turned to Tony and said something in Italian.

Gesturing with both his hands, Tony responded in Italian. Then, the two men laughed.

"Hey," Kaplan said. "English you two. You can speak your native tongue another time."

Francesco said, "Signor Tony said you kidnapped him last night and are holding him hostage, almost got him killed twice, and you need a bath because you stink like hell."

Kaplan raised his arm and gave his armpit a sniff then smiled. "Guilty on all counts."

"I told him you are very good at this kidnapping. Everyone you ever bring here has been kidnapped." Francesco motioned with his arm. "Andiamo Signor Tony, per favore."

Francesco led them to a small room walled off from the main dining area. It was a booth with a side curtain for privacy. "You sit here, signore," he said to Tony.

Kaplan slid in the seat across from Tony.

Tony twisted his head around and then back at Kaplan. "Why do you get to look out the window and all I get to see is the old map of Italy?" He pointed over Kaplan's shoulder.

"Shut up, Tony. All you do is complain. For your information, this window has a mirror on the other side. Bullet proof, or so I've been told. Never been tested that I know of. We use

Francesco a lot and we need to be able to see in the event of a threat."

"Who are *we*?"

"Okay, *I* used to use Francesco a lot. Best of all, we're only three minutes from The B and B."

"Sounds like there's a story there," Tony said.

"There is."

"Just like the woman you're trying to find."

"Yeah, like that."

The curtain parted and Francesco brought two glasses and a bottle of wine. "This is Signor Kaplan's favorite. I hope you approve." He poured a small amount in Tony's glass.

Tony swirled the red liquid around in the glass, raised it to his nose, and sniffed. Then he took a sip and swished it around in his mouth before swallowing.

"Molto buono." Tony touched his fingers to his lips. Francesco filled both glasses. Tony looked at Kaplan. "I am impressed. You have excellent taste in wine."

"You should see his women," Francesco said. "Va voom."

"He does not care to discuss his women." Tony stared at Kaplan.

"No kiss and tell." Francesco wagged his finger. "No kiss and tell."

Francesco turned and left.

"Well?"

"You heard him," Kaplan said.

"Something I've learned over the years, there is that one special woman in every troubled man's heart. It might be the one who got away or it might be a scorned lover. And one thing is for sure, Mr. Gregg Kaplan, you *are* a troubled man. I knew when I met you it was because of a woman."

"Two."

"I beg your pardon."

"Two women," Kaplan said. "One is dead. I don't know where the other is. She might be dead too."

Tony went quiet for a moment. "You want to talk about them now?"

He stared at Tony. In a way it would be nice to talk to someone. Kaplan was a private man and kept his personal life to himself. He refused to talk about the women in his mandatory sessions with the agency shrink and he wouldn't talk about them with the few friends he had. Except one. And he hadn't seen that friend in over two years. They had parted on bad terms and haven't spoken since. Kaplan sure as hell wasn't going to tell Tony anything personal. The curtains parted and Francesco delivered two sampler platters.

He looked at Tony. "You find something you like, I make it special for you next time you come, si?"

"Si," Tony said.

Forty-five minutes later, Kaplan and Tony pushed their platters away as the curtains parted again. It was Francesco. "More vino?"

Kaplan had been getting antsy over the past few minutes. "No, Francesco, thank you, but we really must be leaving."

"No dolce?" Francesco looked at Kaplan. "Signor Tony must have dessert."

"Okay," Kaplan acquiesced. "Then we must—"

A commotion erupted in the main dining area as two Italian men charged through the front entrance brandishing handguns. One man raised his weapon and fired at the mirror. Kaplan yelled, and pulled Tony under the table. He looked up at the glass, his heart pumping. It *was* bullet proof. Spider cracks spotted the mirror although the bullets remained embedded in the glass. Kaplan guided Tony away from the mirror, out of the booth, and toward the side exit from which they entered.

"Signori, hurry," urged Francesco.

Kaplan had explained the risks to Francesco on numerous occasions, as had every other operative who ate in the booth. Risks Francesco was willing to take. After all, it was one of those operatives who had rescued him from captivity when he and nine other Italians were kidnapped while vacationing in Egypt. That operative was the woman Kaplan sought. His way of repaying that debt was taking the risk and making his restaurant available to guests of The B & B.

Kaplan unlocked the car doors with his key fob, shoved Tony in the back seat, and instructed him to stay on the floorboard. He slipped in the driver's seat, started the engine, and gunned the Mercedes into traffic.

In his rear view mirror he saw another car pull out of the restaurant into traffic causing several cars to swerve to avoid impact.

He hit speed dial and called The B and B.

"Kaplan, Alpha One Alert," he said. "Coming in hot."

CHAPTER 29

THIS WAS THE FIRST TIME KAPLAN HAD EVER used the *Alpha One Alert* declaration. It was strictly an internal code for *agent under attack*. Protocol was to make every attempt to evade his pursuers and not lead them to the safe house. Although safe once inside, just like the SSOC, the location was not to be revealed under any circumstances. Under Alpha One Alert, the B & B would intervene at predetermined locations to ensure undetected passage to the safe house.

Located in an older neighborhood on the southwest side of Lexington, the B & B was not far from Washington and Lee University and the Stonewall Jackson House. A thick ten-foot hedge surrounded the brick home situated just northeast of the Lexington Golf and Country Club. Inside the hedge was a brick wall topped with metal spikes. Between the spikes, embedded shards of glass. Inside the wall, a row of razor wire and a ground proximity warning system with automatic tracking video cameras sensitive enough to detect a field mouse.

Every precaution was taken in the event of hostilities. The best weapon, the best layer of protection, was still its secrecy. And that's the reason there had never been a breach event at the safe house. Kaplan knew there had been other *Alpha One Alerts* in the past at the Lexington safe house, but to date, the safe house had kept its anonymity.

From his location at Francesco's restaurant on South Main Street, there was a predetermined maze of turns to be made before approaching the safe house.

South Main Street was a one-way street through downtown—the wrong way—and on a Saturday night, there was plenty of traffic. Too many cars to consider driving head-on against the flow. He'd have to double back on South Jefferson Street, one block over—also a one-way street—the right direction. The car carrying the two gunmen was a quarter-mile behind him when he made the first turn away from Main Street. Now he was running the gauntlet inside the maze. It would take the interference team ninety seconds to get in place since he made the phone call. That time had passed. The team should be ready, he thought, as he raced down the street.

Kaplan took another ninety-degree turn and accelerated. The car behind followed, lost traction in its rear tires and fishtailed as it rounded the corner.

Kaplan had two advantages, the Mercedes and his driving training at the academy. The American car, which appeared to be some model Buick, was no match for his German car. It didn't handle tight fast turns as well, nor did the Buick have the power and performance as the Mercedes. Kaplan needed every advantage possible.

Kaplan followed procedure through the labyrinth of turns, slowly distancing himself from the Buick.

"What's going on?" Tony peeked up from the back floorboard.

"Oh the usual, Tony." He hoped his sarcastic tone would quiet Tony. "I'm trying to keep us from getting killed. Now stay down."

After three more turns, and putting even more distance between his car and the Buick, Kaplan turned onto the longest straight away of the route. It was five blocks from end to end and as soon as he turned onto the road, he saw the interference vehicles at their assigned positions. We made it, he thought, and he began to relax.

As soon as the Buick rounded the corner behind Kaplan, a car backed out of a driveway blocking the road and leaving the Buick with no alternative other than to stop.

But it didn't.

The Buick swerved around the back of the obstructing car, plowed over two mailboxes and narrowly missed a large tree. It bounced back into the road as Kaplan made another turn and accelerated, losing sight of the Buick.

Tony's head popped up again. "Are we almost to the safe house?"

Kaplan said nothing.

"Maybe you should honk the horn to alert people on the street."

Nothing.

"I saw this chase scene on TV once and—"

"Tony, not now. Shut your damn mouth and stay down."

Ten seconds later his phone rang. The voice on the other end informed him that the second vehicle had neutralized his pursuer—a pickup truck pulling a boat on a trailer blocked the entire road, this time forcing the Buick to come to a full stop.

Kaplan made two more turns, pulled through the already open metal gate, and into the driveway. Fifty feet later the driveway split. Kaplan took the fork to the right, which descended below the property to a large underground garage.

There were three people waiting by an elevator, a tall man

who was almost bald, a short woman with wavy brown hair, and a linebacker dressed in a full black tactical uniform holding an AK-47.

Kaplan parked the Mercedes, got out and opened the door for Tony, "Get out," he said in a deep commanding voice as he snapped his fingers.

Tony climbed out of the back of the Mercedes and before he could stand up straight, Kaplan punched him in the chin. Tony fell to the concrete floor, holding his chin. Kaplan leaned down, grabbed a handful of Tony's shirt, and lifted him to his feet. He shoved him against the rear fender of the Mercedes and punched him again. This time the old man's lip split open. Blood oozed from the corner of his mouth.

"What aren't you telling me?" Kaplan yelled.

Tony squirmed across the garage floor trying to get away from Kaplan. "You busted my lip," he said. He cupped his lip with his hand. "What are you talking about? Have you gone crazy?"

"How did these guys find us?"

"I don't know."

"Bullshit. Who are these guys and how did they find us?"

"I have no idea," Tony pleaded. "They must have followed you or traced your phone or something."

"Not a chance. There is no way anyone could have gotten this close to us this fast without some inside knowledge. And if it wasn't me, it had to be you." Kaplan reared his fist back to take another punch but was stopped by the tall, bald man.

"Let him go, Gregg," the man said. "We'll put him in the *quiet room* and check him for tracers."

Kaplan pulled his arm free from the man's clutch. He looked the tall man in the eye. "This son of a bitch almost got me killed. And not just once or twice either." Kaplan released his grasp on Tony's shirt and glowered at Tony. "Lot of thanks I get for saving your ass."

He gave the linebacker a nod. The big man stepped forward, took Tony by the arm, and escorted him toward the elevator. "If he scans clean, I'm going to beat the truth out of him."

"What if he doesn't know anything? What if *you* were compromised and followed?"

"Not a chance, Dick. If there is one thing I know how to do well, it's disappear. I couldn't have been compromised unless someone was tipped off. I don't know how it happened...or why, but my gut tells me that old man knows more than he's telling."

The woman walked up to Kaplan and gave him a hug followed by a kiss on the cheek. "Gregg Kaplan, it's good to see you again."

"Thanks, Susan," he said. "Good to see you too. I hope I haven't caused too much trouble."

"Of course you have." She hooked her arm through his and said, "Try to relax. Come inside and tell me about this old Italian you delivered to me."

CHAPTER 30

ANGELO DELUCA COULDN'T BELIEVE HIS RUN of bad luck. First a car backed out of a driveway causing him to swerve off the road taking out two mailboxes and nearly crashing into a tree. One of the mailboxes dented the hood and left a long scratch across it. Then a pickup truck pulling a boat completely blocked the road and the old man in the Mercedes disappeared around the corner.

For the past thirty minutes he and Bruno had searched every driveway on every road in vain. The Mercedes was gone. Vanished, without a trace. The neighborhood was full of large older homes, most with fences, walls, or at a minimum, a tall dense hedge.

He couldn't rule out the possibility that the Mercedes made its way back to the interstate and was on its way to DC. That would mean the driver changed his plan after he and Bruno made their move a few minutes ago. That thought was unsettling.

Not as unsettling as the thought of telling Martin Scalini the old man had gotten away again. Scalini would see it as another failure. A failure with lethal consequences. Lethal for DeLuca. He was knee-deep in a big pile of shit and needed to shovel his way out fast.

"The boss ain't gonna like this," Bruno said.

DeLuca looked at him. It was as if Bruno the Rat knew exactly what DeLuca was thinking. "You think I'm an idiot?" He raised both hands, palm up, and gestured as he spoke. "We're not telling the boss, capisce? Not right away."

"Yeah, yeah. I understand. So, what do we do next?"

"We keep looking," DeLuca said. "The last message said *safe house-Lexington*. We find the safe house, we find Tony Q. *Then* we call Scalini."

† † †

Kaplan sat on a kitchen stool recounting the past twenty-four hours to Susan when Dick brought him the results of the scan on Tony.

"He's clean," Dick said. "You should think about everything that has transpired. Is it possible you screwed up? Is it possible you were somehow traced and they tracked you here to Lexington?"

"I'll be the first to admit the gap closed on us a few times, uncomfortably so once or twice. But I left nothing traceable. Matter of fact, I went out of my way to send a couple of burn phones in different directions just in case. And I've been through five of them since last night." Kaplan raised his finger and pointed toward the back of the house where the *quiet room* was located.

The *quiet room* was a secure room with copper infused windows and lead-lined walls and ceilings. No electronic signals could get in and no signals could get out. Generally used by operatives for interrogation, the *quiet room* was also used for body scans and strip searches.

"That old geezer has done something to jeopardize our stealth. There is no other reason why our cover could be blown. I don't know what he did and I don't know when he did it but I'm convinced he's behind it."

"You know," Susan said. "I have a connection in the Marshals Service. I can give him a call and find out who Tony's handler is and how to get in touch with him."

"Forget it. His handler's name was Mike Cox…and he's dead."

Dick interrupted, "WitSec would have assigned a new case handler by now, someone who is no doubt searching for him as we speak. It might be to your advantage to contact this person and come up with a game plan for getting the old man safely transferred back into the custody of the U. S. Marshals Service."

Kaplan glanced at Dick. It would be nice to get Tony out of his hair so he could get back on his way to El Paso. But he made a promise to the dying Deputy Mike Cox that he would personally return Tony to a WitSec safe site.

Kaplan had given the man his word. It was an unbreakable contract, not a half empty promise to a dying man. It was a moral obligation. A man who broke his promise was a man without respect. More than just a promise, his word to a fellow Delta Force brother was a sacred bond. *Once in, never out—* Another Delta Force mantra.

He would deliver Tony to the SSOC even if he had to gag and hog-tie the old bastard to keep him from sabotaging his efforts.

Kaplan turned to Susan. "Can you trust him? Will your contact keep this off the books and secure?"

"Of course," Susan said. "Shall I make the call?"

"Thanks, Susan. Please, make the call."

Susan turned and left the room. Kaplan directed his attention to Dick. "Where's Tony now?"

"Still locked in the *quiet room*. You two just ate so I figured he didn't need anything for a while."

"You mean he hasn't been complaining?"

"About what?"

"For one thing, he's got an old man's tiny bladder," Kaplan said. "We had to stop a lot so he could pee. I mean like every couple of hou—" Then it hit him. "That sorry son of a—"

"What?"

"Now I know how he did it."

"Did what? Gregg, what are you talking about?"

"Tony has a connection out there. Someone who isn't trying to kill him. Someone who wants to free him. Whenever we'd stop, Tony would figure out a way to contact them. That explains why I could never get us completely dark."

"I don't know," Dick said. "We found nothing on him. He was clean. How could he have made contact with anyone?"

"He's a mobster. He's used to bribing people. I'll prove it." Kaplan walked back to the *quiet room* and barged through the door. Dick followed him. When the linebacker moved to stop Kaplan's aggressive advance toward Tony, Dick waved him off.

Kaplan raced across the room, collared Tony around the neck, and shoved him against the wall. He pulled out his knife and held the sharp blade against Tony's throat. "You aren't running from Scalini, you asshole. You work for him. You've been alerting him this whole trip. I thought you had a tiny bladder, but what you were really doing was making phone calls?"

"No. No. I promise. I have made no phone calls." Tony's

voice wavered with every syllable. Kaplan could hear the fear in his voice and see the fear in his eyes, which was exactly what he wanted.

"You're lying, Tony."

"No. I swear. I called no one."

Tony winced as Kaplan pushed down on the blade causing blood to drip from the wound. "

"Before your next breath, you need to decide if you want to die or tell me the truth." He pressed harder with the blade.

Tony yelled out in pain. "Ok. But first remove the knife."

"No. That's not how this works. You tell me what you did first."

"I only did it because I thought you were crazy and were going to get us killed. The Marshals Service could not protect me, so I texted an associate for backup."

Tony did have an insider, but wouldn't reveal his identity. He had been sending periodic text messages from random people's phones. Whoever he could bribe, a kid at the gas station, a man at the rest stop, anyone who would take twenty bucks to let him send one text message.

Twenty dollars. One text.

In so doing, though, Tony had repeatedly compromised their safety. His safety. And for that, had committed an unforgiveable wrong against Kaplan. One he would pay the consequences for later.

The door to the *quiet room* opened and Susan stuck her head in and said, "Gregg, I have the info and guess what? The WitSec deputy assigned to Tony is only a couple of hours from Lexington on his way to DC."

Kaplan nodded then turned back to Tony. He pulled the knife blade from the quivering old man's throat, his grip still tight on his shirt. "This isn't over," he said. "I'll be back and you *will* tell me everything." Kaplan relaxed his grip on Tony's shirt and shoved him to the side. The old man slid down the wall to a sitting position. Kaplan turned and followed the other two men out the door.

† † †

Moss was a gambling man and this time he was betting his career he was right. He was all-in.

If he was wrong and Kaplan didn't take the witness to the SSOC, then he'd either be fired or stuck away on some *special projects* detail until he was eligible for retirement. Special projects in the federal sector meant the kiss of death for one's career. The stigma was that a *special projects* detail was assigned to anybody who screwed up so badly that the agency had to stick him in a hole to keep them out of sight. He wasn't about to end his career that way.

After dropping Moore at the Nashville airport, Moss filled up with gas, bought a bag full of greasy fast food, and headed eastbound on Interstate 40. In Knoxville, he picked up Interstate 81, which would take him most of the way to DC. His stomach growled and he belched.

Just outside of Roanoke, Virginia, his cell phone vibrated. The caller ID displayed a phone number with a Tennessee area code and an exchange he didn't recognize. Perhaps it was Nashville PD.

"Senior Inspector Pete Moss."

"Senior Inspector?" a man's voice said. "As in U. S. Marshals Service?"

"That is correct. Who am I speaking with?"

"Are you the replacement for Inspector Mike Cox in Little Rock?"

"Who is this?" Moss raised his voice. "Identify yourself."

"Are you or are you not Mike Cox's replacement?"

"For now. I am taking over one of Inspector Cox's cases."

"The breach in Little Rock?"

"Mister, identify yourself or this call is over."

"You know who I am," the voice said. "And I'm traveling with someone you want."

Moss's heart raced. He didn't speak for several seconds. A thousand questions bombarded his thoughts. "Is this Gregg Kaplan?"

"You found my motorcycle, I see."

"Yes, I did. And all the other clues you left along the way. Is my witness safe?"

Kaplan said nothing.

"Mr. Kaplan? I asked you a question."

"The plate was a mistake."

"Huh?" Moss responded.

"In my haste, I forgot to remove the plate from my motorcycle. That's the only reason you know who I am. The rest of the clues were intentional."

"Gregg Kaplan. Tysons Corner, Virginia. That's all I got. Information from the State of Virginia Motor Vehicles database. Everything else about you requires a higher authorization. Neither the Marshals Service nor the FBI could find out anything more about you. Your identity seems to be protected. Who are you, NSA? CIA?"

Silence.

After several seconds Moss said, "Mr. Kaplan, the U.S. Marshals Service had three deputies trying to locate my witness…and you. I was reassigned from Chicago, Deputy

Jon Hepler from Little Rock was read in, and Inspector April Moore was brought in briefly from the Atlanta office. None of us could learn anything more about you than your name and a post office box number in Virginia. Who are you? Really?"

"Did you say April Moore?"

"Yeah. Showed up unannounced with no paperwork and totally out of protocol. But I let her stay because she knew all the details of the case. Details only WitSec would know."

"Ever met her before Little Rock?"

"No. Like I said, she just showed up out of the blue. Why do you ask?"

"Tall red-headed woman? Fair skin, looks like she could've been a model?"

"That's right. So you've dealt with Inspector Moore before?"

"In a manner of speaking," Kaplan said. "Let me guess, her creds check out but no one has ever seen her."

"That's right, but how—"

"Shit."

Moss heard something strange in Kaplan's voice.

"What is it?" Moss asked.

"This complicates matters."

"Inspector Moore was teamed with me for most of this investigation but she was called off. I'll admit I had bad vibes about her but mostly I felt like I couldn't trust her. How does that complicate things?"

"She's not U. S. Marshals Service and certainly not WitSec," Kaplan said. "Nor is she with any other government agency for that matter. April Moore is an alias she uses from time to time, usually when inside the United States."

"What? Who does she work for then?"

"Nobody. She's an assassin."

CHAPTER 31

"HOW COULD YOU POSSIBLY KNOW THAT?" The voice said on the phone. "I haven't told you anything about her."

Valkyrie's involvement was an unwelcome surprise. Or perhaps not. He had been on the lookout for the killer the better part of a year, as had several other CIA operatives around the globe. He had run into nothing but one dead end after another. Now, it seemed, she had been contracted to kill the old man. And that put her close enough to nab.

What a twist of fate.

Kaplan ignored the deputy's question. "Where is the woman now?"

"I don't know," the deputy said. "I dropped her off at the airport in Nashville a few hours ago. She said she was going back to Atlanta." The deputy paused and then said, "What's this all about?"

"Someone with a lot of clout wants your witness dead," Kaplan said.

"A lot of people with a lot of clout want my witness dead and now you're telling me an assassin has been hired to take him out too?"

"That's exactly what I'm saying, Senior Inspector. If you

had found us, she would have killed you too."

"Lucky for me I never caught up to you then. Are you taking Tony to the SSOC?"

Kaplan wasn't surprised the deputy had figured out his strategy. And since he had, it was a safe bet Valkyrie had as well. "We need to talk. Face-to-face. Where are you?"

"Interstate 81, just outside of Roanoke."

"That's good, meet me in one hour." Kaplan gave the deputy instructions. "And Moss?"

"Yes."

"Don't even think about calling this in. No one knows about this but you, understand? I'll dry clean the area and if you double cross me, I promise you won't like the results."

† † †

Moss did as Kaplan instructed. He wasn't sure if he could trust him, but right now, his choices were limited. Kaplan held all the cards…and his witness. He had kept the witness alive this long, when so many were trying to kill him. Moss had to believe he was genuine. Whatever Kaplan was, whomever he worked for, the man knew the system. Moss would at least give him the benefit of the doubt.

For now.

He parked on the side of the road along U. S. 60 beneath the U. S. 11 overpass. He had moved his car clear of the road with the passenger tires resting against the sloping concrete wall. He checked his watch; according to the time, Kaplan should make contact in two minutes. He thought about what Kaplan had said in his instructions and knew what *dry clean* meant, he'd just never actually heard the term used. It meant Kaplan

would make a thorough sweep of the rendezvous area to make
sure he wasn't under surveillance. It was a Catch 22 for Moss;
procedure required him to call it in to Hepler but doing so and
not trusting Kaplan ran the risk of losing his witness again.

At exactly the one-hour mark, his cell phone rang. "Get out
and stand next to your car," Kaplan said and then hung up.

Ten seconds later a black Toyota 4-Runner pulled beside
the Crown Vic. The passenger window was down and he
recognized the man in the passenger seat by his driver's license
photo—Gregg Kaplan.

"Get in," Kaplan said. He motioned to the back door with
his thumb.

Moss did as requested. Before he could get the door closed,
the driver, a balding white man, punched the accelerator and
drove away into the darkness. "All right, Kaplan, I did what you
asked," said Moss. "I still don't know who the hell you are."

"Pass me your creds and keep your mouth shut until we get
where we're going."

Kaplan's tone infuriated Moss; he wasn't used to taking
attitude from anyone, much less someone he knew nothing
about. "Where are we going?"

"Doesn't listen well, does he?" The driver said.

Kaplan turned around in his seat and gave him a hard
look. Even in the dark car, or maybe especially in the dark car,
Kaplan's eyes told Moss he meant business. It wasn't evil he
saw in the man's eyes, but danger.

Kaplan held out his hand. "Creds."

Moss acquiesced. He reached into his jacket, pulled out his
credentials, and handed them to Kaplan. That was when he
noticed Kaplan pointing a gun at his head.

Kaplan took the creds and said, "Weapon too."

Moss made slow deliberate moves to avoid alarming Kaplan, the last thing he wanted to do was get shot. He withdrew his weapon and handed it over grip first.

"Look, I'm cooperating. Now, how about you cut me a little slack." Moss said.

Neither man spoke.

Moss leaned back in his seat. Kaplan really needed to work on his people skills. The driver made what seemed like two or three dozen turns before he pulled the 4-Runner into a home with a retractable metal gate, brick walls, razor wire, and armed guards. It seemed more like an armored compound than a home. The driveway split and the driver bore right. The driveway descended into an underground parking garage.

The 4-Runner parked beside a silver Mercedes SL55 AMG.

Moss smiled. He had been taken to a spook house.

† † †

Kaplan got out and opened the car door for Moss since the child locks were engaged. He shoved Moss's creds and firearm into his chest. "You check out," Kaplan said.

"Well that's a relief."

"Let's talk first," Kaplan said. "Then I'll take you to see Tony." Kaplan signaled for Moss to follow. "Come on."

When Senior Inspector Pete Moss got out of the car, Kaplan realized for the first time just how big the man really was. He had a good seventy, seventy-five pounds on Kaplan, and solid weight too. His size, coupled with his bald head, gave him a menacing appearance. He didn't look afraid to get physical either. His strong developed neck and shoulders told Kaplan that this guy didn't lose many fights…if any. And even though the man's size was threatening, his face was amicable.

Moss interrupted Kaplan's thoughts as they walked toward the elevator.

"I gotta know. Who do you work for? Why are your file and identity classified at such a high level?"

"CIA," he replied. "Clandestine Service."

Moss smiled. "I figured it was either that or NSA."

For the next hour, Kaplan and Moss discussed the events of the past twenty-four hours. They had both been awake over forty hours; one running from the other, one chasing the other, both with the common goal of keeping Tony alive. After comparing notes, it became clear there were more parties involved than Kaplan originally thought.

Initially, he was hesitant to team up with Senior Inspector Moss. It was too soon to know if he could trust him. He sensed Moss felt the same about him. Perhaps a mutual distrust was the best way to proceed. It might just keep them both honest.

As difficult and dangerous as it was getting Tony to Lexington, the trip from Lexington to the SSOC could potentially be worse. What he needed was more time to figure out the situation and his options.

In light of the recent developments with Tony's pursuers, time was not on his side and the decision to team up with Moss outweighed the risks.

CHAPTER 32

IT DIDN'T TAKE MOSS LONG TO UNDERSTAND why Kaplan had behaved the way he did toward him in the 4-Runner. After Kaplan recounted the past twenty-four hours, including the close calls with Scalini's men, he probably would have been more arrogant if he were in Kaplan's shoes.

He listened as Kaplan outlined his plan to get Tony to the SSOC.

"That's not how the Marshals Service conducts a transport," Moss said. "I should call and have an armored vehicle come pick up Tony and me and take us to a safe site."

"Not going to happen, Senior Inspector."

"Why the hell not?" Moss could feel the anger welling up inside him. This was his business. The U. S. Marshals Service was well equipped to handle situations like this one. "We're going to need more protection. You said Scalini's men were on to you and you had to evade them just to get here. They have had plenty of time to call in reinforcements. There will be more men waiting for us to leave. Then they will feel compelled to make their move."

"First of all, I made a promise I intend to keep. Deputy Mike Cox's last breath was a request that I personally deliver Tony to a Marshals Service safe site. That's a promise I don't intend to break."

"Mike Cox was a friend of mine," Moss said. "I trained him as my replacement. His death pisses me off and I plan on catching the low life bastards responsible for this. Besides, you passed other Marshals Service safe sites to get this far. I think Deputy Cox would think this is good enough."

Kaplan seemed to ignore him.

"Second of all," Kaplan continued. "I'm counting on Scalini's men picking up our trail again."

† † †

Kaplan stared at the deputy. The big man's expression was somewhere between incredulous and frustration. He found it amusing.

"I thought we were trying to keep Tony safe from Scalini's men," Moss finally said.

"We are." The final words of Inspector Mike Cox invaded his thoughts again.

You have to get him to a safe site.

Promise me you'll deliver him to WitSec.

Keeping Tony out of sight hadn't worked so far. His efforts to sequester the old man were being sabotaged. There were entities involved outside a mob boss trying to exact revenge on a stool pigeon. Other players Tony had alluded to wanted to silence the old man and would stop at nothing to keep him from testifying.

There was a leak that needed to be plugged. Perhaps more than one, which could also explain the presence of the assassin known as Valkyrie.

Kaplan looked up at Moss. "We are going to keep Tony

safe, but first…we need to smoke out a few rats."

† † †

Angelo DeLuca made the call he regretted having to make, he called Martin Scalini and requested firepower be sent to Lexington, Virginia.

That firepower came from two locations, Richmond, Virginia and Baltimore, Maryland, both were cities where Scalini owned trucking businesses. Two men were coming from Richmond where the drive was only two and a half hours. Four men in two cars were dispatched to make the drive from Baltimore. Six more men. A total of eight counting Bruno and himself. One more than he had started with two days ago in Little Rock.

Scalini had left him with a foreboding warning. If he failed to capture Tony Q this time, his fate would be death.

A slow and painful one.

By the time the reinforcements from Baltimore arrived, it was already 2:30 a.m. The sky was dark and only the glow of the streetlights illuminated the empty streets of Lexington, Virginia. The past two hours were spent patrolling the area where the silver Mercedes disappeared. With two cars and four men, manpower had doubled and more ground could be covered.

By 4:00 a.m., the results of the reconnaissance gathered was that all but three homes in the neighborhood were completely dark inside and had been for hours. Two of the three homes had open yards, which allowed for closer inspection on foot.

The third home was inaccessible and DeLuca was convinced that was where Tony Q was holed up. Behind a ten-foot high thick hedge of Japanese Ligustrum was an eight-foot brick wall. A metal gate blocked the driveway and DeLuca found the only way to see onto the property was physically climb on top of his vehicle's roof. A quick walk around the perimeter revealed the driveway gate was the only access to the home. Odd place for a fortress unless it also served as some sort of safe house. He'd heard about places like this, but they didn't belong to the U. S. Marshals Service. They serviced much more secretive agencies…or corporations that contracted with these secretive agencies.

The Richmond team was the first to spot the home. They reported movement inside and outside the home for the past hour and a half.

As all the men arrived in Lexington, DeLuca took charge. He couldn't fail again. He ordered the men to make vehicle and foot patrols through the neighborhood.

DeLuca ordered each team to specific locations to sit and wait. He knew whoever had Tony Q wouldn't keep him very long. Eventually they would want to get him back into the hands of the U. S. Marshals Service. Perhaps they were even waiting for the Marshals Service to arrive. Either way, he would end this.

When the gates opened, he and his men would be ready.

CHAPTER 33

KAPLAN AND MOSS SAT AT A TABLE OUTSIDE the *quiet room* drinking coffee. Earlier, Kaplan let Moss talk to Tony alone, a conversation lasting less than ten minutes. When Moss left the sealed room, he took the palm of his right hand and hit his forehead.

"What a pain in the ass," Moss said in exasperation. "I don't know how you kept from shooting him."

Kaplan stared into his coffee and smiled. "I almost did... more than once. Instead, I busted his nose after the old codger thought he could pull a gun on me."

"How'd he get a gun?"

"I gave it to him."

"Why the hell would you do a fool thing like that?"

"I couldn't drive a motorcycle *and* shoot at the helicopter at the same time."

Moss responded, "That explains a few things."

Kaplan swirled the dark liquid around in his cup. "There is something Cox said that has been bothering me. And before we go any further, I want some answers."

"Like what?"

"Like, what did Cox mean when he said the Little Rock PD would only get Tony killed?"

"Little Rock PD means well," Moss explained. "But the Marshals Service has had a couple of jurisdiction issues with them. They aren't the most cooperative department when they think our witness is a criminal. It's that Southern, good-ole-boy mentality, I think. I worked at our Little Rock field office for several years. Matter of fact, I've been gone less than three weeks, so it's like I never left. A year ago or so there was an incident caused by a lack of communication between the departments. A young undercover detective with LRPD recognized one of our witnesses as a wanted criminal, but didn't realize he had entered the WitSec program. It was messy. The detective yelled out the witness's real name and drew a weapon. Thinking his witness's cover had been breached and not realizing he was looking at a plain-clothes cop, the escorting WitSec inspector drew his weapon and fired. The deputy put two rounds in the detective. Fingers were pointed. Blame and accusations flew back and forth. LRPD refused to accept blame for any wrong doing on the part of their officer. Ever since then the relationship between the Marshals Service and Little Rock PD has been...strained, for lack of a better word."

Kaplan looked up for the first time. "How could that happen? Local law enforcement is briefed, right? Didn't he identify himself as a cop? He should have known about the witness, right?"

"She," Moss said. "In this particular instance, she would have been briefed but she had just returned from two weeks leave. First day back on the job. She had stopped at the diner for breakfast before going into the station. That's where she ran into the witness. Eyewitness statements along with the WitSec inspector's testimony claim she never identified herself

as a police officer before she was shot. The politics ran all the
way to the governor, the director of the Marshals Service, and
the Department of Justice. Ultimately the deputy was removed
from WitSec and reassigned to another field office."

"And the undercover cop? What happened to her?"

"She didn't make it. Died enroute to the hospital."

Kaplan studied the big man. His next question was sure to
get a reaction, but he never got the chance to ask.

Dick walked into the room while Susan stood in the
doorway. It seemed an odd match to him. Dick was six-five
and Susan was barely five feet. Dick was all business and Susan
was not.

"We got company," Dick said. "Four cars. Eight men, maybe
more. They've driven by at least a half a dozen times over the
past two hours. Our surveillance cameras spotted a couple of
men walking the perimeter. Could have been the same man
twice, hard to tell in the shadows."

"Gregg," Susan said. "This is new territory for us. This safe
house has never been compromised. We have contingencies in
place, of course, but have never had to use them. Somebody
has gone to a lot of trouble to get to your man."

"Martin Scalini," Moss interjected.

Kaplan looked back at Moss. "Tony said it was Scalini, but
this doesn't seem like wise guy M.O."

Moss hesitated, and then finally said, "Scalini is powerful
and highly respected in the Mafioso. Tony is the one man
who can single-handedly bring down Scalini's entire operation
along with all the drug cartels he does business with. And the
human traffickers. And the gun traffickers. The list goes on
and on. Scalini's top two button men are Angelo DeLuca and
Bruno Ratti, aka Bruno the Rat. We don't know much about

Ratti except that he disappears for a few years at a time and then reappears. Rumor is he spends his time in the Caribbean somewhere. DeLuca is a different story. Angelo DeLuca's got a rap sheet as long as your arm. He's extremely loyal to Martin Scalini. Been with him since he was a teenager. He has a reputation of violence. There is only one person I can think of who is more ruthless and sadistic than DeLuca. And that's Martin Scalini.

"If Scalini takes Tony alive, he will take him to his *room of death*—we don't know exactly where his torture chamber is, only that it exists. There, Scalini tortures his victims. Some are rumored dissolved alive in an acid bath. Some are dismembered. First he starts with the fingers and toes. He breaks them all, one at a time. Slowly. Then, for violating the code of silence, Scalini cuts out the tongue as a symbolic gesture."

"Okay. Enough for me." Susan's face was ashen. "I'm leaving. I don't need to hear this." She turned and left.

"Is this really necessary?" Kaplan watched Susan leave the room. "I'm more than a little familiar with torture."

"Not like this. You know torture when information extraction was the objective." Moss pointed his finger at the man sitting inside the *quiet room*. "This isn't water boarding, this is different. When a member of the family flips and cooperates with law enforcement, a violent message must be sent. Whether it is sadistic torture or being buried alive, the message rings loud and clear throughout the criminal underworld—you don't snitch on the Scalini family. If you do, he will make you beg for death."

CHAPTER 34

THE *CROW'S NEST* WAS A TEN-FOOT BY FIVE-foot rectangular parapet on the roof of the B & B. With its rhythmic breaks in the wall to create a protective pattern of embattlements, the crenellated parapet offered an unobstructed 360° view of the B & B's property. To Kaplan, it looked like a tower on a fortified medieval castle with its notched walls to ward off attackers. Only manned when the safe house was active, it provided high ground so the two armed guards had an advantage against unwelcome intruders.

Kaplan opened the metal hatch and climbed onto the *crow's nest*. Behind the reinforced brick wall, he joined the two men guarding the fortress. According to Dick, both men were former Marines. One was an easy ten years older than the other. Both were dressed in full black tactical uniforms with smudged faces. They had rifles with infrared scopes, night vision goggles, as well as standard binoculars.

"Okay, give me a SitRep," Kaplan said in a hushed voice.

The elder of the two leaned over and gave Kaplan the situation report. "Two cars and two SUVs. Looks like a light colored Buick, maybe a LaCrosse—"

"That's the car with the two goons from Francesco's," said Kaplan.

"It drives by about every fifteen minutes. There is also a Lincoln Town Car and both SUVs appear to be Suburbans. With the exception of the Buick, all the vehicles are dark colored with black out windows. Infrared indicates two men in each vehicle." The guard pointed to the end of the block. "One Suburban parked at the end of the street hasn't moved in forty-five minutes. About every eighteen to twenty minutes, someone from the Suburban gets out and walks down the street and back."

"What about the others?" Kaplan asked.

The man turned and pointed through a break in the trees behind the safe house. "The other Suburban is parked one street back. You can just make out the front grill through there."

"And the Town Car?"

"Wild card. We have no idea. Last time we saw it was over an hour ago. It drove down the street and hasn't been seen since."

"Any chance it's not part of this group?" Kaplan asked.

"No chance, sir. Before its last pass it stopped there." He turned and pointed to the first Suburban at the end of the street. "One man from each vehicle got out and talked for two and a half minutes, both looking in this direction the entire time, then they got back in their vehicles and the Town Car drove down the street and disappeared."

"You think they know you guys are up here?"

"It's possible, but not likely. Heavy cloud cover, no moon, no streetlights on this end of the block. It's pretty dark and we're well hidden behind this wall. Tonight they'd need night vision goggles to know we're here."

"Great." Kaplan opened the metal door and descended

three steps, stopped and turned to the guard. "If anything changes—"

"Yes, sir. You'll be the first to know."

Thirty seconds later Kaplan was standing in front of the *quiet room*. Senior Inspector Moss was back in the room with Tony. Kaplan knocked on the glass and motioned to Moss. The deputy came outside the room. "How long before you can get Marshals protection here to transport Tony?"

Moss looked at his watch. "Three hours. Maybe a little less if traffic isn't bad." He looked up at Kaplan. "Change your mind?"

"Yeah, but three hours is too long. We need to get him out of here ASAP." Kaplan turned and looked at Tony. The old man, with a Band-Aid on his neck, was sitting at the table inside the room glaring at him. "This turned into more than I bargained for."

"What do you want to do?" Moss asked.

Kaplan turned back to the deputy. "All that stuff you said earlier about what Scalini will do to Tony...how sure are you that he'll keep him alive long enough to torture him?"

"It's Scalini's style. Everyone who double-crosses him is tortured first and then killed. Almost without exception. And he's going to want to talk to Tony first. Find out what all he'd told the feds."

"And you know how to find Scalini?"

"More or less," Moss said. "OCRS has plenty of intel on almost all of Scalini's holdings. Putting the finger on him has been the hard part."

"OCRS?"

"The Organized Crime and Racketeering Section of the U. S. Marshals Service."

"How would you like to be known as the man who single-handedly brought down Scalini?" Kaplan asked.

"In a perfect world, what deputy wouldn't?" Moss said. "But right now I'm tasked with bringing in my assigned witness alive." Moss paused and gave Kaplan a perplexed look. "Why? What'd you have in mind?"

"I have a plan," Kaplan said, as he turned and looked at Tony through the window. "It'll give you the chance to kill two birds with one stone. But we'll need Tony's help to pull it off."

Moss followed suit and also looked through the glass. "I'll bet I'm not going to like it."

"No, Inspector Moss, you're going to hate it."

† † †

Angelo DeLuca parked his car around the corner from the safe house giving him a limited view of the front gate. Dark clouds hung in the sky and with no streetlights it was difficult to see anything in detail, but he could still make out the metal gate sandwiched between the two brick abutments of the perimeter wall.

"Boss," Bruno said. He was holding binoculars to his eyes. "You're not going to believe this."

"What is it?"

Bruno passed the binoculars to DeLuca. "Take a look for yourself."

DeLuca twisted the focus until the safe house came into view. Bruno was right; he didn't believe what he saw. The gate had opened a few feet and stopped. The silhouette of a man walked from the opening with hands on top of his head to the middle of the street and stopped. DeLuca zoomed in on the man's face. "Holy shit, it's Tony Q."

The radio crackled and a voice said, "Boss, are you seeing this?"

DeLuca replied, "I'm watching."

The voice said, "Is that Tony Q?"

"Sure looks like him."

The voice asked, "What do you want us to do, Boss?"

"Nothing," Deluca said. "It has to be a trick."

Bruno interrupted, "There's someone else. He's standing at the gate. He's motioning for us to come to him."

"What do you think, Bruno? Think it's a trap?"

"It's that asshole Tony Q. I can smell that two-bit snitch from here."

"It could be a setup," said DeLuca. "Using Tony Q for bait."

"If it is, we whack 'em." Bruno grinned.

DeLuca stared at Bruno. "The boss said alive, you moron."

"Geez, Angelo. Lighten up, I was just kidding. Think logically about this for a second. Of course it's not a setup. Whoever is inside doesn't want to start an all out war in the middle of this neighborhood. It's too risky. The safe house cover would be blown and that's the last thing they want. Besides I'll keep my gun trained on the man at the gate."

DeLuca pulled the car from the curb and crept forward. He rounded the corner and let the Buick roll forward at idle speed until it was only inches away from Tony. The old man hadn't moved. "Tony Q, is that you?"

"Of course, it's me, you dumbass," the old man replied.

Bruno opened his door and got out, keeping his gun trained toward the man at the gate. The man stepped from the shadows. The glow from the headlights outlined the man's face. DeLuca recognized him as the man who escaped with

Tony in Nashville.

"I have a message for your boss," the man said.

"Yeah? What kind of message?" DeLuca said.

"Tell Scalini this favor is on me. Also tell him I plan to collect real soon."

"You think you're some kind of tough guy, huh? Why don't I have Bruno do a number on you right now?" He looked at Bruno and laughed.

"I don't think you'll do that because there is only one scenario where you end up alive and that's you taking Tony back to Scalini unharmed. Go back empty handed, Scalini kills you." Kaplan motioned to the crow's nest. "Make a move on me, we kill you. Your call."

"The boss won't deal with a weasel like you. You show up, he'll kill you on the spot."

"My problem, not yours. All you have to do is leave with Tony and relay the message to your boss."

"Come on, Angelo," Bruno said to DeLuca. "We got Tony Q. Let's get out of here."

DeLuca paused. "Have it your way, tough guy. I'll tell him. But if you do something stupid, like come after Scalini, you better come heavy." Deluca motioned to Bruno. "Put the old man in the back…and make sure he's not wearing a wire."

† † †

Kaplan watched the Buick drive off with Moss's witness in the back seat. Neither Tony nor the inspector was initially onboard with Kaplan's plan. It took a lot of convincing to bring Moss around. The idea of handing over his witness to the very man who wanted to kill him went against everything the Marshals Service stood for…until he understood the plan. Then Kaplan, with Moss's help, finally convinced Tony that his cooperation would be in his best interest.

The Suburban at the end of the street turned around and both vehicles disappeared from sight. One street over he heard another vehicle start and accelerate away.

Across the street a figure emerged from the shadows. He was dressed in full black and walked up to him.

"GPS device in place?" Kaplan asked.

"Yes sir," the man said. "Virtually undetectable and you can track it with your phone."

CHAPTER 35

Twelve Hours Later
Newark Shipping Terminals
Newark, New Jersey

KAPLAN FOLLOWED ANGELO DELUCA TO A
worn-down warehouse inside the Newark shipping terminal
complex. The old Quonset hut style warehouse was a long,
semi-circular cross-sectioned structure with windows near the
apex lending the appearance of a possible upper level on the
inside. Rust had metastasized on the exterior walls through
years of neglect and had mottled the once painted surface.

There was a barrage of background noise at the shipping
terminal, from jet engines at the adjacent Newark International
Airport to the incessant banging and clanging of the never
ending loading and unloading of containers from the twenty-
four hour stream of cargo ships using the port's facilities.

The weather had cleared on the drive from Virginia to
Newark and the northern sky was cloudless. As darkness
descended, the glow from the surrounding mass of bright urban
lights gave the shipping terminal a stereotypical appearance.
Trucks carried cargo into the port where intermodal transfer
cranes loaded the containers from truck to ship. There was

a steady flow of vehicles entering and leaving the shipping terminal complex.

From his vantage point, Kaplan saw the lights on Liberty Island illuminating the Statue of Liberty. Behind it, Ellis Island, Governors Island, and the glow of Battery Park and Lower Manhattan. Farther across the Hudson River, the western shore of Brooklyn seemed closer than it actually was as ships moved in and out of Bush Terminal.

Earlier, Kaplan had called in the location to his handler who verified the warehouse belonged to a shell corporation he painstakingly traced back to a holding company owned by one of Martin Scalini's international investors.

While Moss updated Hepler, Kaplan scouted the perimeter and made his initial assessment of the warehouse before returning to the Mercedes.

The warehouse was a two-story building with upstairs and downstairs rear fire escapes, each door directly above or below the other. All other exits—two truck sized loading and unloading doors and one entrance door—faced the main entrance road to the shipping terminal.

When he and Moss first arrived in Newark, the highways were congested with traffic as if it were rush hour. Thousands of taxis and commuters clogged the roadways. Impatient motorists honked their horns and gave hand gestures expressing their displeasure. The app Kaplan installed on Moss's smart phone displayed the navigation track DeLuca took to the warehouse. It made it unnecessary for Kaplan to keep visual contact with the silver Buick LaCrosse through the maze of surface streets leading to the shipping terminal.

As Kaplan pulled the Mercedes into the complex, Moss spotted DeLuca's vehicle pulling through one of the

warehouse loading doors. The door pulled closed and two
men were stationed outside. Kaplan followed a truck down
the main entrance road, past the warehouse, before selectively
parking the Mercedes on a side street in the shadow of a larger
warehouse, which provided him with two things, a visual of
both the warehouse and access road and a place to conceal the
vehicle in a darkened alley.

Moss looked worried as Kaplan got back in the car. "If
Scalini was already in there waiting, he won't waste much time
going to work on Tony."

"Scalini's not here yet," Kaplan said.

"How do you know?"

"I checked. There is an upstairs fire escape with a row of
windows overlooking the inside of the warehouse. DeLuca's
car is the only one inside. These thugs have another car parked
around back. Scalini won't risk exposure walking in or out
of the warehouse. He'll drive in and drive out in the back
of his limo. In addition to the two men who picked up Tony
in Lexington, I saw one man keeping watch inside. Upstairs
there is a catwalk balcony allowing him to overlook almost the
entire warehouse floor below. And he's packing heavy. Looks
like a silenced Uzi strapped over his shoulder. I saw a couple
of rooms upstairs as well. As far as I could tell, there really
isn't anything located on ground level except open floor space
cluttered with crates, boxes, and metal drums. Tony has to be
in one of the rooms upstairs. Both rear exits have metal doors.
Bolted shut from the inside. Looks like the only way to get in
is through the front door."

Moss pointed to the front of the warehouse. "Those two
look like trouble. They're packing heavy too."

"There's a wino living in a box across the street," Kaplan

said.

"Yeah?" Moss said. "So your plan is to see if the drunk will stagger over and ask them to let us in?"

Kaplan didn't answer. He turned around in his seat and grabbed his backpack. He pulled out two handguns, both with sound suppressors, and two wireless comm sets. "We'll need these." He held up the handguns. "Got clean ones at the B & B. Untraceable."

"You know, Kaplan, we're getting mighty close to the limit of the law."

Kaplan studied the man for a few seconds. Moss thinks too much like a cop. Sometimes laws have to be broken…or at least seriously stretched. "Inspector, before this night is over we might very well cross that line."

Moss pointed toward the complex entrance as a black Cadillac rolled down the main road. "We got company. I thought your plan was to have us in position *before* Scalini arrived."

"It was."

"Well, we're not," said Moss.

"Scalini's early."

Moss turned to Kaplan. "This is not only going to cost me a witness but a career as well. And it might land my ass in jail. Your plan just keeps getting worse."

"Relax," Kaplan reassured. "It'll work."

Kaplan knew the plan was risky. If Moss had known how risky, he was sure the inspector would never have agreed to it. And he knew Tony wouldn't have gone along with it either. But it was too late to back out now.

The limo pulled to the loading door. A heavy-tinted window rolled down and one of the guards leaned over and spoke.

The window rolled up. He saw the other guard lift up the retractable door on the building. The Cadillac drove in and the guard immediately closed the metal door behind it.

"Looks like the clock just started ticking," said Kaplan.

"Just started ticking?" Moss's voice sounded agitated. "The clock started ticking the moment I agreed to let you hand Tony over to those two goons. I can't believe I went along with your harebrained scheme. What was I thinking? We need to call for backup."

"Don't chicken out now." Kaplan stared into Moss's eyes. "We can do this. I've been in situations a lot worse where the odds were stacked against me far more than this. We need to move quickly and not hesitate. Hesitation kills."

Moss looked at his watch. "How long should we wait?"

"We need to move now," Kaplan said. "Or else your witness dies."

† † †

Senior Inspector Pete Moss watched and listened as the wino staggered toward the two men guarding the warehouse entrance. He wore a dirty brown trench coat and a longshoreman's cap with a hole in it. In his left hand he carried a bottle wrapped in a brown paper bag.

"Beat it," one of the guards said. He stepped forward holding up his hand like a traffic cop.

The wino kept staggering toward them.

Based on Kaplan's reconnaissance, Moss calculated there were at least five of Scalini's men inside and now, Martin Scalini himself. Kaplan had counted one man already inside plus Angelo DeLuca and his companion, Bruno the Rat. Then he had to account for the limo driver and one other. And of course, the two men at the entrance. Best case scenario—eight against two. He hoped Gregg Kaplan was as good as Tony said he was during the interview in the *quiet room*.

"Are you deaf or just plain stupid?" the other man said. "Don't make trouble for yourself. Translation…beat it or I'm going to put a bullet in your head." He turned to his buddy and laughed.

The wino stopped less than ten feet from the men and placed his bottle on the ground. He swayed as he said something to the men. The wino turned, faced the building, and unzipped his pants as he prepared to urinate. Both men pulled their guns and rushed to stop him.

The wino attacked with lightning speed. He grabbed the gun barrel of the first man with his left hand pulling the guard closer as his right hand smashed into the man's neck. The man gasped and clutched his windpipe as the wino delivered a knockout blow to the man's head. The guard slumped toward the wino and fell to the ground.

The second man never had a chance. He hesitated, stunned, as his friend fell to the ground. And in that moment of hesitation, the wino delivered a roundhouse kick to the man's head. The second man crumpled to the ground. The wino grabbed both men by the collars and dragged them around the side of the warehouse.

When he returned, he wasn't wearing the overcoat or the longshoreman's cap.

Gregg Kaplan gave Moss the all-clear signal.

Tony was right, Moss thought, Gregg Kaplan was a machine. Perhaps the best he'd ever seen. Certainly the fastest. A dangerous man. His brutal combat martial arts skills made

Moss glad he was on his side.

† † †

Kaplan had placed the unconscious guards in the shadows against the dark side of the warehouse. He flex-cuffed and gagged both men and laid them side-by-side. He poured the five-dollar wine he'd paid fifty dollars for over their bloody faces and dropped the bottle between them. He removed the tattered overcoat he'd paid the homeless man a hundred bucks for and draped it over them.

He motioned for Moss to join him.

When Moss arrived, he handed him one of the weapons he'd taken from the men he'd just immobilized. "Here."

"Uzis," Moss said. "Just like the guy inside?"

"Yep."

After watching you handle those two." Moss motioned with his head. "I'm not sure we'll need reinforcements after all."

"I only need one thing from you Moss." Kaplan said. "I need to know you got my back."

Moss smiled and held up his Uzi. "A hundred percent."

"Good to know. This won't be easy. When we go through that door, you can't think like a cop. From here on out, this is self-preservation. If you hesitate, you're dead. We're dead. It's kill or be killed."

CHAPTER 36

THE FRONT DOORWAY TO THE WAREHOUSE
opened beneath a wooden catwalk overlooking the unlit
warehouse floor. On the upper level behind the catwalk was
a suite of offices or rooms, or something, which occupied
roughly a third of the warehouse's footprint and was built at
the waterfront end of the mammoth-sized building. The only
light inside the warehouse emanated from those rooms. The
dim warehouse provided Kaplan and Moss better cover.

Kaplan looked up and saw a man through the spaces in the
catwalk. He gestured to Moss, his finger over his lips and then
pointed toward the man above.

Moss nodded.

The black Cadillac limo was parked next to the silver Buick
and both bumpers were right in front of a wooden staircase
leading to the rooms upstairs.

Kaplan took in his surroundings. The floor was covered in
sawdust, probably used to absorb spills from the contents of
the dozens of metal drums, some with transfer pumps, crates,
and wooden boxes that occupied most of the warehouse floor
beneath the upstairs offices. Bending low to his knees, he
moved silently, inspecting each item while remaining mindful
of the guard overhead. There were oil drums and solvent

drums with chemical labels he'd never seen before, and some he had, including lead azide, a highly volatile explosive and one he'd used before to set off an explosion at a factory outside of Moscow. At the opposite end of the warehouse he noticed a large fuel tank he assumed was filled with diesel or gasoline.

He and Moss had just invaded a powder keg.

His first order of business was to disable the guard on the catwalk without alerting the others in the rooms upstairs. He gave hand signals to Moss who understood and took up position under the stairs.

Kaplan found a wooden support column beneath the midway point of the catwalk and shimmied up as far as he could without exposing his presence to the man above. He pulled out his knife and clenched it between his teeth. When he was in position he gave Moss a nod—there was no turning back now.

† † †

In the beginning, Moss was skeptical of Kaplan's plan, but now that he'd seen the CIA operative in action, he was confident Kaplan had the skills to pull it off. The guard pacing above Kaplan on the catwalk was armed but not very attentive, which gave Kaplan the upper hand. The man walked back and forth with his Uzi strap draped over his shoulder and his hands in his pockets.

After they had entered the warehouse and made a quick and silent recon, Kaplan grabbed two small bolts on top of a solvent drum, placed the greasy metal objects in Moss's palm, and used hand signals to relay instructions to him. Kaplan laid out his plan to him and then climbed a wooden pole that served as a support column for the wooden catwalk above.

Moss positioned himself beneath the wooden steps leading to the upper level and awaited Kaplan's signal, which came as soon as Moss crouched into position.

Moss took the first bolt, gauged the strength he'd need to hit his target, wound up his arm, and tossed the lightweight object with just enough speed to tumble across the floor and rest against the far wall. The metal bolt bounced unexpectedly and clanged against a metal drum. Kaplan shot him a stern look. The distraction worked, though. The startled man turned and moved swiftly toward the end of the catwalk.

Kaplan started to pull himself over the rail then ducked back down as a voice from inside a room yelled out, "Paulie, you okay out there?"

A man stepped out onto the catwalk. The guard turned around and said, "I'm fine, Joey. Heard something downstairs. Guess I better check it out."

"Probably just a wharf rat. They're all over this filthy place."

"Better check it out anyway," said Paulie.

"Yeah? You think Frankie and Dominic let somebody inside or something?"

Paulie hesitated and then said in a shamed voice, "I guess you're right. Nobody's getting past those two. Like you said, Joey, probably just a rat."

Joey went back inside the upstairs room he came from and Paulie went back to mindlessly pacing the catwalk with his silenced Uzi once again strapped over his shoulder and his hands in his front pockets.

Beads of sweat rolled down Moss's bald head, stinging his eyes. He waited for another nod, which again came too fast for his own comfort and this time with another hand signal to toss the next bolt softer. Moss stretched his arm back and pitched the bolt lower and with less force. It grazed against a wooden crate as it tumbled across the sawdust covered concrete floor.

Paulie turned, walked to the end of the catwalk, and leaned over the railing. He aimed his Uzi down at the noise and pretended to shoot at the fictitious rat. "Damn wharf rats," he muttered under his breath.

Kaplan swiftly hoisted himself over the railing and charged down the walkway with speed and agility. The man was unprepared for Kaplan's surprise attack.

Moss was amazed at how fast Kaplan disabled the threat. The CIA operative collared Paulie from behind, cupped his hand over the man's mouth, and smashed the butt of his gun with exact precision against Paulie's head. Moss expected to hear some noise, but none came as Kaplan slowly lowered the unconscious man to the catwalk planking. Within a minute, Paulie lay flex-cuffed and gagged.

Kaplan motioned for Moss to move to the base of the stairs while he crawled on his hands and knees beneath the windows lining the catwalk. He was vulnerable and wanted someone keeping watch with a gun in case Joey came out to check on Paulie again while he made the thirty-foot crawl beneath the span of windows.

When he reached the end of the catwalk near the staircase, Kaplan checked around the corner and noticed an open and empty foyer with a desk and four cheap red vinyl-covered chairs. They looked like throwbacks from the 70's. Between two chairs on the back wall was an emergency exit door. One he already knew was locked from the inside. The third wall had two doors and what appeared to be a hallway leading deeper into the upstairs space, maybe to bathrooms or other offices.

Kaplan signaled to Moss the all clear. Moss moved up the steps as he kept his eyes fixed on the open foyer above him.

Three steps from the landing, Moss stepped on a loose plank that rocked forward under his heavy foot. He froze and looked at Kaplan who had instinctively hunched at the sound and turned toward Moss. A frozen look of terror filled the big WitSec deputy's wide eyes, but he wasn't looking at Kaplan.

Kaplan turned and saw four gun barrels.

Two pointing at Moss and two pointing at him.

CHAPTER 37

HER PERCH ON THE ABANDONED CRANE platform offered an ideal view down the length of the warehouse. She had an elevated line of sight at anything or anyone entering or leaving the front entrances as well as the rear. Valkyrie scouted the prime location to setup sniper watch after receiving the location of Scalini's warehouse from Shepherd. It was a premium spot for the kill shot.

Her choice of the lightweight .50 caliber Barrett M107A1 rifle with a QDL suppressor was an excellent choice for the one hundred twenty foot vertical climb to the platform. At just over five pounds, the sniper rifle was no burden to carry, unlike her escape kit, which weighed over ten pounds alone.

When she reached the platform, she attached her optics to her rifle, a Barrett Optical Ranging System. Systematically she made her mental and physical preparations for the long-range shot. There was no margin for error. Preparation was an important key to a successful mission. There were countless variables to consider before squeezing the trigger. Range to target, wind direction, air density, and elevation—all factors that influenced the bullet's trajectory and point of impact.

The wind was light, something that would work in her favor. Using the ranging system she determined her shot would be just over nine hundred yards. Not the easiest shot she'd been forced to take. Not the hardest either. She had made longer distance sniper kills with pinpoint accuracy. However, those were daylight shots without shadows or glinting from streetlights.

The long-range sniper shot was Valkyrie's forte. Her trademark. She was a master of stealth with the patience to wait for the perfect shot. It was vital to setup position, verify that position was well camouflaged, establish an escape route with a backup plan, and train both the mind and the body.

The sniper's mind needed to be trained and the skill honed to perfection. As soon as she setup her rifle, she started her relaxation breathing. Proper breathing was another critical step in mental conditioning for the shot. She observed the exits and took mental shots, calculating the options and obstacles. Her line of sight view offered her prey virtually no cover once clear of the building. And, in this instance, clear of the building meant anywhere more than two feet from the exterior walls.

One shot, one kill. A sniper's motto.

Thanks to Shepherd relaying this location from his inside source, she was able to scout the area and get into position on the perch before the Buick LaCrosse arrived. She knew it contained the witness and his captors. Through the crosshairs on her rifle's scope she watched the next two men pull up in a Mercedes, park, and stake out the warehouse. A black limousine appeared and drove inside the warehouse. One of the men from the Mercedes subdued both guards with a quick-hitting strike and dragged their bodies away from the front of the building.

She zoomed the optical in on his face and recognized Gregg Kaplan. He had not lost his skills, she mused. And he was still ruggedly handsome and very dangerous.

Within seconds another man joined him. He stepped in front of Kaplan, blocking her line of sight. It was the man she had met in Little Rock and worked with earlier. And he was now here in Newark.

Senior Inspector Pete Moss, United States Marshals Service.

And by the looks of it, he had teamed up with Kaplan.

The two men quickly disappeared inside the warehouse.

She figured if Moss and Kaplan were together, then Moss's hunch about the man was correct, he was leaving a trail only law enforcement could follow. Something had changed though, because he didn't take the witness to the SSOC in Virginia as originally anticipated. Along the way a new plan must have developed and now all the players seemed to be in Newark and, according to Shepherd, Moss's witness was in the hands of Martin Scalini. And from what she knew of the mob boss, the witness would likely die at the hands of Martin Scalini.

As she settled in to wait for her target to exit the warehouse, she noticed two large black SUVs enter the Newark Shipping Terminal complex and stop a hundred yards from Scalini's warehouse. The vehicles turned off their headlights and idled for several minutes. Even with her high-powered scope she was unable to see through the blackened windows. Traces of steam and exhaust puffed from the tail pipes.

Suddenly, the doors to both SUVs opened and four men from each vehicle exited and rushed toward Scalini's warehouse.

Each man carried an assault rifle and wore an armored vest. Emblazoned on the black vests were three bold white letters.

FBI.

✝ ✝ ✝

Angelo DeLuca waited for Martin Scalini to start torturing the man when they heard the noise on the steps. By the time he and Bruno made it to the landing, Joey and Nicky had the two intruders at gunpoint.

This wasn't the first time DeLuca was going to witness one of his boss's sadistic torture sessions. In fact, he'd had to endure far too many. The victims were tortured until Scalini extracted the information he wanted. If the victim could no longer endure the excruciating pain they would beg for death. The lucky ones got a bullet to the head.

Unless it was personal. Then there were no lucky ones.

And with Tony Q, it was very personal. Scalini would take his time with Tony Q. Make him suffer for two, maybe three days before finally ending it. Driven out of his mind from pain, he too would beg for death. In a way, DeLuca felt sorry for the old man.

As soon as the mob boss arrived, Martin Scalini and Tony Q stood across the torture table from each other without speaking. Scalini, a lanky man with thinning hair had an intense seething glare behind his big black frame glasses with Coke bottle thick lenses.

Tony Q stood straight with relaxed shoulders and a frozen scowl on his face. Odd posture for a man who had an impending date with death. The two men stared at each other, a silent communication that only the two of them seemed to share. Maybe they were sizing each other up for the inevitable. Or maybe Scalini was simply bewildered at Tony Q's demeanor. The mob boss was the most feared and powerful mobster in New York. Instilling fear in others was how he ran his organization. Tony Q did not act panicky or intimidated. Scalini was visibly taken by surprise and shifted his weight back and forth on his feet revealing his obvious agitation.

It was in that moment when they heard Joey yell at the intruders.

† † †

Kaplan looked at Moss and then back to the men pointing guns at his head.

He and the inspector dropped their guns and raised their hands.

An older man with overly thick glasses walked onto the landing and glanced at both men then his eyes settled on Kaplan. He had a cigarette dangling from his lips while he spoke. "Mr. Kaplan, I presume?" He removed the cigarette. "Come to collect on that favor so soon?"

Kaplan recognized two of the men from last night when he handed over Tony in Lexington. "I'm a man of my word," said Kaplan in a terse tone.

"That might very well be your undoing." Scalini looked at Moss. "You must be Senior Inspector Pete Moss."

Moss gave him a baffled look.

"Tony mentioned you to Angelo here." He pointed to Moss. "Plus your belt badge was a giveaway." He smiled. "Pete Moss, not a name one forgets."

Scalini stepped back and took a long draw from his cigarette. He coughed. "Bruno, go get Tony Q and bring him out here. I want these gentlemen to observe what happens when someone double crosses me."

Bruno disappeared into the room and returned leading

Tony by the elbow.

Scalini turned to the old man. Sweat trickled down his forehead. "Tony Q, this breaks my heart. We've been together for forty years. You're like family to me. I gave you your start and what do you do? You stab me in the back. Bastardo. This is how you repay me for all my generosity?"

Kaplan observed the men's body language. Tony stood eerily calm, as if he'd made peace with his impending fate. Scalini, on the other hand, was shaking from pure unmitigated anger. His face was red and more sweat trickled down his forehead and dangled from the tip of his over sized nose.

And then Scalini's phone rang. He looked annoyed until he looked at the caller-id.

"Yeah," Scalini said into the phone. "What? Are you sure?" His eyes took on a panicked look. "When? Now?" He disconnected the call.

If it weren't for the impending threat of being shot by the thugs, Kaplan would have found Scalini's behavior amusing. The already panicked mob boss seemed to unravel at once. And at that moment, all the lights to the warehouse went out.

Scalini gasped and then cursed.

Battery powered backup lights came on at the four corners of the warehouse, barely enough to see but better than pitch black.

Several canisters broke through the windows above them sending shards of glass raining down. The canisters landed on the lower warehouse floor and burst open spewing tear gas into the air.

Kaplan noticed all the men looked at Scalini for instructions.

All, except one.

Bruno.

Scalini looked at the old man. "Tony Q, may you rot in hell." He raised his gun.

Before Scalini could pull the trigger, Bruno turned his weapon on Martin Scalini and fired a bullet into the mob boss's head.

Scalini's face never had a chance to show surprise. His body dropped to the ground. His trusted bodyguard had killed him. Bruno the Rat.

The next projectiles through the broken windows weren't difficult for Kaplan to recognize or prepare for—flash bangs.

Instinctively he and Moss flung themselves to the floor, closed their eyes, opened their mouths, and covered their ears with their hands, pinching off as much noise as possible in preparation for the blast. The last thing he saw before he closed his eyes was Bruno retreat into the back room with Tony…but not before he fired another round at point blank range.

This one into Angelo DeLuca's chest.

CHAPTER 38

IN RAPID-FIRE SUCCESSION, THE STUN GRENADES exploded. The effect was usually brain numbing. Upon detonation, the grenades were designed to emit an intensely loud bang, usually in the range of 170-180 decibels, along with a one million candela plus blinding flash. The immediate result was flash blindness, deafness, tinnitus, and inner ear disturbance. All of which caused disorientation, confusion, loss of coordination, balance, and sometimes even consciousness.

Kaplan's first exposure to the flashbang was in the Army. His Special Forces training had prepared him to use the flashbang against his enemies as well as defend against the grenade being used against him. The use of the flashbang was intended to disorient the opponent and buy the user extra time to gain a tactical advantage. It was a wonderful innovation—unless the mission demanded stealth. Obviously, this one did not.

Scalini's men, Joey and Nicky, groaned as they covered their ears with their hands. They were dazed and blind. Kaplan had a window of at least twenty or thirty seconds before they would recover enough to pose any threat. He also knew the men who launched the grenades into the warehouse would storm through the doors any second and he had no intention of being in the line of fire when they did.

Kaplan grabbed Moss by the arm and herded him toward the back room where Bruno and Tony disappeared.

The smoke from the tear gas canisters was already stinging his eyes. Both he and Moss pulled their neck buffs over their noses to help filter the air and delay the mucus membrane irritation in their lungs as long as possible.

The room was relatively clear of smoke, but in a matter of seconds that would change. He closed the office door behind him and as he did, he heard the sound of the men downstairs breaking through the exterior doors. He turned, expecting to see Tony and Bruno, but no one else was in the room except Moss. Through an open door in the back, Kaplan saw a staircase against the north wall leading to the warehouse floor beneath.

The thunderous sound of the men charging into the warehouse from the main entrance was interrupted by the sound of gunfire as Joey and Nicky had regained their faculties and opened fire on the intruders. The exchange of shooting was close, just outside the office. Below, on the warehouse floor, he heard the invaders yelling halt commands. Bruno and Tony had not gotten away.

"Throw down your weapons," several men yelled from the warehouse floor.

One of DeLuca's men yelled back, "See you in Hell." Then there was a continuous blast from an Uzi followed by an explosion at the far end of the warehouse. *The fuel tank.* Panicked yelling resonated from below and was followed by another salvo of gunfire. Then, everything went silent except for the sounds of boots running and the crackling of a fire in the background. He knew the outcome. Joey and Nicky were dead.

Footsteps pounded up the wooden stairs toward the office. Moss grasped Kaplan and spun him around. Moss looked him in the eyes and placed his gun on the table. He reached into his jacket and pulled out his creds.

The footsteps had reached the landing now and were just outside the door.

Moss snatched off his badge from his belt, turned toward the door, and held up his badge in one hand and his creds in the other.

The door flung open and three men swarmed in, pointing their rifles at Kaplan and Moss while yelling, "Drop your weapons. FBI. On the ground."

Moss yelled back, "U. S. Marshals, U. S. Marshals."

While the first two men in the door were subduing Moss, two others had come up the back staircase and tackled Kaplan from behind. The largest man held him down; pulled his arms behind his back, and held his rifle barrel against Kaplan's head.

"Federal agents," Kaplan shouted over the commotion. "You're making a big mistake."

"Oh, I doubt that," the big man said.

He got off Kaplan, pulled him to his feet, then pushed him over on a table that was bolted to the floor. The table was crudely built with rough-cut lumber and four adjustable leather shackles attached to the tabletop. Its splintery surface had dark red bloodstains from years of use by Scalini.

The man holding him down relaxed his grip and leaned over to speak to him. The other man standing next to him lowered his rifle. Kaplan bolted upright before the man could react and head butted him in the face. He felt the crunch of the man's nose. The crippling blow had momentarily stunned his opponent. Blood streamed down the man's face. With his right leg, Kaplan kicked outward, a powerful blow to the second man's knee. He dropped his weapon and fell to the floor, holding his knee as he did. Kaplan spun his waist in a tight twisting motion, extended his leg, and delivered a crushing blow with his boot to the side of the man's head. The man was unconscious before he hit the floor.

"Kaplan, no," yelled Moss.

Kaplan felt the butt of a rifle bash the back of his head. It sent a paralyzing shockwave through his body. His legs weakened and wobbled. He tried to fight it, but consciousness left him.

CHAPTER 39

WHEN KAPLAN REGAINED CONSCIOUSNESS, his legs and arms were flex-cuffed to the chair behind the table, arms still behind his back but secured to the chair. The chair was bolted to the floor just like the table. He figured Scalini wanted it that way so his victims couldn't move during the torture sessions. His head wobbled as he tried to fight off the fog from the blow to the back of his head. Dazed, he looked up. The room was blurry. He shook his head to clear the cobwebs. Moss's face slowly came into focus.

"Welcome back," Moss said. "I tried to stop them... but they don't take kindly to having their own men beaten up."

Kaplan's head was throbbing. His throat was dry. He could smell smoke but no one seemed in a hurry to get out of the warehouse. "How long was I out?"

"Only a couple of minutes," said Moss. "Barely long enough for them to strap you down."

"Who was the son of a bitch who hit me?"

"One of my men," a strange voice said.

Kaplan turned. Next to the table was a man in a suit and tie with a badge clipped to his belt. He was tall and thin with a ruddy complexion and wire rim glasses. His hair was light brown with a hint of grey. He looked official. There was a man standing behind him with a rifle. "Who are you?"

"Harvey Sturdivant, Assistant Regional Director of the Federal Bureau of Investigation," he said. "And you, Mr. Kaplan, just sent two of my best agents to the hospital. Senior Inspector Moss explained the situation to me and, if you promise to stop killing or disabling my men, I'll have the cuffs removed."

"I haven't killed any of your men."

"Remember the two men who chased you from the restaurant in Little Rock? And then were involved in a car crash near Searcy?" Sturdivant asked. "Those were contract agents. We knew Scalini's men were coming to capture Tony...that's what we wanted to happen, but you interfered. No one knew who you were. They were just trying to stop you."

"Stop, as in shoot me? What am I, a mind reader? No lights, no sirens, no badges," Kaplan snapped back. "And they used sound suppressors."

"Perhaps they didn't handle the situation the way they should have or were trained. Gunfire draws a lot of attention. I authorized the suppressors and since I felt Tony's life was in danger, they were given permission to use deadly force against you if necessary."

"By you?"

"Yes."

"The helicopter?"

"Tragic. Belonged to the contractor as well."

"Your contractors are idiots." Kaplan paused and then asked, "Then you planted the RFID tracking devices?"

"Yes."

"You compromised a witness without the U. S. Marshals Service knowledge?"

Sturdivant looked at Moss and then back at Kaplan. "Correct again."

Moss clenched his jaw and interrupted, "You're telling me you FBI assholes deliberately avoided cooperating with or even notifying the Marshals Service of your intentions? To get your prize you were willing to let civilians and a federal marshal be collateral damage? There is blood on the FBI's hands. I will personally make sure you go down for this and then I'm coming back and kicking your ass."

Sturdivant's voice remained calm as he continued, "Our intel was that Scalini knew the location of your witness and his men were not authorized to shoot, just grab and go. Nobody was supposed to get hurt. We knew your witness," Sturdivant looked at Moss and said, "could lead us to Martin Scalini. That's why we didn't have men inside the restaurant. We didn't alert the Marshals Service because your director would never have agreed to it."

"You're damn right he wouldn't agree to it," said Moss.

"The FBI considered capturing Scalini a higher priority than your witness." Sturdivant turned and looked at Kaplan. "I think it was because of your involvement, Mr. Kaplan, that caused Scalini's men to change their strategy and open fire. When the shooting started, my men scrambled. By then it was too late, the damage had been done."

"Bullshit. I was there," Kaplan began to shout. "Scalini's men had no intention of a simple snatch and run. They came out shooting. If it weren't for Deputy Cox and myself, more people would have died."

Sturdivant was silent. His face had turned red. He motioned to one of his men. "Cut him loose…and give them back their weapons."

The man pulled out a knife and cut the flex cuffs.

"Where is Tony now?" Kaplan rubbed his wrists where the cuffs had been clamped tight against his skin. "And how did you locate us here? Another RFID I didn't find?"

"Tony is downstairs with Bruno Ratti," Sturdivant said. "Both men are fine and in FBI custody. We found the warehouse because Angelo DeLuca called Scalini for backup in Lexington and we were monitoring DeLuca's phone. When we knew we had this chance to nab Scalini, we got authorization to tap and track his phone...that brought us here."

"You're wrong about one thing," Moss said. "Tony is not in FBI custody. His protection was breached and now I'm wondering if the FBI wanted Scalini so bad that it intentionally leaked the info to the mob. I don't know, and at this point, I don't care. Tony is *my* witness and I'm taking him with me."

The door burst open and one of Sturdivant's men entered. "Sir, the fire is spreading. We need to evacuate the building immediately."

Sturdivant nodded and then looked at Moss. "Do whatever you want with Tony." Sturdivant motioned toward the door at the back of the room. "Let's get out of here, we can resume this discussion outside."

Halfway down the stairs Kaplan looked back at Sturdivant. He raised his voice over the increasing background noise of the fire. "This isn't over between you and me," he promised. "Whoever screwed the pooch on this one is going down."

"That's right," Moss chimed in. "Someone will be held accountable."

When they reached the bottom of the stairs, the front door of the warehouse was already engulfed in flames, leaving the rear exit the only safe passage out of the burning building.

Kaplan made a mental note earlier that the warehouse with all the chemicals stored inside was a virtual powder keg waiting to blow. Now he was seeing its volatility first hand. Flames were licking at Scalini's limousine and the heat radiating from the inferno caused a shimmer from the vehicles roof, trunk, and hood. Kaplan figured when the flames reached the north end of the building, the chemicals and solvents stored in the drums beneath the offices would ignite.

A solvent drum next to Scalini's limo caught fire and exploded. Flames swallowed the limo and jumped to the Buick parked next to it. Every man instinctively ducked. Flames from the fire rolled across the warehouse floor devouring everything in its path. The building filled with black hot smoke making it impossible to breathe.

"Move it," Sturdivant coughed twice and yelled as he pointed toward the door. "Now."

Tony and Bruno were ushered through the metal door by two of Sturdivant's men. All four men were wheezing and coughing from smoke inhalation.

Kaplan followed Moss through the door while Sturdivant pulled up the flank. The seven men ran from the raging fire consuming the warehouse. Another explosion rocked the warehouse and blew out all the upper level windows. Flying shards of glass pelted the men on the ground.

The group of men ran out of the burning building into the night. The lights of the city still visible but haloed from the excess moisture in the air. A touch of fog had settled across the Hudson River and Upper New York Bay.

They stopped about a hundred feet from the warehouse. Every man was rubbing his eyes, coughing, and short of breath. Tony fell to his knees, leaned over, and vomited on the ground. Bruno stood next to him. The two men who escorted them out of the warehouse stood watch.

Kaplan stopped beside Tony and put his hands on the old man's shoulder. "Have you noticed that excitement seems to follow you?" Kaplan said to Tony between coughs.

The old man nodded and vomited again.

Sturdivant stopped behind Kaplan and said, "This is far enough."

Moss walked over to Kaplan. "Hell of a forty-eight hours, huh?"

Kaplan nodded and leaned over to cough, cupping his hands over his knees for support. He looked up at Moss. In the corner of his vision, he detected a flash of light.

Behind him, Sturdivant grunted and fell to the ground.

And then the warehouse exploded.

CHAPTER 40

MOSS INSTINCTIVELY DOVE TO THE GROUND as a fireball plumed skyward forming a fiery mushroom cloud over the shipping terminal complex. He'd witnessed Sturdivant go down the same moment the warehouse exploded. His mind barely registered what his eyes had just witnessed. If Kaplan hadn't leaned over to cough, the shot would have struck him in the head. Instead the bullet went over Kaplan's head and struck the man standing behind him.

Sturdivant's men were caught off guard; their gaping mouths an obvious indication of disbelief. Their boss lay dead in an ever-expanding pool of blood. Both men raised their weapons and took up a defensive posture.

The glow from the massive fireball shooting into the sky glistened and sparkled off the crimson liquid.

Moss looked at Kaplan who had turned his head to see Sturdivant lying motionless.

"Take cover," Moss yelled to Sturdivant's men as he stood.

One of them yelled back, "Where?" The two men were back to back, turning and scanning in every direction for the threat that killed their boss.

Moss looked around; there was no cover around them. They were out in the open and easy targets.

"In the water," Kaplan said as he pointed toward the river.

Moss grabbed Kaplan's hand and pulled him to his feet. "We gotta move it."

Sturdivant's two men ran toward the bulkhead next to the water. The ground around them exploded from gunfire. Bruno was already standing on the bulkhead but refused to jump in.

As Moss and Kaplan neared the four men standing on the bulkhead, one of Sturdivant's men took a shot to the head. He crumpled to the ground. Seeing this, the other man pushed Tony off the bulkhead and jumped into the water after him.

Bruno took off running.

Both Moss and Kaplan had their weapons drawn.

Kaplan said, "I saw the flash. The shots came from that crane." He pointed. "That's gotta be a thousand yards. The mob doesn't take shots like that. It's our assassin. The long shot is her specialty."

"Any more good news?" Moss said.

"Yeah, I'm going after her." Kaplan turned and ran toward the shooter.

Sirens grew louder as a line of emergency vehicles turned into the shipping terminal complex. He couldn't let Kaplan go after the assassin alone. He had grievances with her and wanted her alive. She had impersonated a federal law enforcement officer and used him to locate her prey. He didn't like being played by anyone. If Kaplan was going after the red headed woman, so was he.

Moss reached the bulkhead, pulled out his weapon, and yelled down to Sturdivant's remaining man, "Where's Bruno?"

"Took off running, sir." The man pointed.

In the distance Moss could see Bruno running toward the shipping complex entrance. If the cops didn't round him up, then he would go after him later.

Moss looked back at Sturdivant's man. "Stay here until I get back." He pointed toward Tony. "Don't let him get away, understood?"

He didn't wait around for an answer. He was never a fast runner, but he was strong, and ran long distances in high school and college. Of course, those days were long gone, and even though Moss kept up a strict workout regimen, running wasn't part of it.

Initially it was easy to keep Kaplan in sight with the glow from the fire, but the farther he got from the burning warehouse, the darker it became along the waterfront and the harder it was to keep a visual on the operative. Kaplan wasn't running in a straight line either, but a serpentine path toward the shooter's position and keeping himself in a low crouch. And then suddenly Kaplan was gone. Out of sight and Moss had no idea which direction he went.

He came upon a track-hoe and ducked behind it while he scanned the area. His eyes slowly began to adjust to the darkness and he thought he saw movement to his right. He pointed his weapon and strained to see. A hand tapped his arm. He spun around, his weapon leading the way, but the man was faster and deflected it.

"Easy, big guy," Kaplan raised his index finger to his lips. "We're on the same side."

"Son of a bitch. You almost gave me a heart attack."

Kaplan pulled out his phone and dialed.

"Who the hell are you calling?" Moss asked.

"My cavalry."

† † †

Kaplan punched the numbers in his phone, a direct line to his handler at Langley. "You probably shouldn't be here," he said to Moss without looking at the Senior Inspector. "This is a sanctioned hit…not something you want to witness."

"I'm a big boy, Kaplan, I can handle it. I spent a lot of hours alone with that bitch. I know how she operates."

"No you don't," said Kaplan. "She was impersonating a WitSec inspector. Acting. Playing a role. I'll bet she even sweet-talked you. Played you till she got what she wanted." Kaplan paused to let his accusation sink in. "I'm the one who knows how she operates. I've been after her for a year. She's killed twenty-six targets around the globe. Tony was about to be number twenty-seven."

"I got a newsflash for you, pal. She wasn't shooting at Tony. He was puking his guts out at the time and an easy target. That shot was meant for you."

"Bullshit. It was meant for Sturdivant or she just missed hitting Tony. That *was* one hell of a long shot."

"You don't really believe that do you? If you hadn't leaned down when you did, that bullet would have ripped your head off. *You* were the target, my friend. Not Sturdivant. Not Tony. And one more thing." Moss leaned into Kaplan's face and with gritted teeth said, "I want her alive, you hear me?"

Kaplan processed that revelation and concluded the deputy was likely correct. Perhaps Valkyrie *was* shooting at him. "Even if she was, it doesn't change anything. She is still sanctioned, whether you like it or not. She is still my target, so if the two of us are trying to kill each other, then she should be easy enough to find."

"Provided she doesn't kill you first."

"My plan doesn't include dying," Kaplan said as his call went through to Langley.

"No one's ever does."

"Gregg. What the hell is going on?" His handler interrupted.

He turned and looked up at the shooter's position and said, "Valkyrie is here."

† † †

She lost sight of her target as he ran in her direction. He bent down at the same time she fired and her bullet struck a man standing behind him. Then the warehouse turned into a fireball. She randomly fired three more shots before being forced to turn off the night vision feature on her scope due to the blinding effect of the explosion. By the time she spotted the men who ran from the building, two were in the water, one was running away, and two were running in her direction, one several yards behind the other. Her target was in the lead.

Her cover was blown and he was coming after her.

Good. Let the hunted come to the hunter.

The farther he ran from the burning warehouse the harder it was to see him in the darkness without night vision.

Then he was gone.

Both men were gone.

She reactivated the night vision on her scope to scan the area where the men disappeared but was unable to locate either man.

The shipping terminal complex had already turned into a beehive of activity as first responders arrived at the scene to battle the warehouse fire. No telling how many more emergency units had been dispatched to control the blaze.

She used her scope to scan all the exits. Police had already barricaded the roads and all vehicular traffic on the complex was stopped. Two police helicopters equipped with spotlights scanned the warehouse. In the distance, two more helicopters approached yet still maintained a safe distance. Probably newscasters, she thought, trying to be the first to capture the breaking story. Eventually she knew the searchlights would scan the crane where she hid and with all exits blocked, her escape would have to be the river.

But not until her target was dead.

CHAPTER 41

AFTER AN EXPEDITED BRIEFING, KAPLAN connected his phone's Bluetooth to the wireless headset system he and Moss were using. "Alan, meet Senior Inspector Pete Moss, U. S. Marshals Service. Moss, Alan, my handler."

"Okay gentlemen," Alan said. "Let's get down to business. Eyeballs in three, two, one." There was a pause. "Whoa, what a mess. Give me second to locate your phone."

"What does he mean, *eyeballs*?" Moss asked.

Kaplan pointed to the sky. "Spy satellite, what did you think?"

"What if it was cloudy?"

"Then it would be harder."

Alan interrupted, "Pinpointing your location…and I got you. Looks like you are tucked behind some sort of heavy machinery."

"That's us," Kaplan said. "Valkyrie is out by the water somewhere. The flash I saw came from one of those loading cranes at the end of the terminal."

"Bringing the infrared online and, … there she is. She's in the far west crane. Bird's eye view says you have her cornered. Looks like her only escape is down the ladder. That will put her in the open and leave you with a clean shot."

"You're not giving her enough credit, I doubt that's her only escape. She's not that careless." Kaplan paused. "Any cover between us and the crane?"

"Three hundred meters ahead is what appears to be a rock pile," Alan said. "Six meters wide, three meters high. Can you make it there?"

Kaplan looked at Moss and nodded. Moss returned the nod. "No problem," Kaplan said.

"Two assets enroute," Alan said. "Eight and ten minutes out respectively."

"Roger that."

Moss looked at Kaplan, "On three?"

Kaplan nodded.

"One." Moss took a deep breath. "Two. Three."

Both men left the cover of the track hoe and ran for the rock pile.

Bullets peppered the ground.

† † †

When the two men appeared out of nowhere, she saw what they were running toward, a rock pile about halfway between them and her. She fired a few shots to push them back into hiding but they kept running, closing the gap.

She focused on the man to her left. He was slower than the other man. Less agile. An easier target. She zoomed in with her night vision scope—Pete Moss. Not her target, however, still a potential threat. During the time she spent with Moss while impersonating WitSec Inspector April Moore, she grew to like the man. Physically, she was attracted to him, especially his dimples and captivating smile. His voice was deep and authoritative. Somehow Kaplan had recruited him; nevertheless, he was not her target. She would not kill him unless she had to, but she might need to slow him down so she could get Kaplan without Moss's interference.

Valkyrie rotated her scope to the right and scanned for her target. Kaplan's figure ran through the crosshairs and disappeared from her field of vision. As she tried to follow his movements, he kept darting from side to side. At this zoom setting, her scope was tight and Kaplan's serpentine running style and speed made it difficult to keep him in her sights, so she quit trying, anticipated his movements, and fired.

And missed.

Shot after shot, she missed her target until he finally disappeared behind the rock pile. She rotated her scope back to the left and reacquired Moss. He was moving slow. He was huffing and puffing, his chest heaved in and out. He wasn't weaving, an easy shot. She lined up her target and squeezed the trigger.

Through the scope she saw him fall to the ground. Now she could concentrate all her attention on Kaplan.

Kaplan was breathing hard when he dove behind the rock pile. Knowing Valkyrie was trying to pinpoint him in her scope was nerve racking and exhilarating all at the same time. Her reputation as a sniper was well known to him so he ran in random patterns and angles to hopefully throw off her aim. Valkyrie had fired at him several times, missing by a hefty margin each time. He could envision her swinging the barrel left and right trying to keep up with his zigzag route.

He turned to look for Moss. He heard the big man pounding his way toward the rock pile and saw a shadow backlit by the glow from the fire running in the darkness. Kaplan heard the suppressed shot and then Moss grunted. He watched his silhouette reach for his left calf muscle and stumble to the ground. Instinctively and with total disregard of the danger, Kaplan sprinted to Moss, seized him by the arm, pulled him to his feet, and moved them both toward the rock pile. The ground around them erupted from gunfire.

"That bitch shot me," Moss yelled as they raced toward cover.

They both fell to the ground behind the rock pile, breathing heavy, and sweating profusely.

"How bad is it?" Kaplan asked.

"I think it's just a surface wound but it burns like hell."

"I'm surprised Valkyrie didn't shoot you in the chest. As slow as you were running, she could have hit you between the eyes."

"Nice pep talk, Kaplan. It's not me she was paid to kill. Besides, I think she likes me and this is her way of showing it."

"What? Not killing you?"

"You said she was sweet on me."

"No, I said she sweet talked you. She has higher standards."

Kaplan leaned over Moss's leg, whipped open his knife, and said, "Let me take a look, we'll see how much she really likes you."

Kaplan pulled out his penlight, stuck it between his teeth, and sliced the fabric off Moss's pants open just enough so he could see the wound.

"Guess you are right, it's only superficial. She must be sweet on you. Now, take off your neck buff," Kaplan said.

"What?"

Kaplan pointed. "Your neck buff. Take it off and give it to me so I can clean your leg."

Moss pulled it over his head and handed it to Kaplan.

Kaplan took the buff to wipe the excess blood from Moss's leg. "Good news, Deputy, you're going to live. Bullet took a quarter inch size plug out of the side of your leg but it isn't too bad. Bleeding like a stuck pig right now though. No more running for you," Kaplan said. "Not until the bleeding stops." Kaplan folded Moss's neck buff and placed it back on his leg. "Here, hold pressure on it."

Moss clamped his hand over the wound.

Kaplan removed his own neck buff and stretched it around Moss's muscular calf. "Damn," he said. "Not big enough for your fat leg. Give me your belt."

"You're a demanding asshole."

"You know, Moss, I never took you for a whiner." He didn't look up while he worked on the wound. "Cut the crap and give me your belt."

"Your bedside manner really sucks."

Kaplan cinched the belt around Moss's leg, putting enough pressure to slow the bleeding but not enough to act as a tourniquet.

"Still there, Alan?" Kaplan said.

"Still here. Just watching you two Bozos. Like watching Laurel and Hardy. I still have a good heat signature on Valkyrie. Kind of surprising, but she hasn't budged an inch."

"Moss will have to stay here for a while. Took one in the leg. Bleeding won't stop till his heart rate comes down. Field dressing in place. You got a fix on my next cover?"

"Bad news, the next two hundred forty meters, you'll be in

the open. There is a shed at the base of the crane. Can Moss shoot?"

"Yes, I can shoot. I took one in the leg not my trigger finger," Moss interrupted. "And I'm in range to hit the crane from here. At the very least, it will distract her. Never know, I might get lucky and actually hit the crazy bitch."

"How are you two fixed on ammo?"

"Between the two of us," Moss explained. "We have a hundred and two rounds. Three full mags each."

"I'll leave two mags with Moss," Kaplan said. "Leaves me with seventeen rounds. Moss can keep her distracted while I make it to the shed."

"It'll take me a few shots to find the right arc," Moss said.

"No wind," Alan said. "That should help."

"How do you know that?" Moss asked.

"Windsock at Newark International is flat," Alan explained. "Assets are four and five minutes out now."

"Roger that," Kaplan said. "Moss, find your arc."

Moss's first shot hit metal on the lower part of the crane. He adjusted the arc and fired again this time hitting the crane just below the platform the shooter was on.

"Anytime you're ready," Moss said.

Kaplan didn't hesitate. "Now." He vaulted toward the shed as if his life depended on it.

It did.

CHAPTER 42

KAPLAN FELT SLIGHTLY WINDED FROM HIS first sprint when he ran for the small building by the crane. After pulling Moss to safety, his rest break was no more than three or four minutes before he was on the run again. The distance was shorter this time, but not by much. Still, two hundred forty meters was a long haul. Especially in the open with a sniper taking pot shots.

Two hundred forty meters.

Roughly two hundred sixty yards.

Almost eight hundred feet.

And Kaplan's energy was waning.

Halfway to the building Kaplan's pace began to slow. He no longer had the endurance he had in his twenties. The muscles in his legs were fatigued and just wouldn't churn any faster.

Moss had done his job so far and kept Valkyrie from getting off a shot that came anywhere close to hitting him. The closest she had gotten was over six feet.

Then Moss stopped shooting.

Kaplan compensated by increasing the frequency and duration of his serpentine movements. But that also increased his total running distance to the building.

He could see the muzzle flashes in the dark from Valkyrie's

rifle and clearly hear the suppressed pops as well.

"Come on, Moss." Kaplan was breathing heavy. "I sure could use a little help out here."

"Gun jammed. Give me a second."

Each flash was followed by a pop and the ground near him would explode simultaneously.

Valkyrie's shots were getting closer and Kaplan's speed was slowing even more. It was only a matter of seconds before she would hit him. The pendulum had swung to Valkyrie's advantage.

"Got it," Kaplan heard Moss say through his headset and then the firing resumed at Valkyrie's position.

Her return fire was off target. Back to missing by several feet. He could hear Moss's rounds pinging off the metal structure. Sparks sporadically ricocheted off the girders.

Fifty feet and closing.

He knew Valkyrie's shooting angle had changed. She was now shooting down instead of out. The closer he got to the building, the more pronounced her barrel swings were to track his serpentine path. And the more she had to swing her rifle barrel, the better his odds of not getting mowed down by the assassin.

Moss continued firing and suddenly the assassin stopped shooting.

"What happened?" Kaplan asked.

"Don't know," Moss replied. "Maybe I got a hit."

"No, she's not hit," Alan interjected. "She's moving across the crane's lifting arm."

Kaplan reached the side of the building. It was a small maintenance shed used to support the two loading cranes at this remote end of the shipping terminal. He dropped to his knees then fell into a sitting position against the shed.

"I need a minute to catch my breath," Kaplan panted. "What's she doing now?"

"I don't know," Alan said. "She moved out on the crane's arm and hasn't moved since. At least for the past few seconds anyway."

Kaplan pulled out his weapon and scooted to the edge of the building. He took a quick glance around the side of the building and up at the crane. The tall crane structure and the sprinkle of stars in the sky above were all he saw in the darkness.

"I don't get it," Alan said.

Kaplan heard the crane's diesel engine generator fire up and noticed a large rectangular shadow lift off the loading dock.

"I do. She's raising a cargo container."

"She's what?" Alan asked.

"She's in the crane operator's cabin and she's lifting a cargo container."

"It's her escape plan," Moss said.

Kaplan could tell the deputy knew something he didn't by the confident tone in his voice. "Talk to me, Moss. How the hell is she going to escape?"

"Assets are at the terminal entrance trying to clear the roadblock," interrupted Alan. "Looks like the FBI doesn't want to let them in."

"Roger that, Alan. Now let Moss give us his theory. We're all ears, Deputy."

"My guess is she'll drop down to the spreader and use the remote operator's controls to position the container over the water. She'll lower it until she's close enough to jump."

"Moss?" Kaplan said, "What the hell's a spreader?"

"It's a piece of loading equipment on the crane that attaches to the cargo containers."

"One day you'll have to tell me how you know all this crap."

† † †

A good assassin always had an alternative escape plan if things went awry.

Some plans were better than other ones and this time her choices were limited. It was a bad backup plan from the onset and now, her options had dwindled and she was forced to execute it.

She had failed to kill her target tonight although she knew there would be another opportunity. And soon. The unexpected arrival of the FBI and the explosion of the warehouse were unforeseen complications no assassin could have prepared for. Now her target was back on the grid and his movements would be easier to track. And she was like a hound dog following a scent. A week, perhaps as long as a month, she would stay on his trail until another opportunity presented itself. And when that time came, she wouldn't miss.

Now, her first priority was survival. Her only escape route was the water. Crossing the Hudson River in the middle of the night was not something she relished, however it was a necessity if she wanted to stay alive. And free.

She fired up the diesel generator on the gantry crane and activated the equipment. The network of trolleys, and pulleys, and cables tightened, lifting the spreader and the attached cargo container. While the container was in transit, she spun around and used her night vision scope to locate her opponents. Kaplan was still hiding behind the shed and she could see his signature intermittently peeking around the corner. In the distance she saw Moss limping toward her. He was making a straight-line attack as if taunting her to take another shot at him. He held his leg with one hand and with the other, his pistol. She had no ax to grind with the deputy marshal; he was not part of the deal.

In the distance, she saw more emergency vehicles arriving at the shipping terminal and an increasing interest in the activity where she was. Someone had noticed them and that meant cops and helicopters with searchlights and no telling what else. Too much attention, too soon, would come her way. She needed to get away while she had the chance. Ten minutes from now would be too late.

The spreader holding the container came to a stop a few feet beneath her. She exited the Plexiglas enclosed operator's cabin and climbed out on the catwalk until she was directly above the spreader. She grasped a cable with her gloved hands, and lowered herself to the top of the spreader.

Within fifteen seconds she located the remote operator's controls and then she secured her escape kit to the spreader with a locking carabiner so it wouldn't fall.

The first control moved the spreader away from the platform itself and out along the booms of the high-profile gantry crane that extended over the water. When the cargo container was extended along the outreach as far out over the water as she dared move it, she activated another control.

She considered herself a good judge of distance and height so she estimated she was nearly two hundred feet from the gantry and a hundred feet above the water's surface. She hastened her actions at the sounds of more sirens. There was a small window of opportunity to escape…and it was getting smaller.

The container slowly lowered her toward the water.

She removed her escape kit from its tether and unpacked the equipment—a small sea scooter. If she had to cross the Hudson River, she certainly wasn't going to swim. The sea scooter had enough charge to cross the river several times. And that was more than enough to pull her to safety.

She positioned herself behind a steel crossbar that spanned the length of the spreader and took aim at the shed with her rifle while the machine slowly lowered her toward the water. If Kaplan stuck his head around the corner of the shed again, she would not miss.

Kaplan noticed the cargo container shuttle across the outreach arms of the gantry crane until it was almost to the end. Then it slowly descended toward the water below. Moss was right; Valkyrie was going to attempt to escape by water. If, and when, she went into the Hudson, she'd already have a good two hundred foot head start.

He was a good swimmer. By most standards he would even be considered a strong swimmer. Swimming across the Hudson from New Jersey to New York would be much shorter than the last swim he had taken. That one was a nine-mile swim he had to take a couple of years ago when the bullet-riddled boat he was in sank off the northern coast of Spain. Being a strong swimmer didn't automatically relate to being a fast swimmer, which he was not. Unless Valkyrie tired, he might not be able to catch her before she reached the opposite shoreline.

Kaplan needed to get closer to the water's edge and the only way to do that was by leaving the protection of the maintenance shed to seek cover behind the massive tires on the base of the gantry itself. A thirty-yard run, minimum. The opposite corner of the shed offered more protection from the crane structure in the event the woman started firing again. If he weaved when he ran toward the crane's base, she might not have a clear shot at him. At least, that was what he convinced himself. If he was going to do it, though, he needed to move now before the cargo container descended low enough for Valkyrie to jump into the water safely.

Without any further hesitation, Kaplan made a break for it and, as he did, gunfire erupted around him. Valkyrie was pelting the ground with bullets chasing his every step.

Thirty yards to go.

Seemed more like sixty by the time he finally reached the crane. He took refuge behind one of the gantry crane's enormous tires. Bullets pinged and ricocheted around him, but even her rounds weren't going to penetrate his sanctum.

It was dark at this end of the shipping terminal, there were no ships and no lights except the dim red maritime structure lights lining the entire length of the loading dock itself, placed there only to prevent an accidental incursion with the dock.

Every time Kaplan attempted to look around the tire, more bullets fired his way. He was pinned down until the assassin made her move to escape.

At last glance, the container was still thirty feet above the water and he knew she would wait until it got closer. Then he heard everything come to a complete stop. The container had stopped and was suspended ten feet above the water. Moving across the top of the spreader was the shadowy figure of a woman.

Kaplan moved into position to take a shot when the shadow figure raised her weapon. He left his cover and was in the open by the edge of the loading dock with nowhere to hide and nowhere to run. He knew she had him locked in the crosshairs. Exposed, he was a dead man.

A shot rang out before he could fire his weapon. It wasn't from Valkyrie. He turned in the direction of the shot and saw Moss forty feet to his right with his weapon pointed in Valkyrie's direction. He looked back at the container and saw the woman stumble forward. She reached her hand out toward something, the container creaked, and with a loud metal clunk, the spreader released the container.

The spreader swayed from the sudden loss of weight and the figure on top tumbled from her lofty perch toward the dirty river below.

CHAPTER 43

IT FELT A LOT LIKE THE TRAINING SIMULATOR in Chicago except this time it was real life. Now Moss faced a decision much like that from the simulator. His new partner left the protection of the gantry crane in order to capture the assassin known as Valkyrie. The woman Moss had spent so much time with in the Crown Vic traveling the back roads of Arkansas was, in reality, hired to kill the man he had teamed up with now. It was a strange and ironic twist of fate. Kaplan turned out to be the good guy and she turned out to be the villain.

Villainess.

But Moss was a Deputy U. S. Marshal and she posed a threat to Kaplan's life. He knew Kaplan wanted her alive long enough to find out who had paid her to kill him. Then he would kill her. Moss wanted her alive, but if it came down to choosing lives, hers was expendable.

She hadn't seen him approach the loading dock and was so fixated on killing her target that he was able to walk almost to the edge of the water. The clandestine operative and the assassin exchanged gunfire allowing Moss to take aim at the assassin. When she got the drop on Kaplan, Moss took the shot.

† † †

Kaplan had many troubling thoughts as he watched Valkyrie fall toward the water. First and foremost, he needed to get to her before she escaped if he stood any chance of finding out who put the contract on him. If it was even him she was after. Even though Moss was convinced otherwise, Kaplan still had doubts and wondered if perhaps Tony might have been the intended target all along.

Then there was the falling container. If he waited for it to hit the water and the resulting wake to disperse, he would lose valuable time and distance getting to the woman. Moss had shot her, but how badly was she hurt? Could she swim? Was she still conscious? She clutched at her shoulder after the shot rang out and then the container fell.

He decided he couldn't wait for the wake to settle, the cost in time and distance was too great. He secured his weapon and readied himself to dive from the loading dock into the dark water.

The container splashed into the water, stopped, then settled and seemed to rise back to the surface before slowly slipping out of sight. Beyond where the container hit the water, he saw Valkyrie bob up and down in the wake. There was something else in the water and she was trying to swim toward it with one arm.

The wake was higher than he originally expected. As it reached the bulkhead, Kaplan dove over and past the main surge. Then the wake struck the bulkhead at the loading dock and reversed direction, which gave him a short-lived burst of speed through the water as he used the wake to his advantage.

He closed the gap as Valkyrie struggled to swim toward the object floating in the water. The wake had pushed it farther away from Valkyrie. Her determination to reach the floating object seemed undeterred as Kaplan closed in. His strong arms and legs gave him the advantage and he was certain he could catch the assassin.

But, he didn't.

She reached the object floating in the water when he was still ten feet away. She struggled with the object one handed, unable to use one arm, thanks to Moss. She finally flipped it over exposing two handgrips. Kaplan heard the whine of the electric motor and saw a shielded propeller starting to spin. It was a personal water propulsion device, a sea scooter much less powerful than the ones he'd used on some Special Forces missions. Smaller too.

It was cylindrical in shape with a pointed nose cone to reduce friction through the water. Roughly two feet long and eight inches in diameter, the plastic shell held an electric motor with enough power to pull Valkyrie through the water faster than he could swim. If she pulled away from him now, he'd never catch her.

With adrenaline pumping, he kicked and lunged forward in the water extending his strong right arm. As the device started to move Valkyrie through the water, he grasped one of her ankles. If he lost his grip now, she would escape. He felt the pull from the sea scooter dragging them both through the water.

She kicked her leg to free his grip and with her other foot jammed her boot into his wrist. He tightened his grip and refused to let go. He couldn't let go. If he did, she would be gone. He snagged her other foot with his free hand and pulled himself toward her with all his strength.

The combination of him pulling on her feet and the thrust from the sea scooter were too much for the injured Valkyrie. The scooter struggled to accelerate with their combined weight and within seconds Valkyrie lost her grip and the sea scooter floated away.

Valkyrie turned and tried to knee him in the groin but she hit the side of his leg instead. He balled a fist and struck her in the ribs. She groaned and slashed at him with an open hand. Her claws hit his face and he felt his skin tear under her fingernails. The instant burning sensation left no uncertainty that she had drawn blood.

He pushed her hand away and threw a southpaw hook to her jaw. He heard the crunch and felt her jawbone give under the impact. Her head went limp. He spun her around and pulled her to him. He wrapped one arm around her waist and used the other to collar her around the throat from behind.

"It's over," he said.

She elbowed him in the gut. "Let me go," she cried out.

He cinched his grip tighter around her neck. "Who's your target?"

"Go to hell."

Her hand disappeared beneath the water and then reappeared wielding a knife. Not just a knife, a poniard, a tiny dagger. Unable to fend off her knife attack in time, she plunged the small blade into his forearm. His grip loosened and she pushed herself free and moved toward the sea scooter.

He grabbed the poniard and pulled the blade from his forearm muscle. Hot intense pain shot through his arm. He had been in knife fights in the past. Too many to count. A stab in a muscle, though, was much better than having the muscle severed by a slashing blade.

He fought off the pain, tossed the poniard into the water, and lunged toward the escaping assassin, snagging a handful of red hair. He yanked her head backwards, spun her around, and slammed his fist into her face.

She pulled her arm back, made a fist, and swung at his face. He blocked the assault, clamped his hand on her head, and pushed her underwater.

And held her there.

He counted the seconds. She squirmed and kicked. After a full minute, he pulled her head out of the water. "Who's your target?"

"Screw you, asshole."

Without allowing her to take a breath he shoved her head back under. She writhed and grappled until her energy seemed to wane. He had water-boarded prisoners before but all of those were Middle Eastern men, most beaten before being tortured. He wasn't going to torture Valkyrie, but he needed answers so he kept her submerged long enough to let her panic.

He yanked her head out of the water. The Hudson around the shipyards had a foul smell and her hair felt slimy. She coughed and spit and coughed again.

"Who's your target?"

Nothing.

"Who. Is. Your. Target?"

Refusing to answer, he started to push her under again when she cried out, "All right. All right."

"Target? Tony?"

"No." She coughed and vomited into the river. "You," she said. "You are my target."

Moss was right. "Who hired you?"

"I don't know," she said. "I never met him."

"Give me his name."

"I don't know his name," she replied.

He shoved the weakened woman underwater again, counted to thirty, and then pulled her head out of the water by her hair. "Give me a name now or the next time I pull you out of the water you'll be dead."

"A code name," she said. She was gagging and spitting river water. "That's all I know. A code name."

"I'm listening."

"Shepherd."

"What?" He was taken by surprise.

"He called himself Shepherd."

"I'll be damned," he muttered to himself. "Çoban."

He started pulling Valkyrie back toward the loading dock.

"Shepherd," she said. "What does that mean?"

"Two things," he said. "First, you get to live. And second, it means I'm going back to Lebanon."

CHAPTER 44

TWO CIA ASSETS WERE STANDING NEXT TO Moss when Kaplan reached the loading dock with the injured Valkyrie in tow. They pulled her from the water and field dressed her gunshot wound. She had lost a lot of blood in her struggle with Kaplan so he decided to send her with the two operatives to a secure CIA site in Manhattan that also housed an agency run trauma medical unit.

According to Valkyrie, Shepherd got his information about Kaplan from a paid informant at the agency. Not only did the United States Marshals Service have a leak, so did the CIA.

Identifying the mole at the CIA could prove a challenge. Whoever was on the payroll of the Hezbollah Sheik had covered his tracks well…or her tracks. Kaplan knew the CIA's own secret version of Internal Affairs would soon be hard at work digging and prying into anyone who might have had access to Kaplan's movements. In a sense, its tactics resembled the infamous Nutting Squads of the Irish Republican Army more than it did Internal Affairs. The Nutting Squad was known for putting bullets, or *nuts* as they were called in Belfast, in people's heads if suspected of passing information.

Of course, the agency had its own *official* Internal Affairs, but that group wouldn't be involved in ferreting out this mole. There would be nothing *official* about this investigation. Nothing legal about the secret team's methods and procedures for getting to the truth either, although the end result was often the same as the Nutting Squad—death.

No one in the agency would be safe from the exhaustive approach. And the first one under the microscope would be the man who knew the most about Kaplan's movements, his handler.

Kaplan and Moss started the long walk back to the burning warehouse while the two assets hauled Valkyrie away. Kaplan's clothes were soaked. While Kaplan was still in the water, Moss had removed the belt from his leg and allowed one of the assets, the same one who treated Valkyrie, to clean and apply *QuikClot* to his wound. After applying a clean dressing, he secured it by wrapping duct tape around the deputy's calf. Moss barely showed any signs of a limp as he walked next to Kaplan.

"I thought you said she was a sanctioned kill," said Moss.

"I did."

"Then why is she still alive?"

"Something changed."

"While you were in the water?"

Kaplan turned and looked at the taller deputy. "Yes."

"Well? What changed?"

"She told me I was the target."

"And *that* changed your mind? Hell, I already told you that you were her target."

"That wasn't the only thing. It was *who* hired her to kill me that changed my mind. And the agency will want to interrogate her about him."

"Okay, the suspense is killing me," Moss said. "Who hired her to kill you?"

"Valkyrie called him Shepherd. He calls himself Çoban, which literally means shepherd. His real name is Hakim Omar Khalil."

"As in the terrorist Hezbollah Sheik Khalil?" Moss queried. "The same Sheik in the news lately?"

"One and the same."

"What the hell did you do to piss him off?"

"I killed his cousin a few months ago."

"That might do it." Moss smiled. "What did his cousin do to make the CIA want him dead?"

"I don't know if you knew this or not since it didn't get a lot of fanfare in the media, but last summer a suicide bomber blew up a café in Damascus killing twenty-six people at a wedding reception. Bride and groom killed along with the entire wedding party, several of whom were U. S. citizens. The Sheik's cousin orchestrated and ordered the bombing."

"How did Khalil know it was you who killed his cousin?"

"Damn good question." Kaplan turned and looked Moss in the eyes. "And I intend on finding the answer."

Once out of the Hudson River, Kaplan had field dressed the wound to his arm inflicted by the slender blade of Valkyrie's poniard in the same manner as the asset treated Moss. Clean, *QuickClot*, dressing, duct tape.

When they reached the warehouse, the blaze was almost under control. Firefighters were unable to control the massive inferno fueled by so many barrels of combustible material and were forced to let it burn down. All that remained of the warehouse structure were the metal girders, which glowed red from the intense heat of the conflagration. There were two-dozen people gathered around where Sturdivant was lying dead in a pool of blood along with the accompanying ambulances, law enforcement and rescue vehicles.

A man stepped forward to intercept Kaplan and Moss as they approached. He held up his credentials and identified himself as FBI Regional Director Mark Bruder. He demanded their identification and when they reached for their creds, several FBI special agents drew their weapons. After Bruder reviewed the credentials, he motioned for his men to lower their weapons.

"Where is my witness?" Moss demanded.

"First I want to know who killed my men," Bruder said as he pointed toward the bodies.

"Your men," said Kaplan, "were already dead when we went after the shooter."

Moss stepped in front of Bruder. "Where. Is. My. Witness?"

"The old man?" Bruder pointed. "He's over there, with my men."

"Have your men bring him to me."

"Who is he?"

"You know I can't reveal that," Moss said. "Besides, I think you already know his identity."

"You better come up with an explanation pretty quick because I have a dead assistant regional director, a dead agent, a burned down warehouse with five crispy critters inside and two on the outside." He pointed to the spot where Kaplan left the first two guards. "To top it off, the man this raid was supposed to nab is nowhere to be found. I got nothing to show for it."

"Sure you do," Kaplan interrupted. "Martin Scalini is dead. Moss and I personally watched Bruno Ratti put a bullet in his head. Pull the dental records. You'll see he's one of your crispy critters. And if there had been even so much as an inkling of inter-agency communication, then this whole mess could have been avoided."

The regional director did not seem to appreciate Kaplan's attitude. Kaplan didn't care. It had been a long three days. Tony was alive and in custody, Bruno was missing, and this dipshit from the FBI was about to read them the riot act. Kaplan stepped back and let Moss take a turn with the man. The discussion would heat up, with threats from the director about hauling them in for questioning followed by more threats of interfering with a federal investigation. After a few minutes, it was nothing more than background noise droning in his ears.

He was done.

Done with Tony.

Done with trying to fulfill his promise to the dead Deputy Mike Cox. If the CIA rat squad ruled out his handler as the mole, then Kaplan would be free to locate the elusive Çoban and eliminate him once and for all.

Of course, he knew he couldn't do it, just forsake his word to Inspector Mike Cox. His word to a fellow Delta Force soldier—*Once in, Never out.* Deep down, he knew he'd finish the job. His word was his bond. And whether Moss or the U.S. Marshals Service liked it or not, he was going to see Tony delivered to the SSOC.

After fifteen minutes, most of which was spent shouting, Moss and Bruder parted ways. Moss walked over to Kaplan. "Let's get Tony and get the hell out of here," the deputy grumbled.

CHAPTER 45

The Next Morning
Alexandria, Virginia

THE ARMORED MARSHALS SERVICE SUBURBAN picked the three men up from a fortified hangar at the Ronald Reagan Washington National Airport. The passenger compartment had black out windows. Totally opaque. Not to keep someone on the outside from looking in but to keep whoever was on the inside from seeing out. Kaplan sat in the seat next to the driver. Tony, Moss, and another WitSec deputy sat in the blacked out compartment.

Witness Security Safe Site and Orientation Center had been veiled in secrecy since its inception; only the U. S. Marshals Service and a select few other authorized and well-vetted individuals knew its location.

Supposedly.

In reality, though, plenty of people without clearance knew the location. Local rumors of the facility spread soon after construction. Now in the digital age if someone knew its general location, the facility wasn't difficult to locate with a quick satellite view search on *Google Maps*. How hard could it be to pick out an oddly shaped compound stuck out in the marsh?

The SSOC itself was a secure area inside a secure area. There was no easy access due to the isolation. No one could *accidentally* wander up to the place. It was well guarded and no one entered without proper authorization and identification. The octagonal shaped complex was under constant surveillance. Kaplan had been there before. The other men had been there before as well, although Tony had never seen the outside.

The octagon was double-fenced with razor wire topping. Between the fences was a ground proximity system. At each point of the octagon was a light pole with mounted closed-circuit cameras. A network of electronic anti-intrusion equipment and sophisticated communications systems protected the entire facility and its occupants. It was the same MAID-MILES system used by the Air Force to protect nuclear weapons, another government acronym that stood for Magnetic Anti-Intrusion Detectors and Magnetic Intrusion Line Sensors. It seemed the government had an acronym for everything. In Delta Force they joked that somewhere in Washington D.C. there was a lonely man in charge of creating acronyms for the government. He would have an acronym for his job title as well—Joint Acronym Control Officer—or JACkOFF for short.

Inside the SSOC, Kaplan remembered, cameras were spaced every few feet along the quiet corridors. All exterior and interior cameras were under round-the-clock monitoring. Interior doors opened and closed automatically. Every room was the same temperature and same humidity. To him, living there would be like being incarcerated.

Kaplan had insisted on going with Moss and Tony to the SSOC. In his mind, it was the fulfillment of his promise to the departed Deputy Mike Cox, the man who begged him to personally deliver Tony to a WitSec safe site. It was the handshake oath—*I give you my word*—although there was no handshake.

Raised in the Deep South, keeping his word was part of his upbringing. His father taught him at an early age not to make veiled promises; he had no respect for people who broke their word. Kaplan respected his father and his ideal, that a man's word was his bond.

As a soldier in Delta, a man's oath was his sacred vow. Each man in the squadron depended on the other—*I got your back, you got mine.* A code of honor that extended well past military service, it was a lifetime oath among fellow Delta comrades.

The Suburban drove through Alexandria and intercepted Telegraph Road on the south side of town. A few minutes later, the Marshals Service vehicle entered a military installation identified by the sign as *U.S. Coast Guard, Alexandria, Virginia.* The soldier at the guardhouse checked the driver's identification and waved the Suburban through. The Marshals Service vehicle drove down a long straight road until it reached another gate at the end of the road. The gate opened and the Suburban drove into a secured holding area. The gate closed behind them and then the driver pulled forward to a physical barrier.

Two men scrambled to the vehicle and checked the underside with mirrors on extended poles and other electronic detection devices. After a few minutes, the interior gate opened and the driver weaved around the barriers and through a double gate. Guards, presumably deputies, patrolled the perimeter.

The Suburban pulled into the complex and up to a garage door. The driver waited for the door to open and then drove inside a windowless garage. It wasn't until the garage door had completely closed that Kaplan was given the okay to exit the vehicle.

The deputy in the blacked-out compartment with Moss opened the back door and Tony followed him out of the vehicle.

"Same as I remember it," Tony said.

Moss was last to exit the vehicle.

Moss and Kaplan escorted Tony inside for processing. Tony signed several documents and was issued a toiletries package. After he finished *in-processing*, the old man walked over to Moss and Kaplan.

"I guess this is goodbye fellows," he said. He shook hands with both men.

"I'll be seeing you in a few days," Moss said to Tony. "For the hearing." He looked at Kaplan. "I'll go get us a ride."

After Moss was out of earshot, Kaplan leaned forward and said to Tony in a low but harsh voice, "If you screw this up or double-cross Pete, I *will* track you down and kill you."

Tony jerked his head back in apparent disbelief.

Kaplan smiled. "And you of all people know I can do it."

"Have you ever heard of the Sicilian word *Quattrocchi?*"

Kaplan shook his head and said, "Does it mean lying piece of shit?"

"On the contrary. In Sicily, it implies a binding agreement between two men. A covenant made with four eyes. A promise that cannot be broken. A trust. A bond. An agreement. It is stronger than your piece of paper." Tony held up his documents. "It is as strong as a blood oath, only without the blood. To break it, is the ultimate dishonor."

Kaplan said nothing at first. Then he stepped closer to Tony. Kaplan's face flushed, the creases in his forehead deepened, his eyes narrowed. "You mean like risking my life to save an ungrateful blood-sucking leech just because a dying man asked me to? A man I didn't know. Is that the kind of bond you're talking about, Tony?"

The two men stared at each other for several seconds without speaking.

"Mr. Kaplan," Tony finally said. "You have my word, I will honor my obligation with Inspector Moss."

A deputy walked forward. "Sir," he said. "I'll take you to your room."

Tony gave Kaplan one last look.

"Remember what I said." Kaplan pointed at his eyes and then at Tony's eyes. Four eyes. Quattrocchi. "That's a promise. And I never break a promise."

And then Tony was gone.

Moss returned with the keys to a government sedan, a Crown Vic. *What else?* After they folded themselves into the vehicle, Moss started the Crown Vic and pulled up to the gate.

The process was reversed. Through the double gates, stop at the barriers, through the next gate, and down the long straight road to the guardhouse at the exit of the Coast Guard facility.

"Where to now, Inspector Moss?" Kaplan asked.

"Little Rock."

"Figure out your mole?"

"Yeah." Moss revealed the identity of the mole.

"Why don't you just have him picked up?"

"Oh hell no." Moss held up the mob boss's phone. "I plucked this off Scalini's body on the way out of the warehouse and scrolled through the call log. That last call, the warning call, came from him. This is personal now. He stabbed me in the back, I want to slap the cuffs on that scumbag myself."

Moss's face revealed his true emotions. He was angry and hurt, and he had a right to be both. A trusted ally had betrayed him, had lied to him, and had used him. Kaplan knew that feeling all too well. He'd been betrayed in the past too and vowed never to trust anyone again. He guessed some wounds never heal.

"What about Bruno?"

Moss didn't answer at first. He seemed to be searching for the right words. Then he said, "I figure you'll help me track him down later."

"It's a tempting offer, but Bruno will have to wait."

"Where will you go now?" Moss asked. "Finish your trip to Texas?"

"No, not yet. First there is a flock of sheep in Lebanon that will soon be in need of a new shepherd."

CHAPTER 46

IT WASN'T LEBANON WHERE KAPLAN HAD to travel to locate Çoban; it was Cyprus, an unlikely place for Hezbollah leader Sheik Hakim Omar Khalil to seek refuge. Unlikely in that the two main religious groups dominating the island were Greek Orthodox and Islam—Sunni Islam—and Hezbollah was a Shiite militant group.

Expedited vetting by the agency's secret internal affairs team found Kaplan's handler, Alan, had no involvement in the leak. Kaplan was relieved. Alan was a good handler and he now knew he had his back.

Alan was able to locate the Sheik on a small seaside compound outside the town of Paphos. Over the years, the island's Sunni population had migrated to the northern end of Cyprus, which explained Çoban's seclusion on the southwestern side. He couldn't run the risk of being recognized by his sworn enemies. In a way, it was a wonder he'd taken up refuge on Cyprus at all. On the other hand, it was brilliant. Who would think to look for the Shiite Sheik amongst an island full of Sunnis?

After Çoban was located, Alan deleted the search from CIA's databases. No evidence of Kaplan's new destination could be known until the agency's leak was located and plugged. For that matter, with the one exception of communications with his handler, as soon as Kaplan left the U. S. Marshals Service Safe Site and Orientation Center in Alexandria, Virginia, he went off the grid.

Again.

He and Moss parted ways at Washington National Airport. The deputy booked a flight from DC to Memphis where he planned to drive to Little Rock and put the pinch on the traitor. Kaplan felt he had been successful in helping Moss channel his anger. The big man seemed ready, if not eager, to confront his Judas.

He couldn't worry about Moss anymore though, he had his own mission to plan and execute. After he took care of his business with the Sheik, or Shepherd as Valkyrie referred to him, he had agreed to meet with Moss and together they would go after Bruno the Rat.

Kaplan called in a favor from a Mossad operative whose life he had saved eight months ago in Egypt. His gesture had gone a long way in strengthening the relationship between Mossad and the CIA. It didn't hurt that she also happened to be the niece of the Mossad director himself.

Al Qaeda terrorists shot Marla Farache last Christmas when she tried to exfiltrate an Israeli tourist who had been kidnapped by the radical group. Kaplan pulled Farache and the tourist to safety after mounting a one-man rescue mission that resulted in the deaths of their captors. He applied a makeshift triage on her wounds and carried Marla on his back five kilometers to safety.

From there, he was sent to Lebanon to assassinate the Sheik's cousin.

After he parted company with Moss, Kaplan took a

taxi from the terminal to a General Aviation hangar on the other side of the airport. As a precaution, his weapons were surrendered prior to boarding and secured in a lockbox. It was standard Mossad protocol.

Kaplan climbed the air stair to the business class jet and found Marla Farache sitting on a leather couch talking on her cell phone. She was still as exotically beautiful as he remembered. Her long black hair draped across one shoulder and her rich brown eyes set off her dark skin.

She looked up when he entered the aircraft and smiled. She waved him in. "He just arrived," she said into her phone. "I'll call back once we're in the air."

She grabbed the cane propped against the seat next to her and pulled herself to her feet. "Gregg Kaplan, come in."

He walked over to her and held out his hand.

"We're on a handshake basis now?" she said. "After everything we've been through? I want a hug."

She opened her arms and they shared an embrace. "Marla, how are you?" he asked. Her eyes sparkled when she looked at him. "Wounds all healed?"

"My back healed fine but this leg isn't up to Mossad field standards yet." She held up her cane as she spoke. "Doctors say I might not ever have enough strength to work in the field again."

As she spoke, he noticed the sparkle in her eyes was replaced with sadness.

"You're in the States, you must have some duties."

"Uncle named me Mossad Deputy Director of American Affairs."

"Sounds important. What does that mean?"

"Not much," she sighed. "I spend a lot more time in the

U.S. now as liaison to NSA, CIA, and DoD. I think Uncle just wanted to no longer worry about me."

"I hope this favor won't land you in hot water."

"Not at all. On the contrary." Her tone changed, more upbeat. "Gives me a chance to go back home for a few days. I owe you this one...and a lot more. Besides, Uncle said he wants to see you again too." She lowered herself to the couch and patted her hand on the seat next to her. She leaned over and pulled a packet out of her briefcase and handed it to Kaplan. "This contains everything Mossad knows about Çoban. We were surprised you found his location, Mossad has been searching for his hideout ever since his cousin was executed."

Kaplan broke eye contact and fidgeted in his seat.

"Did you have something to do with that?" She asked. "Hezbollah blamed Mossad."

"Yeah," Kaplan dragged out the word. "I was afraid there might be some blowback aimed at Israel."

"I have to wonder," she said. "Why Çoban? And why now?"

"Remember Valkyrie?" Kaplan asked.

Marla Farache nodded.

"Çoban hired her to kill me as retribution for his cousin."

"Then why aren't you dead? She's never missed a target."

"She did last night," he said. "I collared her in New Jersey. We got her tucked away in a holding station in Manhattan until the agency can figure out what to do with her."

"Gitmo?"

"That's my guess. For a while anyway."

Farache gently put her hand on Kaplan's arm. "Gregg, you look like hell. Your eyes are bloodshot and you have dark circles under them. When was the last time you slept?"

"Do naps count?"

"No. When was your last full night's sleep?"

"Four days ago."

"No wonder you look so tired. There is a queen sized bed in the back." She pointed to a door at the back of the cabin. "After we get in the air, you can eat and I'll put you to bed."

"If I recall correctly," Kaplan said as a smile crept across his lips. "Last time you did that neither one of us got much sleep."

She smiled and lowered her head pretending embarrassment. "Are you complaining?"

"More like bragging," he said. "Seems like such a long time ago."

"It does." There was a long awkward silence. She patted her leg where the bullet had entered and said, "Night before this happened."

CHAPTER 47

U. S. MARSHALS SERVICE SENIOR INSPECTOR Pete Moss thought about how he was going to handle the issue with the traitor. He should have followed procedure and reported what he found on Scalini's phone to his superiors, however he couldn't bring himself to do it. Not yet anyway. Not because of loyalty either, just the opposite. He wanted to confront the man and personally take him down.

The past twenty-eight hours had been the most tension filled of his career. Out of the chaos, Gregg Kaplan had emerged as an unlikely ally and partner. As their bond grew, so did their admiration for each other and their respective abilities. Of course, Kaplan seemed to be skillful at everything. His tradecraft training far surpassed anything the Marshals Service had to offer. Moss let his past dealings with the traitor cloud his judgment and derail his main objective, but Kaplan was able to rein him in and help him focus on the task at hand. Since Moss refused to turn everything over to his superiors and let them handle it, the objective was getting the turncoat to confess his involvement with Scalini.

Moss and Kaplan brainstormed some of the different techniques to make the man talk. The simplest, he thought, was to basically beat a confession out of him. That was his first option, but Kaplan tossed it off the table. He said it was self-defeating. Kaplan was right but it would have made Moss feel better.

After his flight landed in Memphis, he rented a vehicle from one of the vendors, stopped by an electronics store, and then made the two-hour drive to Little Rock. He had a gut feeling this confrontation would not turn out well. When he finished with the traitor, one way or another, he was finished. Being betrayed had taken the last bit of enthusiasm for the job away from him. He would find a hole somewhere within the Marshals Service and ride out his last few months until he was eligible to retire. When that day came, he'd turn in his paperwork and walk out the door.

In the back of his mind, he'd already tossed around the idea of starting a private investigation firm in the Chicago area where he could pick and choose his case load and be his own boss. That idea appealed to him. Now it was on the forefront of his mind as the job with the Marshals Service seemed to have sucked the life out of him. He was tired of the bureaucracy and wanted a new start.

As he arrived in Little Rock, his stomach churned. In a matter of minutes he would be face to face with the traitor and, at that precise moment in time, their relationship would make an irrevocable turn. Actually, it already had. Moss would become the man's enemy for life, which was probably the prison sentence the traitor would get when the courts were finished with him.

Moss pulled into the Little Rock Federal Courthouse, flashed his creds, and was waved through by a guard he'd known for several years. It was a formality. Even though the guard recognized the face, a cred check was always required or else the guard would find himself, or herself, out on the streets looking for employment. Since 9/11, security at all federal buildings and courthouses had been permanently ramped up and in many instances, unnecessarily so, and all at taxpayer expense.

Before he drove through he held out a piece of paper. "Do me a favor, Gus?"

"Sure, Inspector Moss. Anything for you."

Moss handed the guard a piece of paper. "Self explanatory."

Moss made his way to the Marshals Service office as he had countless times before.

When he reached Deputy Jon Hepler's office, Moss stopped, took a deep breath, and walked inside.

Hepler hung up the phone when Moss walked in, smiled and said, "Dirt Man. Hell of a weekend, huh?" He pointed to his phone. "Been trying to call you for two days."

Moss held up his phone. "Battery died."

"Last time you checked in, you and Gregg Kaplan were on your way to Jersey. Sit down and tell me what happened."

Moss took a seat. "What have you heard?" Moss asked.

"All I know is the FBI raided a warehouse, Martin Scalini is dead, the warehoused burned down with Scalini in it, and your witness is tucked away at the SSOC." Hepler leaned in and said, "How'd it go down?"

"Turns out Bruno Ratti works for Tony Q. He shot Scalini in the head at point blank range and then offed Angelo DeLuca."

"No shit? Bruno the Rat and Tony Q. Who would have seen that one coming?"

"I don't know if they've released this yet," Moss said. "But an FBI Regional Director was shot and killed by an assassin."

"An assassin wanted the regional director dead?"

"Not just any assassin. And her target wasn't the director."

"*Her* target?

"Remember Inspector April Moore?"

"How could I forget that red-headed pain in the ass?"

"Turns out she was an imposter. She's the international assassin known as Valkyrie. Number six on Interpol's top ten most wanted list. Kaplan said he'd been chasing her for over a year."

Hepler leaned back in his chair. "How do you know all this?"

"We caught her," Moss said. "Actually Kaplan did most of the catching, all I did was shoot her."

"Where is she now?"

"I don't know. Tucked away in a CIA jail somewhere in Manhattan, I guess." Moss leaned back in his chair. He finally felt relaxed...or as relaxed as possible. "Funny thing though, Scalini got tipped off about the FBI raid just seconds before they kicked in the doors."

Moss was always good at reading people, and Jon Hepler just gave up *a tell*. Moss noticed the tiny face twitch and skin flush. Body language was a good indicator. The man was guilty. A dirty cop. Now, he really did want to jump on the man and beat him to a pulp.

"You know, Jon." Moss paused long enough to get Hepler to react. "Scalini's men had the drop on me and Kaplan. We were almost killed. *I* was almost killed by Scalini's men. So I guess I owe you a debt of gratitude. Your call to Scalini saved my life."

"What are you talking about?" Hepler's voice cracked. "What call?"

Moss reached into his pocket and pulled out Scalini's phone.

"The one you placed to Scalini. If it hadn't been for you, I'd be dead right now. And so would Kaplan. So we both owe you a debt of gratitude."

"Look, Pete. I don't know what the hell you're thinking and I don't like what you're insinuating. I had nothing to do with any of this. I haven't made any calls to Martin Scalini. Ever."

"Sure you have," Moss said as he held up Scalini's phone log. "See, right here. Deputy Jon Hepler. And it's a 501 area code."

"That's not even my number," Hepler defended. "Someone is trying to set me up. Look, Pete, you must believe me, I would never do that. You're my best friend, I would never betray you."

"As much as I want to believe you, Jon, I can't. See, Kaplan called in a few CIA favors and had the number run through their computers. He located the store where the phone was purchased and had the surveillance footage pulled. Guess whose mug showed up buying the phone?"

The expression on Hepler's face changed. His eyes darkened and his brow furrowed. "You WitSec boys always think you're better than everyone else. Always bossing around the PODs. Hell, it was probably one of you high and mighty WitSec inspectors who came up with *plain ole deputy* in the first place. What a slap in the face. You're nothing but a bunch of pompous assholes." Hepler pulled his weapon and pointed it at Moss. "You know, Pete, we had some good times before you went off to Chicago." He motioned with his gun. "Give me that phone."

Moss placed Scalini's phone on Hepler's desk and slid it toward him. "Jon, you're just making this worse."

"Worse? How could it get any worse?" Hepler put the phone in his pocket.

"Why'd you do it, Jon?" Moss asked. "Why did you turn?"

Hepler smiled. "What is it they said in the movie? Oh yeah, he made me an offer I couldn't refuse. You only get to say *no* one time to Martin Scalini, and then you're dead. I didn't want to be dead, Pete. I didn't want to die."

Hepler stood. "Now you just stay right where you are, Pete, and you won't get hurt. I'm going to leave now."

"Jon." Moss's voice changed. It was deep, strong, and authoritative, as if he were giving orders. "Sit down, Jon. It's over." Moss looked at his watch. "I'm wearing a wire...and that's not really Martin Scalini's phone. The real phone is in DC. Since there was no way you could know what Scalini's phone looked like, I had a similar one duplicated. You're going down, Jon."

Hepler took two steps back, still pointing his weapon at Moss. "No, Pete, I'm leaving. I'm not going to jail." Hepler backed out of his office, his gun still aimed at Moss.

"Freeze," a voice called out. "Drop your weapon."

Moss knew the voice. It was FBI Special Agent Richard Small.

Moss watched Hepler turn around.

His former friend pointed his gun at Small.

And just like that...it was all over.

CHAPTER 48

SLEEP CAME SO FAST KAPLAN BARELY remembered lying down on the bed.

Marla Farache had a meal prepared for him then insisted he get some sleep. He didn't resist. So much had happened in such a short span of time, he'd not been able to reflect on the events of the past few days.

He'd been asleep almost eight hours when he felt Marla's warm body curl up beside him. Her hand gently stroking his bare chest. He rolled over and faced her.

"How much longer till we land?"

"Little over two hours," she said. "It will be morning when we arrive in Tel Aviv. Uncle sent a message saying he'd meet us at the airport. He wants to personally take you to the harbor."

"Did he say why?"

"No, there were no details. Just that he wanted to talk to you alone."

Kaplan wrapped his arm around her, placed his hand in her lower back, and pulled her naked body against his.

She arched her back and tilted her head. "What? No foreplay?" she said with a smile.

He placed his hand behind her head and pulled her lips to his and kissed her softly. He rolled her on her back, climbed on top, and gazed into her eyes. "Nope."

The jet landed in Tel Aviv around 5:00 a.m. local time and he reset his internal clock. Marla reviewed with him the arrangements her uncle had made for his passage to and from Cyprus. He would have twelve hours from the time he arrived in Limassol to travel to Paphos, eliminate his target, and travel back to Limassol before the boat hoisted anchor and sailed out of the harbor. It was the kind of rogue mission he'd grown accustomed to with the CIA.

It was where he excelled.

Sex with Marla was as exciting and passionate as it was the first time in Egypt. It happened the night before he saved her life. They had shared a spontaneous moment of unrivaled passion. And even now, nearly eight months later, he could recall every vivid detail of their lovemaking.

Her skin was smooth as silk and her body toned and tight. With the exception of the two small scars from the al Qaeda terrorists' bullets, she was still a flawless beauty.

The Mossad jet taxied into a guarded hangar inside a razor wire perimeter fence. Every precaution was taken, as Mossad was always a target from one militant group or another.

After the jet's engines shut down, the cabin's air stair lowered. When Kaplan reached the exit, his weapons were returned. He stood in the exit door and glanced back at Marla who flashed him a guarded smile. He understood its meaning.

Kaplan reached the bottom of the air stair and was greeted by a man in his early seventies. He'd met the man once before, Marla Farache's uncle, Mossad Director Eli Levine.

Levine extended his hand. "Mr. Kaplan, welcome to Israel."

Kaplan shook the director's hand and said, "Thank you,

Director Levine, for your assistance and cooperation in this matter."

The gray-haired man turned around and motioned to the armored limo waiting for them. "Think nothing of it, my son," he said. "It is the very least I can do for the life of my niece. How is Marla anyway?"

Kaplan motioned back to the aircraft as the two men walked toward the limo. "She's fine, Director, she's ins—"

"Let us go," Levine interrupted. "You have much work to do and we have many things to discuss."

There wasn't much discussion enroute to the harbor since Levine did most of the talking. Levine didn't mention anything about Kaplan's upcoming mission, which was why he thought Levine wanted to speak to him alone. The Hezbollah leader had been a thorn in Israel's side and Levine likely saw this as another favor Kaplan and the CIA were doing for him. At least equal to saving the life of his niece. Perhaps more so.

Instead, Levine talked about family, or in his instance, the lack of a family. His wife and three young children had been killed twenty years ago by a suicide bomber on the streets of Jerusalem. The only family he had left was his sister and niece.

"You did more than simply save my niece, Mr. Kaplan." Levine's voice filled with remorse. "You saved our bloodline. My sister has been barren since Marla's birth. The only hope for our bloodline to continue rests solely with my niece."

The limo pulled up to a dock and came to a stop in front of a familiar looking yacht.

Levine said, "I believe you have been on this boat before, yes?"

Then Kaplan saw the name emblazoned on the transom—
The Toymaker. It was the same boat he rendezvoused with in

the Red Sea after rescuing a woman held prisoner in a palace located in the mountains of Yemen. An operative who eventually became his partner at the agency.

After returning with her to the United States they engaged in a passionate love affair. Then one day, without an explanation, she disappeared. It was that operative the CIA had tasked him to locate and his starting point was El Paso, Texas.

He never made it.

"Yes, Director, I believe I have."

"Go then," said Levine. "I pray for your safe return." The director placed his hand on Kaplan's arm as he opened the door. "One more thing, I understand you have business to finish in the United States after Cyprus."

"Yes, Director. I have a few loose ends to tie up."

"When your business is complete, I would consider it an honor for you to return and be a guest in my country. I think Marla might take pleasure in that too."

Levine released his grip on Kaplan's arm as a deck hand from the yacht approached, "Mr. Kaplan, we are ready to set sail."

Kaplan looked at the director and gave a respectful nod. "I would like that very much, Director."

Kaplan boarded the yacht and was greeted by the captain. "Welcome aboard, Mr. Kaplan. Or should I say welcome back aboard?"

"Thank you, Captain." Kaplan noticed this wasn't the same boat captain as the last time he was on this vessel. The captain he met last time was American. This captain had a British accent. Or perhaps it was Aussie.

The Toymaker was a one hundred twenty-five foot yacht that resembled a live aboard dive boat with some specialized enhancements designed by the owner. "How soon will we be in Limassol?"

The blond-haired captain smiled and said, "We've had a slight change in plans, I'm afraid. We won't be dropping you off in Limassol as planned."

"Oh?" Kaplan said. "Why is that?"

"Your connection in Limassol was involved in an unfortunate accident last night and will be unable to fulfill his obligations."

"What's the plan now, then?"

"About a mile offshore from your destination is the shipwreck Achilleas. We will sail to the Achilleas and anchor for the night. I will put divers in the water for several night dives on the wreck. You know, in case anyone is watching. You will swim to shore, complete your mission, and return to the ship. You're okay with swimming, aren't you?"

Little did the captain know, less than twenty-four hours ago Kaplan was in the Hudson River capturing an assassin. "Cakewalk," said Kaplan. "I just boned up on my swimming yesterday."

"Beg yours, what is a cakewalk?"

"Just an expression. Means it will be easy."

"No worries," the captain said. "You will have a total of four hours to complete your mission and be back on board or get left behind."

The cruise to the shipwreck Achilleas took all day and into the night. *The Toymaker* arrived over the sunken ship at 2200 hours. It had been another long day. There wasn't much for him to do except review the architectural plans of Çoban's compound, eat, and sleep. By the time the captain dropped anchor, Kaplan was well rested, well fed, and had memorized every detail of the Hezbollah leader's hideout. He felt good and his strength had returned. He was mentally focused, something he hadn't felt for several days.

Kaplan wanted to hit the compound between the hours of 0200 and 0400 local time. It was during that time period when the guards would be most vulnerable. Those early morning hours were a time when typically there was a lull in one's awareness. It would be quiet and boring. The guards' senses dulled from a lack of stimulation. Their recognition of danger would be slow and their reaction time even slower. Kaplan would have the clear advantage.

At midnight the captain woke Kaplan from another nap.

"Divers go in the water at 0100," he said. "You have until 0500 to get back on board. If you're not back, my instructions are to consider you dead. If there is a disturbance at the compound, I am to recall my divers, go dark, and leave immediately whether you have returned or not. These are my orders, Mr. Kaplan. Good luck."

"Understood, Captain. I will be back onboard by 0500 hours."

† † †

Kaplan placed his hand over his mask and regulator and took a giant stride from the dive platform into the water with the rest of the divers. The water was brisk but not cold. He took a compass heading to the designated spot on the shoreline and then descended to fifteen feet. It took him twenty-five minutes to reach shore. It was a darkened portion of the rocky shoreline free from any lights. An area of slight coastal indentation surrounded by twenty-five foot rocky cliffs.

Intel reports indicated two men typically guarded the stone

perimeter wall and one sharpshooter positioned on top of the building. He located all three as soon as he surfaced. His Delta Force training kicked in as he slowly approached the shore. Using his hands, he felt for the bottom. When his hands found it, he removed his fins, looped them over his non-firing hand, and let the waves bring him to shore. If anyone were to spot him on this moonless night, he'd look like a piece of driftwood floating in the water.

The two perimeter guards were smoking and standing beneath floodlights. *Who trained these idiots?* Standing near lights killed night vision. There was virtually no chance either one of them could spot him before he was on top of them.

Then it would be too late.

For them.

When he reached shore, he pulled off his fins, mask, and tanks and securely stored them amongst the rocks along shore. He pulled off his wet suit and draped it over his equipment. He opened one of the two dry bags he had towed behind him. His weapons.

He made a quick weapon check. All dry, loaded, and silenced. He slipped on his boots and prepared himself for action. He looked at his watch to verify his internal clock, almost two. Check. He wanted to make his move at 0230 hours so he sat on the rocky shoreline and waited.

Kaplan focused on the sharpshooter in the tower on top of the main compound building. Take him out first, if he could. Without his night vision goggles, Kaplan could see the man's rifle perched on top of the whitewashed wall. Through his NVGs, he saw the man slumped in a chair—asleep. Kaplan was stunned at the incompetence of Çoban's men. It wasn't yet 0230, but Kaplan couldn't afford to miss this window of opportunity.

Kaplan opened his other dry bag and pulled out his sniper rifle with its night vision scope. The most critical shot was the man in the tower. If Kaplan missed or only wounded the man, the mission would be compromised. If successful, the other two targets, the men under the lights with no chance at night vision, would be simple to take out.

He lined up the crosshairs on the man in the tower, zoomed in with his night vision scope, and saw the man's head hung across the backrest leaving Kaplan with a perfect profile view. The man had a full beard and his mouth gaped open. Kaplan could see his chest expanding and contracting with each breath, the deep relaxation of slumber. Kaplan locked the crosshairs with the center of the man's cranium, took five deep breaths, and gently squeezed the trigger. A mist flew from the man's skull.

He moved quickly to the guards. He had a good angle for rapid-fire succession kill shots. He dropped the first guard. The second guard heard the man fall and turned. Before the man could react, Kaplan squeezed off another round.

Fifteen seconds, three shots, three kills.

CHAPTER 49

KAPLAN BROKE DOWN HIS RIFLE AND SECURED
it in the dry bag. Later, when he returned to the boat, there
could be no trace he was ever here...other than the dead
bodies. If all went according to plan, even the bodies would
not lead back to him.

Kaplan scaled the twenty-five foot rock wall and located
the dead guards. Each fell under a light. He removed the slugs
from the whitewashed exterior, dragged the dead bodies clear
of the lights, and tossed them over the sea wall to the rocky
beach below. With any luck, the outgoing tide would drag their
bodies out to sea.

His brain retrieved the details of the architectural design of
the compound from his short-term memory. Intel indicated
the possibility, although unlikely, of another guard inside the
compound residence so Kaplan, as usual, erred on the side of
caution always assuming there was a threat around every corner
and hoping there wasn't. He moved through the compound
with his weapon ready, poised, and steady.

Mossad reports indicated the Sheik traveled to Cyprus with
his entourage, never with his family. His wife and children
remained in Lebanon. However, the Hezbollah leader was
rarely alone when in Cyprus and intel speculated he had been

involved in some sort of clandestine sexual affair. A practice conflicting with Islamic law.

Kaplan entered the only exterior door that was unlocked. It emptied into a mudroom of sorts, and from there, the hallway led to a great room that branched out into several adjoining bunkrooms and offices. Kaplan knew the bunkrooms held imminent danger, the remainder of Çoban's traveling entourage, including the rest of his bodyguards, all peacefully sleeping until morning.

Sheik Hakim Omar Khalil had a separate, private wing in the compound and, according to Kaplan's intel, no one was allowed to enter without permission. The leader's official business was conducted elsewhere on the compound.

The countdown timer in his head told him he still had two and a half hours.

With feline-like stealth, Kaplan negotiated his way through the compound's maze of halls and corridors. At each room, he opened the door and shot the occupants in the head with the throw-down weapon he brought with him. If his mission was to be successful, there could be no one left alive in the compound. When he reached Çoban's wing, as expected, the door to his bedroom suite was locked, but the rudimentary mechanism was easy enough for Kaplan to pick. He quickly aligned the tumblers and unlocked the door.

Çoban was not alone.

He had his lover in the bed with him and his lover was awake, covers pulled over her head. He could tell she was very petite. Slowly the covers lowered. The Sheik's lover was nothing like Kaplan had expected. She had olive skin, cropped black hair, and two brown eyes that gazed at him in fear.

Not Lebanese as expected.

Cypriot.

She glanced at him and then at the sleeping Çoban and then back to him before her eyes locked on his. He stepped forward and realized she was a child, perhaps no more than twelve or thirteen. His anger for the Hezbollah leader increased tenfold. A pedophile terrorist.

The child was trembling.

Kaplan put his finger to his lips and slowly reached for the covers to remove the girl from harm.

And then it happened.

The covers dropped.

A knife was clenched tight in the naked child's hand.

And it wasn't a girl.

It was a young boy. His body bruised from repeated beatings.

Çoban had been keeping the boy as a sex slave and forcing him to have sex.

The Sheik was guilty of an ultimate Islamic sin.

Punishable by death.

A sentence Kaplan was about to carry out.

Kaplan stepped back and motioned to the boy to move away while he kept his gun aimed at Çoban. Without warning, the boy lunged with the knife. Not at Kaplan, at the Sheik. The boy plunged the knife into Çoban's chest.

This complicated matters.

Çoban woke up in a startle. Kaplan knew the wound was not fatal. The Sheik cried out, at first in pain, then in anger at the boy. Then he saw Kaplan with his gun pointed at his head and went silent. Kaplan lodged his gun firmly against the Sheik's forehead and pushed him back down on the bed. Kaplan took a strip of duct tape and strapped it over the Sheik's mouth. The Hezbollah leader never moved, his eyes full of terror. Kaplan restrained the Sheik's arms behind his back with flex-cuffs and then placed a rag over Çoban's face and waited for the fumes to take effect. Çoban kicked and bucked in the bed, but with his mouth taped shut, he had no way to avoid breathing the fumes and quickly succumbed.

Kaplan communicated to the boy to get dressed by pointing to the pile of the boy's clothes on a chair and nodding.

He secured a bed sheet to a post and beam rafter. Kaplan hoisted the unconscious Çoban over his shoulder and wrapped the bed sheet around the leader's neck. He lowered the Sheik until the sheet pulled taut.

Çoban snapped awake. Oxygen deprivation overpowered the mild sedative. He jerked and squirmed. The rafter squeaked under the Sheik's weight. In a little over a minute, the squirming slowed and Çoban's body went limp. Kaplan waited until the Sheik had no pulse then removed the flex-cuffs and tape and left the man hanging from the rafter. He wrapped Çoban's fingers around the handgrip of the gun, and then tossed it on top of the bed. He wiped the boy's prints from the knife and placed it in the grip of one of the dead members of Çoban's entourage.

When the investigation of the Sheik's death was completed, there would be more questions than answers.

Kaplan looked at his watch to confirm the urgency he was feeling inside. 0345 hours. One hour fifteen minutes until the boat left. He could not leave the boy. He was a witness. And he would not kill the innocent boy, which left him only one option, take the boy with him.

The boy was dressed and still trembling. Kaplan scooped the boy in his arms and carried him from the compound.

By the time they reached the cliff, descended the rocks to

shore and gathered his equipment for the return swim it was already 0400 hours. It took twenty-five minutes to swim alone, now he had only one hour to swim the same distance with a child and his equipment in tow.

He kicked hard and swam as fast as he could. After thirty minutes he was breathing heavy. His legs felt like they were on fire, but he could not slow down. He was still over a quarter of a mile away when the boat flashed its underwater lights to recall the divers.

Kaplan doubled his efforts carrying the boy on his back and towing his equipment behind him. Equipment he couldn't leave behind. His orders were clear, *no trace left behind.* Which also meant the boy.

His internal clock said he had five minutes when he noticed there were no more divers climbing out of the water and onto the dive platform. While several men were showering on the platform, Kaplan heard the engines fire up.

Five minutes later he heard the rattling of the anchor chain as the captain retracted it from the sea bottom.

A hundred yards to go and he and the boy were surrounded by total darkness. Even though they could clearly see the boat, nobody on the boat could see them. He began to wonder how they might survive if the boat left them

As if the young boy recognized their plight, he started screaming. Seconds later the engines shut down and the spotlight from *The Toymaker* found them in the water.

CHAPTER 50

KAPLAN GAVE THE CAPTAIN INSTRUCTIONS ON caring for the young boy. His decision to rescue the young boy and bring him onboard was not questioned. The captain wasted no time returning to Tel Aviv.

Mossad director Eli Levine picked Kaplan up at the same dock he'd dropped him off the day before. "To a most successful trip," Levine said as he held up a glass of wine in the back of the limo. "Israel is once again in your debt. As am I." Levine bowed his head. "The captain says you rescued a young Cypriot boy from the Sheik's compound and brought him back with you. Do you think that decision wise?"

"It was never open for discussion, Director. The boy could not remain in Cyprus. Not after what he'd been through."

"Perhaps you are right. I will ensure he is taken care of."

Marla Farache was waiting inside the jet when Kaplan and Levine arrived. Once again he surrendered his weapons for the duration of the flight. This time Levine boarded the aircraft with him claiming business in DC that required his presence. Marla remained understandably indifferent toward Kaplan with her uncle onboard, a tremendous contrast from the flight yesterday from DC to Tel Aviv. Like Francesco told Tony in Lexington, *no kiss and tell*. It was none of Levine's business.

Immediately upon arrival at Dulles, an agency representative met Kaplan and escorted him to Langley for a debriefing. As it turned out, Çoban had extorted a CIA analyst to reveal everything he could gather on Kaplan, assignments, locations, personnel file—the works. The analyst had run up gambling debts at a casino in Atlantic City. Debts he failed to disclose to the agency as required. Çoban capitalized on the man's weakness and threatened to expose his debts unless he cooperated by providing detailed information about Kaplan and all his movements. In return, Çoban would pay off the analyst's gambling debts.

Also included in that data was the FBI's first attempt to learn Kaplan's identity when the two contract agents in Little Rock, the ones who died in the Crown Vic, called in the license plate from his Harley. Now he knew how Valkyrie was able to locate him so fast.

In the end though, it had cost them all. They had gotten their due…and that was all that mattered. Valkyrie would never see freedom again and, once tried and convicted, could very well end up with a needle in her arm. Assuming she ever saw a trial. The CIA employee who leaked information to Çoban would spend the rest of his years locked away in Fort Leavenworth for treason.

It was midnight East Coast time when Kaplan's debriefing ended, but his long day had started on eastern Mediterranean time and grew longer as he traveled west to the U.S. He was tired and ready for some rest. Right now, all he wanted was to get a good night's sleep in his own bed.

An agency car dropped him off at his Tysons Corner residence. When he got out of the car and headed up the walk he saw the man sitting on his front porch. The man made no attempt to hide his gun or his badge.

"Well, Inspector Moss, I'm surprised you haven't been arrested," Kaplan said. "Neighbors around here are kind of nosy. Big black man with a gun hanging around my house in the middle of the night might make them a little nervous."

"So I noticed. Real friendly place you got here. Already had to show my creds twice. Once to a local LEO and another time to one of your CIA boys. By the way, did you know the agency kept your house under surveillance?"

Kaplan smiled. "Yeah, I knew. I don't think I'm supposed to know, but these knuckleheads aren't very subtle. All clandestine operatives' homes are monitored…especially when we're out of town."

Kaplan pulled out his keys and unlocked the front door. He entered the code and disarmed his alarm system. "Come on in," Kaplan said as he motioned to Moss. "Since you're here, I assume you have something you want to discuss."

Moss walked through the doorway and closed the door behind him. "How did your mission go?"

"Just another day at the office." Kaplan smiled. "All right Moss, spit it out. You didn't show up on my doorstep in the middle of the night to shoot the breeze about my mission."

"Never one for chit-chat, are you? I guess your lack of tact is growing on me." Moss hesitated and then said, "Have you seen the news?"

"No, I've been a little busy and out of the country?"

"Something big went down today and Tony's involved."

"Doesn't surprise me, but perhaps you could elaborate unless you want me to play twenty questions."

"Still the perennial smart ass." Moss walked over to the sofa. "This might take a while." He sat down.

"Please, have a seat."

Moss just stared at him.

Kaplan pulled a chair from the dining room table and sat in it backwards, resting his arms on the backrest. "I'm all ears, Inspector."

"In light of Tony's breach in Little Rock, a federal judge allowed Tony to present videotaped testimony from the SSOC to a Grand Jury. Tony provided supporting documentation and everything."

"I know. I heard that was the way it was going down right before I left."

"Then Tony was immediately sent to his new relo area. Based on his testimony, the Grand Jury acted fast and issued indictments against *the* five major crime families in the country along with two other members of the Scalini family. Six arraignment hearings were held today. The Abruzzi family in Chicago, the Giordano family in Miami, Romano in New Jersey, Esposito and Scalini in New York, and Lombardi in Los Angeles."

"A real family affair. What's your point?"

"Point is," Moss continued and then took a deep breath. "In a well orchestrated and coordinated attempt by the D.O.J., all of the crime family bosses were hauled into federal courts across the country at the exact same time."

"All of them? At the same time?"

"The Department of Justice, in its glorious wisdom didn't want the families conferring when the first indictments were handed down so they ordered all hearings at the same time. 1:00 Eastern, 12:00 Central, and so on. That way, Justice believed the element of surprise would work in their favor."

"Did it?"

"Oh yeah. Every federal judge slapped the cuffs on the men and hauled them off to jail. All of them are being held without bond."

"And that's a bad thing? Is there a problem?"

"Tony."

"You said he was in his relo area. Which is where exactly?"

"Fort Collins, Colorado."

"And the problem is...?"

"He disappeared fifteen minutes before the hearings were scheduled to begin. Went to the bathroom and was never seen again. We have deputies looking all over for him."

"Maybe one of the bosses, or all of them, had him taken out. What makes you think he's not a victim?"

"Because Tony Q is a lying weasel and my gut tells me he's involved in this up to here." Moss held his hand in front of his eyes.

Kaplan thought about it for a second. "Everyone calls him Tony Q. Why? What's the Q stand for?"

Moss looked at Kaplan. "It's his true identity. I can't reveal that."

"Give me a break, Moss. Everybody *but me* seems to know already. If my security clearance is high enough for the U. S. Marshals Service to let me into the SSOC, then it's damn well good enough to know Tony Q's true identity."

Moss was silent for a few seconds, obviously reflecting on Kaplan's argument. "Anthony Quattrocchi."

"Quattrocchi?"

"Yep."

Kaplan rubbed the three-day old stubble on his chin. He stood and paced the floor. "Back in Little Rock, when all this started, one of the goons I shot muttered *four eyes* right after

I asked him who he worked for. I just assumed it was Scalini because of those Coke bottle thick glasses of his."

"Yeah," Moss said. "We've all heard Scalini called *four eyes*."

"But *four eyes* isn't Scalini...it's quite literally Quattrocchi."

"Wait. What?" Moss asked. "Why do you say that?"

Kaplan continued, "Tony told me the meaning of the word at the SSOC, while you were getting us a car. Said in Sicily the term Quattrocchi means some sort of covenant between two people, like an oath or contract, and their four eyes seal the deal. I didn't know it was his last name at the time. Now I'm wondering about a lot of things."

"For instance?"

"For instance," Kaplan continued. "Why would Bruno let Tony be tortured by Martin Scalini? He wouldn't. We never saw Tony strapped to that table. There were no bruises on his wrists to indicate he'd been restrained either."

"That's right," Moss agreed. "If Bruno worked for Tony... which we now know he does...he would never have allowed the situation to develop that far."

"But Scalini *was* going to kill Tony."

"Remember. Scalini said something to Tony about breaking his heart. Maybe Scalini and Tony were more than boss and employee—"

Kaplan interrupted, "Maybe Scalini and Tony were partners."

CHAPTER 51

"YOU HAVE A 7:00 A.M. FLIGHT OUT OF DULLES," Alan said through the speakerphone. "Connecting through San Juan to the island."

Kaplan replied, "Wow, you have been busy."

Earlier, Kaplan had called his handler, Alan, to enlist his help in locating Tony. He and Moss briefed Alan with every bit of information they thought could be relevant in their search. The call took a couple of hours but Alan was able to piece together a logical location for the missing Sicilian.

"It's getting late, gentlemen," Alan said. "Or early. You guys need to leave for the airport in thirty. I'll sit and monitor the bait and let you know if we have a hit." Alan hung up before he or Moss could respond.

"You never told me," Kaplan said to Moss. "How'd it go with Hepler?"

"Tragic." His voice sounded strained. "Suicide by cop."

"You shot him?"

"No. An FBI agent moved in when Jon became threatening. JP drew on the agent and the agent pumped three rounds into his chest. I was wearing a wire so it's all on tape. His confession, the shooting, everything."

"That's a shame." Kaplan lowered his head and said softly,

"I'm truly sorry, Pete."

"Don't be. JP was a fool corrupted by money. He sealed his own fate when he cut a deal with Scalini."

"Root of all evil."

"Yep. He was a dirty cop. No telling how many other times he'd taken a bribe. Sooner or later, he was going to get caught. It was just a matter of time."

Kaplan yawned and stretched his arms. "No rest for the weary, huh?"

"I thought you were the *Energizer* bunny, this should be a walk in the park."

"I am starting to think this job is strictly for the young," Kaplan grumbled. "I'm gonna take a shower and change then we can leave." He walked halfway across the room and then said, "Maybe you should have asked Tony what I'm like without sleep."

"Buck it up," Moss said with a smile. "You can sleep on the plane."

Neither Moss nor Kaplan was able to sleep on the plane.

It was the peak of hurricane season and the entire East Coast was impacted by an extra large tropical system in the Atlantic churning its way westward with an expected landfall of Savannah, Georgia. The cyclonic spread of the system had created high altitude turbulence from Virginia all the way to the southern end of the Bahamas. By the time the turbulence subsided, their flight was already starting its descent into San Juan.

After an hour and half of being jostled in his seat, Moss

finally gave up trying to sleep when they were somewhere over North Florida. Every time he tried to rest his head against the window, turbulence would rock the regional jet and he would bump his head on the glass.

He watched Kaplan try to sleep, but the frequent updrafts and downdrafts kept the operative's eyes open most of the trip. That was compounded by the fact almost half of the occupants of the flight had gotten airsick. Every few minutes he would catch a waft of a *sic sac* being filled by yet another nauseated passenger.

Moss wasn't particularly fond of flying but fortunately he didn't get airsick. He favored wheels on the ground modes of transportation. The regional jet from DC to San Juan was small. The aircraft waiting for them in San Juan was even smaller, a Saab 340 turboprop. Moss was a very large man crammed into a very small seat. Even walking down the aisle to his seat was physically uncomfortable since he had to remain hunched over while he moved.

The flight was long, loud, and tiring. The pilot never seemed to bother syncing the pitch of the propellers and the drone reverberated from ear to ear in a constant *wa-wa wa-wa* sound. After two hours in the turboprop, Moss had had enough.

When he and Kaplan deplaned, the Fort-de-France CIA Station Chief met them at baggage claim—even though neither one of them checked bags. In reality, the Chief was a one-man show on the island of Martinique. There was no real *station*, just equipment and weapons stored at the man's home. It was that equipment and those weapons Moss and Kaplan needed.

He simply called himself Nat. He was a native of Martinique and said his real name was too difficult for *Yankees* to pronounce. The CIA recruited him over ten years ago. Although Nat spoke

English, his native Creole tongue made it difficult for Moss to understand many of his words. He dropped most of his *r*'s and inserted *w*'s. He sounded like the islander that he was.

When Nat stopped the car and turned off the ignition, Moss was sure they were at the wrong house. Nat's bright aqua colored shanty had only one inviting feature, a front porch overlooking the Caribbean. There was laundry hanging on a droopy line strung from a power pole to the corner of the rusty metal roof. A barbed wire fence protected a garden in the front yard. He was surprised the run-down shanty had withstood the tropical storms and hurricanes for all these years. Nat took Moss and Kaplan to a back room. The windows were barred and the door was fortified. He opened a vault, pulled out a duffle bag, and tossed it on a table in the middle of the room. Inside was an assortment of handguns and rifles and ammunition.

"Pick your pwoison, gentlemen," Nat said.

While Moss and Kaplan were sorting through the weapons, Nat brought out a wireless communication system and placed it on the table next to the duffle bag. "State of art." Nat smiled and looked at Kaplan. "The Company be listening...Mashuls Suvice too." He glanced back at Moss.

After the two men *gunned up*, Moss pulled out the briefing packet and showed Nat where they needed to go.

"Îlet Antonio, yes," Nat said. "Heavily guarded. Helicopter fly in two days past."

Moss and Kaplan looked at each other and smiled.

"Antonio?" Kaplan questioned.

"Yes. Îlet Antonio. Three miles east of Baie du Simon."

"What is that?" Moss asked.

"Bay of Simon." Nat pointed to the spot on the map. Then

he ran his finger to the right until he reached the unmarked island. "Three miles to Îlet Antonio. I take you to boat. You make it there by dark."

"You're going with us, right?" Moss asked Nat.

"No way, mon. No one who go there eva come back. Island elders say evil man live there. You go alone. I stay and monitor radio."

"An evil man does live there," Kaplan explained. "But not evil in a voodoo kind of way, more like a criminal kind of way. We would appreciate any manpower assistance you could provide."

"Is okay." Nat tapped a large radio sitting on top of a desk. "Everything be okay in a few hours."

Moss asked Kaplan, "Shouldn't we wait till morning so we can scout during the daylight?"

"No," Kaplan replied. "Too risky. We need to go at night."

"What if we rest and go tomorrow night?" Moss said. "Then we can scout it during the day and return after dark. You were the one whining about rest. This way you'll get some."

"Yeah? And you said I was the *Energizer* bunny." Kaplan tapped his fingers on the briefing packet. "We already have the topo maps and satellite photos, we know the lay of the land. There will be no scouting. We have our orders. We storm the castle tonight."

CHAPTER 52

JUST LIKE HE HAD MEMORIZED ÇOBAN'S
Cyprus compound, Kaplan committed every minutia of this
mission briefing to memory, including the detailed satellite
photos of the rocky island. Topographic images provided
by his handler depicted an amoeba shaped island roughly a
mile in diameter at the center. The south and the east end of
the island jutted out in a finger-like peninsula and offered the
lowest elevation and the only potential spot to come ashore
undetected. With a pebble beach and a grassy flat, the elevation
rose to the west and north along a forested promontory to a
rugged ridge approximately five hundred fifty feet above the
Atlantic Ocean. It was nothing more than a huge volcanic rock
sticking out of the water.

A palatial home was built on the western apex of the
island. Dense tropical trees wrapped tight around three sides
of the mansion leaving only a grand vista of the big island
of Martinique to the west. Briefing photos indicated three
outbuildings, several satellite dishes, a helicopter pad, and a
one-acre solar panel farm.

A self-contained retreat.

Or fortress.

The boat Nat had provided for their mission was a fifteen-foot wooden skiff with a flat bottom, dirty yellow hull, and teal gunwales. It was propelled by an underpowered, manual steering outboard motor that looked like the engine on the old fishing boat his father had when he was a kid. That engine was now in the junkyard and this one should be too. To start the engine, Kaplan wrapped a rope around a spindle on the top of the old engine and pulled. If it didn't start on the first pull, he had to repeat the laborious process until it did.

Nat was wrong about making it to Îlet Antonio before dark. The water was rough. Too rough and too wet to proceed at anything above a fast idle. Traversing the rocky waters in the dark added an extra element of danger. There was no light in the sky or on the horizon in front of him making it nearly impossible to detect the rocky obstacles until the boat was almost on top of them. Moss sat on the bow scouting for rocks in the water.

"I can't see squat," Moss said in a hushed voice.

Moss had told him earlier that he didn't like water and didn't like boats. "Not much further, I think," Kaplan reassured Moss. "That is if this old engine will make it."

Finally, about two hours after complete darkness swallowed them, the island came into view and when it did, they were almost close enough to touch the western cliff. Kaplan negotiated the boat around the northern side of the island to the eastern end where he could pull the boat onshore. There was a dock on the south shore but, not knowing if it would be guarded, he avoided going anywhere near it.

He reached the predetermined landing spot and slowly aimed the boat's hull toward shore. When the bow struck the gravelly bottom, Moss jumped out, pulled the boat on shore, and tied it to a boulder. Kaplan killed the engine and followed.

Moss pulled out his silenced weapon and ensured a round was in the chamber. "You ready for this?"

"Don't worry about me. But just so we're clear, if you get shot again, I'm not carrying your big ass out of here."

"Check your memory, old man. I believe I was the one who saved your ass from Valkyrie."

"Turn on your comms and let's go."

Moss reached down and powered up his voice-activated communication system. "Test 1-2."

"Five by," Kaplan responded as they performed a comm system check.

The grassy area along the east and south shoreline was narrow and flat. Kaplan motioned to Moss's left. "Bogey on the dock smoking. Good thing we didn't chance it."

The terrain rose quickly from that point. Using his NVGs, Kaplan noticed a path around the south side of the island rising toward the complex. It was a more gradual climb than the northern shore, but the trail was also monitored every couple hundred yards by more guards.

"No telling how many men Tony has guarding this place."

"Definitely has quite the payroll," Moss agreed.

The climb up the spine of the ridgeline was brutal. It was steep and rough and full of loose rocks that moved under foot. Each step was a high step with hands extended on the rocks ahead for stability and within minutes he felt the burn in his thigh muscles. It was more like rock climbing or bouldering than uphill hiking. "How ya doing, Moss?"

"I'm pretty much a flatlander, this is killing me."

"Don't be such a wuss, we're not even a third the way to the top."

"You never mentioned anything about climbing Mount

Everest."

"Look up. Only another fifty feet or so to the solar farm. It should level out some up there."

"I hope so or I'll never make it." His breathing seemed labored.

The terrain did plateau at the solar farm, which gave Kaplan a welcome breather too, although he would never admit that to Moss.

Solar panels spanned an area roughly the size of a football field. At one end, the opposite end from where they were standing was one of the outbuildings. It housed two diesel generators, one of which was running. Kaplan could see the heat signature in his NVGs. What he couldn't see were the fuel tanks that fed the generators. A fuel supply line ran into a wooded area. He and Moss followed it and found a large camouflaged tank not visible in the satellite photos.

There was another guard patrolling the area next to the tank. He had a rifle strapped to his shoulder and a cigarette dangling from his lips. There was no way past him without being detected.

"I'll take this one," said Kaplan. He dug around in his pocket and fished out a mini-syringe. The chemical was designed to disable its victim for twelve hours leaving them with nothing more than a bad headache when they finally woke up. It had an automatic delivery system built in so all he needed to do was get close enough to stick the victim.

"What Rambo, no knife?"

Kaplan held up the syringe. "You want to do it?"

"No, he's all yours. I'll be here for backup."

Kaplan maneuvered around and behind the guard with silent precision, clamped his hand over the man's mouth, and inserted the needle into the man's neck. Within seconds, the guard collapsed into unconsciousness. Kaplan cradled his fall and started to drag the man out of the opening when Moss gave him an urgent warning over his comm system.

"Duck."

Kaplan dropped the guard and dove to the ground. He heard Moss's silenced weapon pop as he fired a round past him. He looked over and saw a man fall to the ground. He got up and brushed the dirt from his clothes and gave Moss a thumbs up signal. Before he could turn around he heard the sounds.

Dogs.

All at once, barking seemed to resonate from every part of the island.

So much for stealth.

The first dog had been with the man Moss shot and lunged at Kaplan's throat. He fended off the snarling dog's teeth with a forearm block, knocking the large animal to the ground. He reached for another syringe, but the dog attacked again knocking it from his hand. Kaplan was toppled flat on his back as the dog pounced again clamping his sharp teeth into his forearm, still sore from Valkyrie's poniard. While wrestling the guard dog he saw a shadow reach down and the dog released his grip and fell limp.

Moss tossed the spent syringe on the ground. "I hate mean dogs," Moss said as he pulled Kaplan to his feet.

Not just any dogs, Rottweilers. Kaplan didn't care for them either.

"You okay?" Moss asked.

"Kind of slow for backup, don't you think? Why didn't you just shoot the dog?"

"I could have missed while you two were rolling all over the ground. And don't bother to thank me for saving your ass… yet again."

"Let's get out of here," Kaplan said, "before more mutts show up."

"Right behind you."

"Let's head for the ledge and regroup." Kaplan's handler had located an escarpment on the north side ridge with a winding ledge about thirty feet below the crest of the bluff. It was the same escarpment where the satellite dishes were fenced. It actually took them away from the residence but offered a protected refuge in the event of potential detection.

Ahead Kaplan saw another guard and two dogs running toward them. The man pointed and both dogs charged. Kaplan's first shot sent the lead dog tumbling down a steep hill. Moss dropped the second dog and then the man with the rifle fired.

Moss grunted and fell to the ground.

Kaplan fired a return volley and the man toppled like a bowling pin, following the dog down the hill.

"Son of a bitch," he said, "shot me in the same leg."

Kaplan ran back over to Moss. Up the hill he could hear more men pounding toward them. He could hear boots sliding across loose rock. From below, he saw two more men running up the steep grade with flashlights. The gap was closing fast.

He pulled Moss to his feet. "I already told you, I'm not carrying your ass out of here. Can you run?"

"Run? Seriously? You really do have a sense of humor," said Moss. "This one isn't a flesh wound. It hit square in my thigh."

Three more shots rang out, but missed the mark. Kaplan found the ledge. It started just below their position overlooking the north side of the island. To get to the ledge, he and Moss would have to slide down a twenty-foot embankment of rock and gravel and then make a ten-foot vertical drop to the ledge below.

Barking got closer.

Their options dwindled.

Kaplan looked back and saw the Rottweiler within a few feet. It snarled at him, bared its teeth, and lunged.

Kaplan sidestepped the dog's leap and shoved the dog over the side of the cliff barely missing Moss.

Moss slid down the hill while Kaplan picked off the two men running up the hill. He dropped to his belly and lay in wait for the other men.

Moss called out. "Kaplan. Get your ass down here."

When more men appeared above him, Kaplan squeezed off three well-placed rounds. Each shot found its intended target. Two armed men. One mean-ass growling dog.

"Kaplan."

Kaplan turned and skidded down the hill on his backside. Rocks and pebbles rolled under him. When he stopped next to Moss, he was inches from the drop-off to the ledge.

"Can you make this?" Kaplan asked.

"What's my second choice?"

"I'll go first," Kaplan insisted. "When you hit, try not to roll toward the edge of the cliff."

"Now why didn't I think of that?" Moss said.

"I plan on saving both our asses if we survive this jump." Kaplan knew they were rapidly running out of time. He dropped to his belly and slid his feet off the rocky edge. "Try not to land on top of me, okay?"

Without waiting for a reply, Kaplan dropped to the ledge

and almost lost his balance when he did. Now he really was worried that the injured Moss wouldn't be able to control his landing and would tumble over the edge and drop five hundred feet to the rocky shoreline below.

Or worse yet, take Kaplan over the edge with him.

CHAPTER 53

IT FELT LIKE A HOT BRANDING IRON HAD been jabbed into his left thigh. The burning sensation from the bullet wound was ramping in intensity. Moss looked down at the ledge and wondered if the momentum of his landing wouldn't just carry him over the cliff and to his death. The pain in his leg made him think death wasn't his worst option.

He heard Kaplan in his earpiece, "Come on, Moss, we don't have all day."

The mission laid out by Kaplan was supposed to be fail-safe. Now it was beginning to look like a fiasco. Murphy's Law was chasing them and had finally caught up. Perhaps Kaplan should have anticipated that Tony would have attack dogs guarding his compound. Maybe Alan should have seen evidence in those ultra high-resolution spy satellite photos. This wasn't at all what he'd expected to happen on this mission. Kaplan made it sound easy, almost fun. That should have been a red flag. Fact of the matter, the entire mission was falling apart. And it was getting worse by the minute.

Moss heard two men in the distance trying to figure out which way he and Kaplan went and what had happened to their dogs.

He rolled over onto his belly and slid his legs down slowly

lowering himself over the ledge until he was hanging on by just his fingertips. He glanced once more at his landing spot and pictured which direction he needed to roll when he landed. He released his grip and fell.

When his feet hit the ledge, his left leg collapsed, unable to support his weight. Pain shot through his body and he strained to suppress sounds of his agony. He fell to his side and his momentum rolled him away from the wall toward the drop-off. His big hands clawed the rocky ground, searching for a handhold, anything to keep him from falling off the cliff. He felt the edge of the ledge beneath him when his hand found a hold.

Kaplan had reached out, clasped his hand at the last second, and pulled Moss toward him.

"Damn, you're heavy," Kaplan said. "Ever thought about *Weight Watchers*?"

"You're just jealous."

Kaplan stood, gripped Moss's hand, and helped him to his feet.

"This way."

Moss followed the CIA operative, both men keeping their backs against the wall as they side-shuffled along the ledge. With each step, Moss dragged behind his injured left leg. For the first time, he felt the warm blood cascading down his leg to his boot.

"How's the leg?" Kaplan asked, almost as if he knew what Moss was thinking.

"I think I need to stop the bleeding."

"The ledge should be a little wider up ahead. We'll stop there and I'll take a look."

Moss and Kaplan were still wearing their NVGs, which

enabled them to locate the ledge. Without the night vision goggles they would still be aimlessly searching for it. Or dead.

Oddly though, it seemed no one was chasing after them now. After they rounded the first turn on the ledge, everything grew quiet. No more yelling. No more barking. The only sounds filling the night air were the waves crashing against the rocks below and the whistling of the wind against the rocky cliff.

The wide spot in the ledge Kaplan referred to wasn't very wide at all. Maybe four feet at its widest juncture. It was enough room, however, for Moss to sit against the rocky wall and let Kaplan inspect his wound. Kaplan took out his knife and cut a long slit in Moss's pants. He put his hands inside the slit and wrapped them around Moss's leg.

"No exit wound. That's good."

"What do you mean, *good?*"

"It's good because the entrance wound is small. Exit wounds generally are larger and more destructive. We need to apply pressure and stem the bleeding though. You're lucky."

"How the hell do you call this lucky?"

"Could've hit the artery and you'd be dead already."

"Can you take the bullet out?"

"Hell no, Moss. This isn't the Wild West. I can't just dig out the bullet with my knife and patch you up. That's a job for a doctor. I might do permanent damage."

"What about infection?"

"Quit your belly aching. First, we need to stop the bleeding, so you need to hold pressure on the wound."

"Then what?"

"And then I need to find a way to get us off this ledge."

✝ ✝ ✝

He and Moss had been on the ledge for hours without hearing a sound. Neither man had spoken in over two. They had moved to the precipice of the escarpment. The three-foot wide ledge rounded a corner in both directions and led back toward the main section of the island.

Kaplan field dressed Moss's leg wound and wrapped a makeshift dressing around the man's huge thigh. The last time he'd checked the bleeding had stopped. The deputy kept his big hand clamped around the wound to help with the bleeding or maybe because of the pain. Perhaps both. Every few minutes Kaplan would hear Moss's breathing stop and when he'd glanced over at him, the big man was grimacing. He suffered in silence, refusing to make any audible sound. The man was tough and would not allow his pain to give away their position.

Kaplan leaned over and looked down into the dark abyss below. Earlier, he and Moss had removed their NVGs so he already knew what was down there, five hundred feet below. Rocks. Certain death for anyone who fell from this narrow ledge.

It had been nearly forty-eight hours since he'd slept. Focus diminished with every blink. His eyelids grew heavy and his field of vision narrowed. He rubbed his eyes and shook his head in a futile attempt to clear the cobwebs. Anything to stay awake. Sleep was not an option. Sleep was certain death.

His forearm still throbbed from the crushing force of the Rottweiler's bite. That damn dog was *not* man's best friend. He would rather have been shot.

Fatigue was taking its toll. More so on Moss who wasn't accustomed to the washout effects of adrenaline overload. The effects were not so pronounced for Kaplan; he'd learned to cope with it years ago.

Kaplan noticed Moss's eyes close and his torso start to waiver. He jabbed the deputy in the ribs and the big man jumped almost losing his balance and falling off the ledge. Kaplan's arm was all that stopped the man.

"What the hell?" Moss said. "Are you trying to kill me?"

"Just the opposite. Trying to keep you alive."

"By pushing me off this ledge?"

Kaplan smiled. He had raised the man's alertness level. Temporarily snapped his mind awake.

"How long have we been on this ledge anyway?"

"Too long," Kaplan replied.

"What do you think the odds are of us getting out alive?"

"We both can agree jumping is out, right?"

Moss nodded.

"We're trapped in the middle and, I figure, outgunned at least six or eight to two...so, I'd say the odds are still in our favor."

"We should have waited on backup."

"I made a promise to Tony that I intend to keep."

"Kill him? No wonder you were so anxious to get here right away."

Kaplan said nothing in reply. He made Moss aware of his intentions from the beginning.

Kaplan watched the big man feign a smile and then grimace. "Hurt much?" Kaplan knew it was a stupid question as soon as the words passed his lips.

"Nah," Moss said in a sarcastic tone. "After Valkyrie shot me I thought to myself, *hey, why not try this again.* Kinda feels like someone sliced my leg open and poured hot sauce inside. You should give it a try."

"Been there, done that. First bullet I took was in the gut."

"Special Forces?"

"No, never got shot in the Army. Happened in civilian life where the enemy was a little harder to recognize."

Kaplan heard the sounds coming in both directions along the ledge. He glanced at Moss. He'd heard them too. Their position was no longer safe. They would soon be discovered and they had nowhere to go. He and Moss were trapped. Their chance of getting off the ledge alive had seemingly dropped to zero.

He glanced again into the abyss and then to each side as the danger approached.

He and Moss looked at each other and instinctively knew what had to be done. They picked up their silenced weapons, leaned into each other, and pushed themselves to their feet.

How in the hell it came to this was beyond him. Less than a week ago he was loading his Harley for a two-day ride to El Paso, Texas. If he'd minded his own business and not gotten involved, if he'd only stopped somewhere else to eat, if he'd only passed Little Rock by, then none of this would have happened.

And if it did, he wouldn't be the one involved.

Or maybe he would.

Maybe some perverse predestination had drawn him in and this was his fate all along.

Either way, it ended now.

He heard the voices and then shadowy figures appeared on both sides.

He heard the voices again, but this time they were calling his name.

CHAPTER 54

"MR. KAPLAN," THE VOICE RANG OUT. "MR. Gregg Kaplan."

There were many things he expected. Like a shootout on the ledge, or being shot, or falling into the abyss, but he didn't expect someone to approach in this manner.

"Mr. Kaplan, please respond."

Kaplan glanced at Moss. The deputy shrugged his shoulders and whispered into the comm system, "What have we got to lose?"

Kaplan turned toward the direction of the man calling his name. "This is Kaplan."

"Mr. Kaplan, please drop your weapon. Tony Q wishes to speak to you. To you, and Senior Inspector Moss."

"And if I don't?"

"Mr. Kaplan, my instructions are not to harm you, but to help. We saw blood, one of you is injured and in need of medical attention and Tony Q told me to tell you that neither of you are in any threat of harm. Actually, he says he wants to help."

"Bullshit," Kaplan said. "If that's true, then throw me *your* weapons."

"That won't be happening, Mr. Kaplan, but please believe

me, we mean you no harm."

"What do you think, Moss?" Kaplan asked in a hushed voice. There was no response. Kaplan turned and saw Moss sliding down to his seat. He was losing consciousness and perilously close to falling off the ledge. Kaplan grappled for the deputy and pulled him against the wall.

He looked in each direction and could see both men.

"Please, Mr. Kaplan," the man said. He pointed at Moss. "That man needs our help."

† † †

Moss was strapped in a harness and lifted to safety from above, he was conscious, but barely. Kaplan followed the man who spoke to him around the ledge and back to the top of the escarpment where Moss had been lifted. That man was Bruno Ratti.

The last time he'd seen him, Bruno was escaping from the raging warehouse fire in New Jersey. Right after he killed Martin Scalini and Angelo DeLuca.

Kaplan and Moss were relieved of their handguns and were taken to a sterilized room beneath the main level of the residence. A man Bruno claimed was a doctor cleaned and bandaged the puncture wounds from the dog bites on his arm. Moss was pumped full of painkillers and antibiotics, both of which temporarily restored most of his strength and lucidity.

Moss was given some old crutches by the doctor while Bruno held them at gunpoint with an AK-47. Kaplan looked at Bruno who was pointing the assault rifle at him. "I thought you said you meant us no harm."

"Yeah, I did. Tony Q warned me about you. Said not to get

too close. Stay more than arm's length and to shoot you if you moved."

Bruno then escorted the two men to the main floor.

When the doors opened, Kaplan was staring out of a large plate glass window overlooking the island of Martinique. Dawn was breaking and the sky was getting lighter.

The old man appeared in the doorway and walked in.

"Mr. Kaplan, Inspector Moss," Tony said. "Welcome to Villa de Quattrocchi."

"Hell of a greeting party, Tony," Kaplan said. "I should have killed you when I had the chance."

Tony stared at Kaplan then turned to Moss. "I was not expecting either of you. I take intruders seriously…as you well can understand when so many want to kill me. One can never be too careful, you know."

"You should have expected me," said Kaplan. "I warned you at the SSOC."

"Yes. Yes." Tony laughed. "To hunt me down and kill me if I double crossed Inspector Moss here." Tony pointed at Moss. "So you did, Mr. Kaplan. So you did."

Tony walked over to the large window and gazed outside. "The thing is, I did not double cross anyone. I lived up to my part of the agreement. I provided testimony. I produced evidence." Tony looked at Moss. "Your Department of Justice got what they wanted."

Moss raised his voice. "You disappeared from your relocation area. You cost the U. S. Government a lot of money."

"What I should have done, what I wanted to do, was kill every one of those bastards I testified against. That would have saved the government millions of dollars. Just think, no court costs, no appeals, no legal wrangling. Hell, I could have done your government a favor. Only the risk of getting caught and sent to prison kept me from this. Instead, I did the right thing…in accordance to my contract with Justice. And what do I get in return? You track me down, trespass on my property, kill several of my men, and then have the audacity to come in here and threaten me. A lot of thanks I get for saving your life."

Kaplan took a few steps toward the window. Bruno raised his gun as a warning but Tony waved him off. Kaplan stopped at the opposite end of the large window, still fifteen feet from Tony.

"All this because of Scalini's son?" Kaplan asked.

Tony looked at Kaplan for a few seconds and then a hint of a smile crept across his lips. "I might have lied to you about that."

"What do you mean?"

"That's not the reason Scalini was after me. Martin and I were partners."

Kaplan and Moss looked at each other.

"Had been for many years," Tony continued. "He gave me my start and I eventually made enough money to buy half interest in the family business. A silent partner if you will. He knew his son was a worthless piece of crap. The first and only time that little punk drew a gun on me, Bruno whacked him. Did Martin a favor actually. Believe it or not, he harbored no ill will, not about his son anyway."

Tony kept talking. As if he was trying to justify his past.

"I had been skimming Martin's share for years. Decades really. How do you think I could afford all this?" Tony waved his arms. "When Martin finally figured it out and came for me, I knew I had to do something or I'd end up in Martin's acid bath. So I cut a deal with the Marshals Service and the Department of Justice. The only reason I agreed to go with Angelo DeLuca that night was because I knew Bruno was my protector." The old man stared at Kaplan. "Like you had your gun, I had Bruno."

"But you did kill Martin," Moss said.

"Technically, no. Bruno killed Martin before Martin killed me. I'll give you that. As my bodyguard, that was his job. I think I have a good argument for self defense...especially with two federal law enforcement officers as witnesses."

"What about the men in the restaurant?" asked Kaplan. "One of them muttered four eyes...did he work for you?"

"Very astute, Mr. Kaplan. That was Marco, and yes he worked for me. As do many others. At least two with each of the six families."

Then it occurred to Kaplan what this was all about...every bit. From the beginning, it was orchestrated by the old man. And it was a brilliant move.

Almost.

"In reality though," said Kaplan. "This has been one big takeover scheme."

"You're on a roll, Mr. Kaplan. And thanks to you two, I am now in a position to seize control of all six family businesses and turn them into one giant corporation. As I explained in the car a few days ago, I devised this plan decades ago. A long-range plan with a vast and intricate corporate structure with so many failsafe layers, that it can never be brought down entirely. Yet it seems I was the only one with enough patience to wait and make it work."

Moss hobbled on the crutches next to Kaplan, followed closely by Bruno brandishing his assault rifle. "The men are your Trojan horses," Moss said. "Get them inside the gates and wait for the villagers to fall asleep and then attack."

Tony smiled. "A crude analogy, but close enough. It's all about trust. My men had to be trusted by their families and that meant years on the inside as a sleeper. Without trust, I could never have gotten the information I needed to take them down and see my plan come to fruition."

"You used the U. S. Marshals Service to protect you while the Department of Justice moved in and eliminated your competition," Kaplan said. "That's a very sly move."

"Another Sicilian meaning for the word Quattrocchi," Tony said as he looked at Kaplan. "Someone who is particularly shrewd or diligent."

"It seems the United States government played into your hands," Moss moved closer to Bruno and stopped.

"They did make it quite easy," the old man replied.

There was an awkward moment of silence and then Kaplan asked, "Did you not think anyone would come for you?"

"Actually," Tony said. "No." He looked at Moss. "Senior Inspector, my agreement with the U. S. Marshals Service was to testify. I have done that." He paused. "Martin Scalini is dead, the others are all locked away. Quite frankly, I don't consider the Marshals Service witness protection even remotely close to adequate so I opted out…which, by the way, I have the right to do. Your WitSec inspectors have reminded me of that numerous times. My number one priority was to seek safety, and that meant here." He waved his arms at the glass window overlooking the big island. "Which brings up another issue." He looked at Kaplan. "How did you find out about this place?"

"Something you said in the car," Kaplan responded. "About French Creole cuisine and Martinique."

"But that didn't cinch it," Moss added. "It was that rare stamp you purchased this morning. Your WitSec file mentioned your prior involvement with several philatelic societies and your reluctance to give up your stamp-collecting hobby after you entered the program. So we did some digging." Moss turned to Kaplan.

Kaplan finished. "You see, you're not the only one who can devise a sinister plan and have the patience to wait it out. The stamp was a setup. The CIA put that stamp on the market as bait. When you bought the stamp, it confirmed your location."

All four men turned when two dogs barked outside. Then the animals went silent.

"I almost balked but I could not resist. It was a once in a lifetime buying opportunity."

"And now it will cost you your life," Kaplan added. "And just like everything else in your life, the location of your secret hideout has been blown."

"I have heard all I care to hear." Tony turned to Bruno and said, "Kill them. And then throw their bodies off the cliff. Let the birds peck away at their dead carcasses."

Bruno raised his AK-47 and swung the barrel toward Kaplan. Moss countered by throwing a crutch at Bruno's gun. The impact was enough to deflect Bruno's shot and the bullet shattered the large plate glass window. Wind swirled through the room.

Kaplan dropped to one knee and retrieved the knife from the specially designed pouch in his boot. Tony's men failed to search his boots when they confiscated his handguns. He grabbed the old man and used him for a shield, holding the tip of the blade against Tony's throat.

Bruno pointed the barrel of the assault rifle at Kaplan and

then turned it on Moss.

"Let him go or I'll shoot," Bruno shouted over the wind whistling through the broken glass window.

"Hand over your weapon or I'll kill him. You have my word." Kaplan countered. He pressed the blade tip firmly against Tony's throat, enough to draw blood. "And I always keep my word."

Tony screamed. A trickle of blood ran down his neck.

Kaplan leaned near Tony's ear and said, "Tell him to give up the gun or I swear on everything you hold sacred, I will slash your throat from ear to ear and let you watch your own blood spill from your neck. We're not in the quiet room at the B & B. There is no one here to stop me from killing you this time." He yanked up on the old man's body. "Tell him now."

"Give him the gun, Bruno. For God's sake…give him the gun."

Bruno hesitated then released his grip on the trigger and held the AK-47 out to the side with one hand on the stock.

Moss limped over to Bruno, took the rifle, and pointed it at him. He took a few steps back.

Kaplan lightened the blade's pressure from Tony's neck yet held it in place. He kept a tight grip on the old man. "Remember our Quattrocchi, old man. I warned you not to double-cross Deputy Moss." Kaplan pressed the knife blade just below Tony's left ear.

"Kaplan, no," Moss yelled without taking his eyes off Bruno. "Let him go. There's no need for this. You got your man. Why kill him when you can let him rot in prison?"

Moss was right. He knew that. But he'd made a promise to the old man. One he desperately wanted to keep.

"Let the Marshals Service take it from here," Moss urged.

"The old man will get what's coming to him...I give you my word."

Kaplan relaxed his grip and allowed Tony to push himself a few inches away.

Moss glared at Kaplan and as he did, Bruno reached behind his back, drew a handgun, and pointed it toward Kaplan.

Kaplan yanked Tony's arm and pulled the old man toward him.

Bruno's gun fired.

Kaplan felt a stabbing pain in his left shoulder. His shirt turned red and he felt the instant flow of warm sticky blood streaming over his armpit. He and Tony fell to the floor.

Moss turned toward Bruno, took aim, and fired three shots.

Tony's body went limp in Kaplan's arms. Blood oozed from a gunshot wound to the old man's chest. Dead center of the heart.

Kaplan lowered the dead witness to the floor and then clutched his own shoulder. He groaned as he pushed himself to his feet and walked to where Moss was standing. The two men hovered over Bruno the Rat.

Kaplan looked down at the man's dead body and was once again reminded of his Special Forces mantra. *Two in the chest, one in the head works 100 % of the time.* Moss did okay.

Ten seconds later, six men stormed the mansion.

They weren't Tony's men.

They were dressed in black.

They wore helmets and carried rifles.

And badges.

Emblazoned on their armored vests was a now familiar and relieving sight.

U. S. Marshals.

EPILOGUE

Little Rock, Arkansas
One week later

KAPLAN WASN'T SURE WHY HE WAS STILL IN town.

Maybe he needed to say a few goodbyes. Or make a few apologies. He owed them that much. Jeff and Kam claimed they were happy to help an old friend. Deep down he knew how much trouble he'd caused, how much anxiety his intrusion had created. Jeff said given the circumstances, he'd do it again. That's what being a true friend was all about—and Kaplan didn't have many friends left.

Life in his secret world was lonely. And thankless. The job was full of deceit and danger where most would question his sanity for not getting out of his clandestine job at a younger age. There were times he had questioned it too, but he knew why he stayed.

Patriotism.

At least that was part of it. Deep down, though, he knew he craved the thrill of the chase. Bringing evildoers to justice—or simply just eliminating them.

A large man with a cane limped into the restaurant; Kaplan

raised his hand and motioned to him.

"Got your message." Moss leaned his cane against the table and carefully sat in the chair. "Surprised you're still in town. Figured you'd be long gone by now."

"Me too, but sometimes I surprise myself." Kaplan looked at Moss's leg and motioned with his head. "How's the leg?"

"Sore as hell, but better." Moss paused. "Why are you still here, really?"

Kaplan picked up his glass and swirled the ice. "Felt like I still owed you a drink."

"You owe me a hell of a lot more than a drink," Moss scoffed. "Your harebrained scheme almost cost me my life... and my career."

Kaplan waved the waitress to the table. "I'm buying so order something and quit whining."

Moss looked at the waitress. "Since he's paying, I'll have the New York Strip, medium, baked potato, loaded, and the house salad." Moss looked at Kaplan's glass. "A glass of water and whatever he's drinking."

"You're that hungry? At three in the afternoon?"

"I'm always hungry." Moss patted his belly. "How else am I going to keep this rock solid body?"

Both men laughed.

It felt good to laugh. Moss had become a good friend in a short time and he wanted to touch base with the deputy one last time before he rode out of town.

"I hear you're on administrative leave. Word on the street is you don't follow orders and went rogue. I'll bet you've always been a pain in the CIA's ass." Moss unfolded his napkin and removed the silverware hidden inside. "What now? Continue your trip to Texas to find that woman Tony Q told me about?"

"Tony Q talked too much."

"Not anymore," Moss said.

Kaplan smiled. "No, I guess not. So what about you? When will you be headed back up North?"

"I have been remanded to stay in this WitSec office until a new inspector is permanently assigned."

"How long will that take?"

"Couple of weeks," Moss replied. "Then I've been ordered to take a long vacation and think about my future with the Marshals Service."

"What are you talking about?" Kaplan asked.

"Didn't you hear? I put the Director in a pickle. I got slapped with a list of Marshals Service infractions from willfully endangering the life of a witness to breach of WitSec protocol, and a whole lot more. The list was long and extensive. Fortunately, though, the end result washed away most of my sins and I got off with nothing more than a reprimand."

"Got any vacation plans?" Kaplan asked. "Go to a beach? Work on your tan?"

"Nah. Never was much of a beach person. Too much sand. Plus I don't like the water. And, in case you haven't noticed, I already have a tan."

"If you get bored, you can always join me in Texas."

"I hear black men in cowboy boots and hats are the rage in Texas these days. The women can't resist them."

Kaplan pursed his lips, took a long draw from his drink, and then said, "Perhaps you heard wrong."

The pretty young waitress returned with Moss's drink. Kaplan stood, fished a hundred dollar bill from his pocket, and gave it to the waitress. "This should cover everything."

The waitress took the money. "Mister, this is way too much.

Let me get your bill."

Kaplan pointed at Moss. "Get him whatever else he wants and keep the rest for yourself."

Kaplan looked down at Moss and stuck out his hand. "Deputy Moss, I'd say it's been a pleasure working with you, but then I'd be lying."

"Likewise." Moss gripped his hand and gave it a firm shake. "I never realized what a pain in the ass you CIA spooks were until I met you."

There was a moment of awkward silence and then Moss said, "If you ever get to Chicago..."

"You can count on it." Gregg Kaplan turned and walked out of the Little Rock restaurant, leaving behind his newest friend, Deputy U. S. Marshal Pete Moss.

CHUCK BARRETT

ACKNOWLEDGMENTS

First things first, to my wife Debi, who always gets first read and the first shot at keeping from seriously embarrassing myself. With each manuscript she reads, she claims it will be her last. So I'm honest and tell her that her input makes it a much better book. Thank you for keeping me in line, on track, and for reeling me in when I need it. Thank you for your ideas, your suggestions, and your criticism. Without your valued input, these books would always be lacking. Lastly, thank you for your patience and support, as the arduous task of cranking out stories must seem like a never-ending process. I love you with all my heart and soul.

With each new book I write, the list of acknowledgements grows. I am indebted to those who have graciously volunteered their time and energy to steer this author in the right direction. Perhaps it's their occupational expertise or a past experience that has provided me, through our interviews and discussions, a rudimentary foundation to write about things I know nothing about. To each of those listed below, you have my sincerest gratitude. Thank you for making *Blown* a better book.

Special thanks to Mary Fisher Design, LLC who always creates awesome covers; this time with the special artistic touch of Kelly Young. She patiently listened to my ideas and used her talents to take this cover well beyond my expectations.

Thanks to the following subject matter experts who graciously allowed me to pick their brains and kept me out of trouble on topics I know nothing about. Whether it is health care fraud, police procedures, Aikido moves, Special Forces, farming, or background on the Mafioso. In no particular order—David Raines, Artie Lynnworth, G. J. 'Cos' Cosgrove, Ruth Corley, Doug Wilson, and Francesco Milana.

A special thanks to a U. S. Marshal, who must remain anonymous, for his insight on the inner workings and procedures of the U. S. Marshals Service and WitSec.

Some authors call them *test-readers*. Others call them *beta-readers*. Whatever the title, every author understands the true value of extra eyes reading their material. Thanks to Cheryl Duttweiler, Terrence Traut, Ruth Corley, and Early McCall for your honest, unbiased, and unabashed input.

Whenever real people get their names in fiction stories, they run the risk of being cast as good, bad, and sometimes downright evil characters. Thank you to the *real* J.P. 'Jon' Hepler, Tony Quattrochi-aka Tony Q, Jeff and Kam Harrell (and for the use of your home in this story), and lastly to April J Moore for making such a wonderful villainess/assassin. I hope your characters met your expectations.

Lastly I want to thank you, the reader, for buying this book. It is my genuine hope that you found this story entertaining and that those unexpected twists and turns left you smiling…or perhaps cussing… either way, it works for me.

WRITER'S NOTE

On April 27, 2014, an EF-4 tornado cut a 41-mile swath of destruction through Arkansas destroying much of the town of Mayflower. Fortunately, my friends' home was spared and received only minor damage in comparison, however most of their neighborhood was not. Many homes were completely demolished and lives were lost. Weather is unpredictable at times, and certainly pinpointing exactly when and where a tornado will form is impossible with today's technology. However, meteorologists can predict when conditions are right and the likelihood of tornados is high. These warnings should not be taken lightly. When a tornado forms, seconds count. Seconds that could mean the difference between life and death.

The United States Marshals Service Witness Security Program (WitSec) has been in place since 1970. For the sake and safety of the witnesses in the program, WitSec procedures and safe-site locations are shrouded in secrecy. However, with today's technology, most of that shroud has been removed. Even the location of the U. S. Marshals Service Safe Site and Orientation Center (SSOC-pronounced "sock") can be determined by some savvy Google Earth searches of the Alexandria, Virginia area. Rumors of a new site have surfaced and funding authorized by Congress. It is currently called the Alternate Safe Site and Orientation Center. You guessed it, ASSOC. Location not publicly revealed.

The B & B (CIA safe house) in Lexington, Virginia is a fabrication of this author's imagination. Although these types of facilities exist, this isn't one of them.

The Big Dam in Little Rock, along with the Arkansas River Trail and Emerald Park quarry, are accurately depicted.

The fortress of Tony Q's on Isle de Antonio is all a fabrication. However, Martinique is real…and beautiful.

CPSIA information can be obtained
a ...
Pr...
...
...PQX786886